RING

KOJI SUZUKI

Translation
Robert B. Rohmer
Glynne Walley

KODANSHA

Ring

A VERTICAL Book

English language version produced by Kodansha USA Publishing, LLC, 2024.

Originally published in Japan as *Ringu* by KADOKAWA CORPORATION, Tokyo, 1991.

Previously issued in English in paperback in 2007.

ISBN 978-1-64729-465-6

Printed in the United States of America

Special Edition

www.kodansha.us

KODANSHA

PART ONE *Autumn*

1

September 5, 1990, 10:49 pm
Yokohama

A row of condominium buildings, each fourteen stories high, ran along the northern edge of the housing development next to the Sankeien garden. Although built only recently, nearly all the units were occupied. Nearly a hundred dwellings were crammed into each building, but most of the inhabitants had never even seen the faces of their neighbors. The only proof that people lived here came at night, when windows lit up.

Off to the south the oily surface of the ocean reflected the glittering lights of a factory. A maze of pipes and conduits crawled along the factory walls like blood vessels on muscle tissue. Countless lights played over the front wall of the factory like insects that glow in the dark; even this grotesque scene had a certain type of beauty. The factory cast a wordless shadow on the black sea beyond.

A few hundred meters closer, in the housing development, a single new two-story home stood among empty lots spaced at precise intervals. Its front door opened directly onto the street, which ran north and south, and beside it was a one-car garage. The home was ordinary, like those found in any new housing development anywhere, but there were no other houses behind or beside it.

Perhaps owing to their inconvenience to mass transit, few of the lots had been sold, and For Sale signs could be seen here and there all along the street. Compared to the condos, which were completed at about the same time and which were immediately snapped up by buyers, the housing development looked quite lonely.

A beam of fluorescent light fell from an open window on the second floor of the house onto the dark surface of the street below. The light, the only one in the house, came from the room of Tomoko Oishi. Dressed in shorts and a white T-shirt, she was slouched in a chair reading a book for school; her body was twisted into an impossible position, legs stretched out toward an electric fan on the floor. Fanning herself with the hem of her T-shirt to allow the breeze to hit her bare flesh, she muttered about the heat to no one in particular. A senior at a private girls' high school, she had let her homework pile up over summer vacation; she had played too much, and she blamed it on the heat. The summer, however, hadn't really been all that hot. There hadn't been many clear days, and she hadn't been able to spend nearly as much time at the beach as she did most summers. And what's more, as soon as vacation was over, there were five straight days of perfect summer weather. It irritated Tomoko: she resented the clear sky.

How was she supposed to study in this stupid heat?

With the hand she had been running through her hair Tomoko reached over to turn up the volume of the radio. She saw a moth alight on the window screen beside her, then fly away somewhere, blown by the wind from the fan. The screen trembled slightly for a moment after the bug had vanished into the darkness.

She had a test tomorrow, but she was getting nowhere. Tomoko Oishi wasn't going to be ready for it even if she pulled an all-nighter.

She looked at the clock. Almost eleven. She thought of watching the day's baseball wrap-up on TV. Maybe she'd catch a glimpse of her parents in the infield seats. But Tomoko, who wanted in the worst way to get into college, was worried about the test. All she had to do was get into college. It didn't matter where, as long as it was a college. Even then, what an unfulfilling summer vacation it had been! The foul weather had kept her from having any real fun, while the oppressive humidity had kept her from getting any work done.

Man, it was my last summer in high school. I wanted to go out with a bang and now it's all over. The end.

Her mind strayed to a meatier target than the weather to vent her bad mood on.

And what's with Mom and Dad anyway? Leaving their daughter all alone studying like this, covered in sweat, while they go gallivanting out to a ball game. Why don't they think about my feelings for a change?

Someone at work had unexpectedly given her father a pair of tickets to the Giants game, and so her parents had gone to Tokyo Dome. By now it was almost time for them to be getting home, unless they'd gone out somewhere after the game. For the moment Tomoko was home alone in their brand-new house.

It was strangely humid, considering that it hadn't rained in several days. In addition to the perspiration that oozed from her body, a dampness seemed to hang in the air. Tomoko unconsciously slapped at her thigh. But when she moved her hand away she could find no trace of the mosquito. An itch began to develop just above her knee, but maybe it was just her imagination. She heard a buzzing sound. Tomoko waved her hands over her head. A fly. It flew suddenly upwards to escape the draft from the fan and disappeared from view. How had a fly gotten into the room? The door was closed. Tomoko checked the window screens, but nowhere could she find a hole big enough to admit a fly. She suddenly realized she was thirsty. She also needed to pee.

She felt stifled—not exactly like she was suffocating, but like there was a weight pressing down on her chest. For some time Tomoko had been complaining to herself about how unfair life was, but now she was like a different person as she lapsed into silence. As she started down the stairs her heart began to pound for no reason. Headlights from a passing car grazed across the wall at the foot of the stairs and slipped away. As the sound of the car's engine faded into the distance, the darkness in the house seemed to grow more intense. Tomoko intentionally made a lot of noise going down the stairs and turned on the light in the downstairs hall.

She remained seated on the toilet, lost in thought, for a long time even after she had finished peeing. The violent beating of her heart still had not subsided. She'd never experienced anything like this before. What was going on? She took several deep breaths to steady herself, then stood up and pulled up her shorts and panties together.

Mom and Dad, please get home soon, she said to herself, suddenly sounding very girlish. *Eww, gross. Who am I talking to?*

It wasn't like she was addressing her parents, asking them to come home. She was asking someone else....

Hey. Stop scaring me. Please....

Before she knew it she was even asking politely.

She washed her hands at the kitchen sink. Without drying them she took some ice cubes from the freezer, dropped them in a glass, and filled it with coke. She drained the glass in a single gulp and set it on the counter. The ice cubes swirled in the glass for a moment, then settled. Tomoko shivered. She felt cold. Her throat was still dry. She took the big bottle of coke from the refrigerator and refilled her glass. Her hands were shaking now. She had a feeling there was something behind her. Some *thing*—definitely not a person. The sour stench of rotting flesh melted into the air around her, enveloping her. It couldn't be anything corporeal.

"Stop it! Please!" she begged, speaking aloud now.

The fifteen-watt fluorescent bulb over the kitchen sink flickered on and off like ragged breathing. It had to be new, but its light seemed pretty unreliable right now. Suddenly Tomoko wished she had hit the switch that turned on all the lights in the kitchen. But she couldn't walk over to where the switch was. She couldn't even turn around. She knew what was behind her: a Japanese-style room of eight tatami mats, with the Buddhist altar dedicated to her grandfather's memory in the alcove. Through the slightly open curtains she'd be able to see the grass in the empty lots and a thin stripe of light from the condos beyond. There shouldn't be anything else.

By the time she had drunk half the second glass of cola, Tomoko couldn't move at all. The feeling was too intense, she couldn't be just imagining the presence. She was sure that something was reaching out even now to touch her on the neck.

What if it's...? She didn't want to think the rest. If she did, if she went on like that, she'd remember, and she didn't think she could stand the terror. It had happened a week ago, so long ago she'd forgotten. It was all Shuichi's fault—he shouldn't have said that.... Later, none of them could stop. But then they'd come back to the city and those scenes, those vivid images, hadn't seemed quite as believable. The whole thing had just been someone's idea of a joke. Tomoko tried to think about something more cheerful. Anything besides *that*. But if it was...If that had been real...after all, the phone did ring, didn't it?

...Oh, Mom and Dad, what are you doing?

"Come home!" Tomoko cried aloud.

But even after she spoke, the eerie shadow showed no signs of dissipating. It was behind her, keeping still, watching and waiting. Waiting for its chance to arrive.

At seventeen Tomoko didn't know what true terror was. But she did know that there were fears that grew in the imagination of their own accord. *That must be it. Yeah, that's all it is. When I turn around there won't be anything there. Nothing at all.*

Tomoko was seized by a desire to turn around. She wanted to confirm that there was nothing there and get herself out of the situation. But was that really all there was to it? An evil chill seemed to rise up around her shoulders, spread to her back, and began to slither down her spine, lower and lower. Her T-shirt was soaked with cold sweat. Her physical responses were too strong for it to be just her imagination.

...Didn't someone say your body is more honest than your mind?

Yet, another voice spoke too: Turn around, there shouldn't be anything there. If you don't finish your coke and get back to your studies there's no telling how you'll do on the test tomorrow.

In the glass an ice cube cracked. As if spurred by the sound, without stopping to think, Tomoko spun around.

September 5, 10:54 pm
Tokyo, the intersection in front of Shinagawa Station

The light turned yellow right in front of him. He could have darted through, but instead Kimura pulled his cab over to the curb. He was hoping to pick up a fare headed for Roppongi Crossing; a lot of customers he picked up here were bound for Akasaka or Roppongi, and it wasn't uncommon for people to jump in while he was stopped at a light like this.

A motorcycle nosed up between Kimura's taxi and the curb and came to a stop just at the edge of the crosswalk. The rider was a young man dressed in jeans. Kimura got annoyed by motorcycles, the way they wove and darted their way through traffic like this. He especially hated it when he was waiting at a light and a bike came up and stopped right by his door, blocking it. And today, he had been hassled by customers all day long and was in a foul mood. Kimura cast a sour look at the biker. His face was hidden by his helmet visor. One leg rested on the curb of the sidewalk, his knees were spread wide, and he rocked his body back and forth in a thoroughly slovenly manner.

A young lady with nice legs walked by on the sidewalk. The biker turned his head to watch her go by. But his gaze didn't follow her the whole way. His head had swiveled about 90 degrees when he seemed to fix his gaze on the show window behind her. The woman walked on out of his field of vision. The biker was left behind, staring intently at something. The "walk" light began to flash and then went out. Pedestrians caught in the middle of the street began to hurry, crossing right in front of the taxi. Nobody raised a hand or headed for his cab. Kimura revved the engine and waited for the light to turn green.

Just then the biker seemed to be seized by a great spasm, raising both arms and collapsing against Kimura's taxi. He fell against the door of the cab with a loud thump and disappeared from view.

You asshole.

The kid must've lost his balance and fallen over, thought Kimura as he turned on his blinkers and got out of the car. If the door was damaged, he intended to make the kid pay for repairs. The light turned green and the cars behind Kimura's began to pass by into the intersection. The biker was lying face up on the street, thrashing his legs and struggling with both hands to remove his helmet. Before checking out the kid, though, Kimura first looked at his meal ticket. Just as he had expected, there was a long, angling crease in the door panel.

"Shit!" Kimura clicked his tongue in disgust as he approached the fallen man. Despite the fact that the strap was still securely fastened under his chin, the guy was desperately trying to remove his helmet—he seemed ready to rip his own head off in the process.

Does it hurt that bad?

Kimura realized now that something was seriously wrong with the rider. He finally squatted down next to him and asked, "You all right?" Because of the tinted visor he couldn't make out the man's expression. The biker clutched at Kimura's hand and seemed to be begging for something. He was almost clinging to Kimura. He said nothing. He didn't try to raise the visor. Kimura jumped to action.

"Hold on, I'll call an ambulance."

Running to a public telephone, Kimura puzzled over how a simple fall from a standing position could have turned into this. He must have hit his head just right.

But don't be stupid. The idiot was wearing a helmet, right? He doesn't look like he broke an arm or a leg. I hope this doesn't turn into a pain in the ass.... It wouldn't be too good for me if he hurt himself running into my car.

Kimura had a bad feeling about this.

So if he really is hurt, does it come out of my insurance? That means an accident report, which means the cops....

When he hung up and went back, the man was lying unmoving with his hands clutching his throat. Several passers-by had stopped and were looking on with concerned expressions. Kimura pushed his way through the people, making sure everybody knew it had been he who had called the ambulance.

"Hey! Hey! Hang in there. The ambulance is on its way." Kimura unfastened the chin strap of the helmet. It came right off: Kimura couldn't believe how the guy had been struggling with it earlier. The man's face was amazingly distorted. The only word that could describe his expression was astonishment. Both eyes were wide open and staring and his bright-red tongue was stuck in the back of his throat, blocking it, while saliva drooled from the corner of his mouth. The ambulance would be arriving too late. When his hands had touched the kid's throat in removing his helmet, he hadn't felt a pulse. Kimura shuddered. The scene was losing reality.

One wheel of the fallen motorcycle still spun slowly and oil leaked from the engine, pooling in the street and running into the sewer. There was no breeze. The night sky was clear, while directly over their heads the stoplight turned red again. Kimura rose shakily to his feet, clutching at the guardrail that ran along the sidewalk. From there he looked once more at the man lying in the street. The man's head, pillowed on his helmet, was bent at nearly a right angle. An unnatural posture no matter how you looked at it.

Did I put it there? Did I put his head on his helmet like that? Like a pillow? For what?

He couldn't recall the past several seconds. Those wide open eyes were looking at him. A sinister chill swept over him. Lukewarm air seemed to pass right over his shoulders. It was a tropical evening, but Kimura found himself shivering uncontrollably.

2

The early morning light of autumn reflected off the green surface of the inner moat of the Imperial Palace. September's stifling heat was finally fading. Kazuyuki Asakawa was halfway down to the subway platform, but suddenly had a change of heart: he wanted a closer look at the water he'd been looking at from the ninth floor. It felt like the filthy air of the editorial offices had filtered down here to the basement levels like dregs settling to the bottom of a bottle: he wanted to breathe outside air. He climbed the stairs to the street. With the green of the palace grounds in front of him, the exhaust fumes generated from the confluence of the No. 5 Expressway and the Ring Road didn't seem so noxious. The brightening sky shone in the cool of the morning.

Asakawa was physically fatigued from having pulled an all-nighter, but he wasn't especially sleepy. The fact that he'd completed his article stimulated him and kept his brain cells active. He hadn't taken a day off for two weeks, and planned to spend today and tomorrow at home, resting up. He was just going to take it easy—on orders from the editor-in-chief.

He saw an empty taxi coming from the direction of Kudanshita, and he instinctively raised his hand. Two days ago his subway commuter pass from Takebashi to Shinbaba had expired, and he hadn't bought a new one yet. It cost four hundred yen to get to his condominium in Kita Shinagawa from here by subway, while it cost nearly two thousand yen to go by cab. He hated to waste over fifteen hundred yen, but when he thought of the three transfers he'd have to make on the subway, and the fact that he'd just gotten paid, he decided he could splurge just this once.

Asakawa's decision to take a taxi on this day and at this spot was nothing more than a whim, the outcome of a series of innocuous impulses. He hadn't emerged from the subway with the intention of hailing a cab. He'd been seduced by the outside air at the very moment that a taxi had approached with its red "vacant" lamp lit, and in that instant the thought of buying a ticket and transferring through three separate stations seemed like more effort than he could stand. If he had taken the subway home, however, a certain pair of incidents would almost certainly never have been connected. Of course, a story always begins with such a coincidence.

The taxi pulled to a hesitant stop in front of the Palaceside Building. The driver was a small man of about forty, and it looked like he too had been up all night, his eyes were so red. There was a color mug shot on the dashboard with the driver's name, Mikio Kimura, written beside it.

"Kita Shinagawa, please."

Hearing the destination, Kimura felt like doing a little dance. Kita Shinagawa was just past his company's garage in Higashi Gotanda, and since it was the end of his shift, he was planning to go in that direction anyway. Moments like this, when he guessed right and things went his way, reminded him that he liked driving a cab. Suddenly he felt like talking.

"You covering a story?"

His eyes bloodshot with fatigue, Asakawa was looking out the window and letting his mind drift when the driver asked this.

"Eh?" he replied, suddenly alert, wondering how the cabby knew his profession.

"You're a reporter, right? For a newspaper."

"Yeah. Their weekly magazine, actually. But how did you know?"

Kimura had been driving a taxi for nearly twenty years and he could pretty much guess a fare's occupation depending on where he picked him up, what he was wearing, and how he talked. If the person had a glamorous job and was proud of it, he was always ready to talk about it.

"It must be hard having to be at work this early in the morning."

"No, just the opposite. I'm on my way home to sleep."

"Well, you're just like me then."

Asakawa usually didn't feel much pride in his work. But this morning he was feeling the same satisfaction he'd felt the first time he'd seen an article of his appear in print. He'd finally finished a series he'd been working on, and it had drawn quite a reaction.

"Is your work interesting?"

"Yeah, I guess so," said Asakawa, noncommittally. Sometimes it was interesting and sometimes it wasn't, but right now he couldn't be bothered to go into it in detail. He still hadn't forgotten his disastrous failure of two years ago. He could still clearly remember the title of the article he'd been working on:

"The New Gods of Modernity."

In his mind's eye he could still picture the wretched figure he had cut as he'd stood quaking before the editor-in-chief to tell him he couldn't go on as a reporter.

For a while there was silence in the taxi. They took the curve just left of Tokyo Tower at a considerable speed. "Excuse me," said Kimura, "should I take the canal road or the No. 1 Keihin?" One route or the other would be more convenient depending on where they were going in Kita Shinagawa.

"Take the expressway. Let me out just before Shinbaba."

A taxi driver can relax a bit once he knows precisely where his fare is going. Kimura turned right at Fuda-no-tsuji.

They were approaching it now, the intersection Kimura had been unable to put out of his mind for the past month. Unlike Asakawa, who was haunted by his failure, Kimura was able to look back at the accident fairly objectively. After all, he hadn't been responsible for the accident, so he hadn't had to do any soul-searching because of it. It was entirely the other guy's fault, and no amount of caution on Kimura's part could have warded it off. He'd completely overcome the terror he had felt. A month...was that a long time? Asakawa was still in thrall to the terror he'd known two years ago.

Still, Kimura couldn't explain why, every time he passed this place, he felt compelled to tell people about what had happened. If Kimura glanced in his rearview mirror and saw that his fare was sleeping then he would give up, but if not, then he'd tell every passenger without exception everything that had occurred. It was a compulsion. Every time he'd go through that intersection he was overcome by a compulsion to talk about it.

"The damnedest thing happened right here about a month ago...."

As though it had been waiting for Kimura to begin his story, the light in the intersection changed from yellow to red.

"You know, a lot of strange things happen in this world."

Kimura tried to catch his passenger's interest by hinting in this way at the nature of his story. Asakawa had been half-asleep, but now he lifted his head suddenly and looked around him frantically. He had been startled awake by the sound of Kimura's voice and was now trying to figure out where they were.

"Is sudden death on the increase these days? Among young people, I mean."

"Eh?" The phrase resonated in Asakawa's ears. Sudden death.... Kimura continued.

"Well, it's just that...I guess it was about a month ago. I'm right over there, sitting in my cab, waiting for the light to change, and suddenly this motorbike just falls over on me. It wasn't like he was moving and took a spill—he was standing still, and suddenly, wham! And what do you think happened next? Oh, the driver, he was a prep school kid, 19 years old. He *died*, the idiot. Surprised the hell out of me, I can tell you that. So there's an ambulance, and the cops, and then my cab—he'd banged into it, see. Quite a scene, I tell ya."

Asakawa was listening silently, but as a ten-year veteran reporter he'd developed an intuition about things like this. With instinctive, reflexive quickness he made note of the driver's name and the name of the cab company.

"The way he died was a little weird, too. He was desperately trying to pull off his helmet. I mean, just trying to rip it off. Lying on his back and thrashing around. I went to call the ambulance and by the time I got back, he was stiff."

"Where did you say this happened?" Asakawa was fully awake now.

"Right over there. See?" Kimura pointed to the crosswalk in front of the station. Shinagawa Station was located in the Takanawa area of Minato Ward. Asakawa burned this fact into his memory. An accident there would have fallen under the jurisdiction of the Takanawa precinct. In his mind he quickly worked out which of his contacts could give him access to the Takanawa police station. This was when it was nice to work for a major newspaper: they had connections everywhere, and sometimes their ability to gather information was better than the police bureau's.

"So they called it sudden death?" He wasn't sure if that was a proper medical term. He asked in a hurry now, not even realizing why this accident was striking such a chord with him....

"It's ridiculous, right? My cab was totally stopped. He just went and fell on it. It was all him. But I had to file an accident report, and I came this close to having it show up on my insurance record. I tell ya, it was a total disaster, out of the blue."

"Do you remember exactly what day and time this all happened?"

"Heh, heh, you smell a story? September, lemme see, fourth or fifth must've been. Time was just around eleven at night, I think."

As soon as he said this, Kimura had a flashback. The muggy air, the pitch-black oil leaking from the fallen bike. The oil looked like a living thing as it crept toward the sewer. Headlamps reflected off its surface as it formed viscous droplets and soundlessly oozed into the street drain. That moment when it had seemed like his sensory apparatus had failed him. And then the shocked face of the dead man, head pillowed on his helmet. What had been so astonishing, anyway?

The light turned green. Kimura stepped on the gas. From the back seat came the sound of a ballpoint pen on paper. Asakawa was making notes. Kimura felt nauseated. Why was he recalling it so vividly? He swallowed the bitter bile that had welled up and fought off the nausea.

"Now what did you say the cause of death was?" asked Asakawa.

"Heart attack."

Heart attack? Was that really the coroner's diagnosis? He didn't think they used that term anymore.

"I'll have to verify that, along with the date and time," murmured Asakawa as he continued to make notes. "In other words, there were absolutely no external injuries?"

"Yeah, that's right. Absolutely none. It was just the shock. I mean...I'm the one who oughta be shocked, right?"

"Eh?"

"Well, I mean...The stiff, he had this look of complete shock on his face."

Asakawa felt something click in his mind; at the same time a voice in him denied any connection between the two incidents. *Just a coincidence, that's all.*

Shinbaba Station on the Keihin Kyuko light-rail line loomed up in front of them.

"At the next light turn left and stop there, please."

The taxi stopped and the door opened. Asakawa handed over two thousand-yen notes along with one of his business cards. "My name's Asakawa. I'm with the *Daily News* company. If it's all right with you, I'd like to hear about this in more detail later."

"Okay by me," said Kimura, sounding pleased. For some reason, he felt like that was his mission.

"I'll call you tomorrow or the day after."

"Do you want my number?"

"Never mind. I wrote down the name of your company. I see it's not far away."

Asakawa got out of the taxi and was about to close the door when he hesitated for a moment. He felt an unnameable dread at the thought of confirming what he'd just heard. *Maybe I'd better not stick my nose into anything funny. It could just be a replay of the last time.* But now that his interest had been aroused, he couldn't just walk away. He knew that all too well. He asked Kimura one last time:

"The guy—he was struggling in pain, trying to get his helmet off, right?"

3

Oguri, his editor, scowled as he listened to Asakawa's report. Suddenly he was remembering what Asakawa had been like two years ago. Hunched over his word processor day and night like a man possessed, he'd labored at a biography of the guru Shoko Kageyama, incorporating all his research and more. Something wasn't right about him then. So bedeviled was he that Oguri had even tried to get him to see a shrink.

Part of the problem was that it had been *right then*. Two years ago the whole publishing industry had been caught up in an unprecedented occult boom. Photos of "ghosts" had swamped the editorial offices. Every publisher in the country had been deluged with accounts and photographs of supernatural experiences, every one of them a hoax. Oguri had wondered what the world was coming to. He had figured that he had a pretty good handle on the way the world worked, but he just couldn't think of a convincing explanation for that kind of thing. It was utterly preposterous, the number of "contributors" that had crawled out of the woodwork. It was no exaggeration to say that the office had been buried daily by mail, and every package dealt with the occult in some way. And it wasn't just the *Daily News* company that was the target of this outpouring: every publisher in Japan worthy of the name had been swept up in the incomprehensible phenomenon. Sighing over the time they were wasting, they'd made a rough survey of the claims.

Most of the submissions were, predictably, anonymous, but it was concluded that there was no one out there who was sending out multiple manuscripts under assumed names. At a rough estimate, this meant that about ten million different individuals had sent letters to one publisher or another. Ten million people! The figure was staggering. The stories themselves weren't nearly as terrifying as the fact that there were so many of them. In effect, one out of ten people in the country had sent something in. Yet not a single person in the industry, nor their families and friends, was counted among the informants. What was going on? Where were the heaps of mail coming from? Editors everywhere scratched their heads. And then, before anyone could figure it out, the wave began to recede. The strange phenomenon went on for about six months, and then, as if it had all been a dream, editorial rooms had returned to normal, and they no longer received any submissions of that nature.

It had been Oguri's responsibility to determine how the weekly of a major newspaper publisher should react to all this. The conclusion he came to was that they should ignore it scrupulously. Oguri strongly suspected that the spark which had set off the whole thing had come from a class of magazines he routinely referred to as "the rags." By running readers' photos and tales, they'd stoked the public's fever for this sort of thing and created a monstrous state of affairs. Of course Oguri knew that this couldn't quite explain it all away. But he had to approach the situation with logic of some sort.

Eventually the editorial staff from Oguri on down had taken to hauling all this mail, unopened, to the incinerator. And they dealt with the world just the way they had, as if nothing untoward were happening. They maintained a strict policy of not printing anything on the occult, turning a deaf ear to the anonymous sources. Whether or not that did the trick, the unprecedented tide of submissions began to ebb. And, of all times, it was then that Asakawa had foolishly, recklessly, run around pouring oil on the dying flames.

Oguri fixed Asakawa with a dour gaze. Was he going to make the same mistake twice?

"Now listen, you." Whenever Oguri couldn't figure out what to say, he started out like this. Now listen, you.

"I know what you're thinking, sir."

"Now, I'm not saying it's not interesting. We don't know what'll jump out at us. But, look. If what jumps out at us looks anything like it did that other time, I won't like it very much."

Last time. Oguri still believed that the occult boom two years ago had been engineered. He hated the occult for all he'd gone through on account of it, and his bias was alive and kicking after two years.

"I'm not trying to suggest anything mystical here. All I'm saying is that it couldn't have been a coincidence."

"A coincidence. Hmm..." Oguri cupped a hand to his ear and once again tried to sort out the story.

Asakawa's wife's niece, Tomoko Oishi, had died at her home in Honmoku at around 11 p.m. on the fifth of September. The cause of death was "sudden heart failure." She was a high school senior, only seventeen. On the same day at the same time, a nineteen-year-old prep school student on a motorcycle had died, also of a cardiac infarction, while waiting for a light in front of Shinagawa Station.

"It sounds to me like nothing *but* coincidence. You hear about the accident from your cab driver, and you remember your wife's niece. Nothing more than that, right?"

"On the contrary," Asakawa stated, and paused for effect. Then he said, "The kid on the motorcycle, at the moment he died, was struggling to pull off his helmet."

"...so?"

"Tomoko, too—when her body was discovered, she seemed to have been tearing at her head. Her fingers were tightly entwined in her own hair."

Asakawa had met Tomoko on several occasions. Like any high school girl, she paid a lot of attention to her hair, shampooing it every day, that sort of thing. Why would a girl like that be tearing out her precious hair? He didn't know the true nature of whatever it was that had made her do that, but every time Asakawa thought of her pulling desperately at her hair, he imagined some sort of invisible *thing* to go along with the indescribable horror she must have felt.

"I don't know.... Now listen, you. Are you sure you're not coming at this with preconceptions? If you took any two incidents, you could find things in common if you looked hard enough. You're saying they both died of a heart attack. So they must have been in a lot of pain. So she's pulling at her hair, he's struggling with his helmet.... It actually sounds pretty normal to me."

While he had to recognize that this was a possibility, Asakawa shook his head. He wasn't going to be defeated so easily.

"But, sir, then it would be the chest that hurt. Why should they be tearing at their heads?"

"Now listen, you. Have you ever had a heart attack?"

"Well...no."

"And have you asked a doctor about it?"

"About what?"

"About whether or not a person having a heart attack would tear at his head?"

Asakawa fell silent. He had, in fact, asked a doctor. The doctor had replied, *I couldn't rule it out.* It was a wishy-washy answer. *After all, the opposite sometimes happens. Sometimes when a person experiences a cerebral hemorrhage, or bleeding in the cerebral membrane, they feel stomach discomfort at the same time as a headache.*

"So it depends on the individual. When there's a tough math problem, some people scratch their heads, some people smoke. Some people may even rub their bellies." Oguri swiveled in his chair as he said this. "The point is, we can't say anything at this stage, can we? We don't have space for that stuff. You know, because of what happened two years ago. We won't touch this kind of thing, not lightly. If we felt fine about speculating in print, then we could, of course."

Maybe so. Maybe it was just like his editor said, it was just a freak coincidence. But still—in the end the doctor had just shaken his head. He'd pressed the doctor—do heart attack victims really pull out their own hair? And the doctor had just frowned and said, *Hmmm*. His look said it all: none of the patients *he'd* seen had acted like that.

"Yes, sir. I understand."

At the moment there was nothing to do but retreat meekly. If he couldn't discover a more objective connection between the two incidents, it would be difficult to convince his editor. Asakawa promised himself that if he couldn't dig up anything, he'd just shut up and leave it alone.

4

Asakawa hung up the phone and stayed there like that for a while, motionless, his hand still on the receiver. The sound of his own unnecessarily excited voice, hanging on the other person's reaction, still echoed in his ears. He had a feeling he wasn't going to be able to do this. The person on the other end had taken the phone from his secretary with a suitably pompous tone, but as he'd listened to Asakawa's proposal the tone of his voice had softened somewhat. At first he'd probably thought Asakawa was calling about advertising. Then he'd done some quick calculating and realized the potential profit in having an article written profiling him.

The "Top Interview" series had begun running in September. The idea was to spotlight a CEO who had built up his company on his own, focusing on the obstacles he'd overcome and how. Considering that he'd actually succeeded in getting an appointment to do the interview, Asakawa should have been able to hang up the phone with a little more satisfaction. But something weighed on him. All he'd hear from this philistine were the same old corporate war stories, boasts about what a genius he was, how he'd seized his opportunities and clawed his way to the top.... If Asakawa didn't thank him and stand up to leave, the tales of valor would go on forever. He was sick of it. He detested whoever had come up with this project. He knew, all too well, that the magazine had to sell ad space to survive, and that this kind of article laid the necessary groundwork for that. But Asakawa himself didn't much care if the company made money or lost it. All that mattered to him was whether or not the work was engaging. No matter how easy a job was physically, if it didn't involve any imagination, it usually ended up exhausting you.

Asakawa headed for the archives on the fourth floor. He needed to do some background reading for the interview tomorrow, but more than that, there was something that was bothering him. The idea of an objective, causal relationship between those two incidents fascinated him. And then he'd remembered. He didn't even know how to begin, but a certain question had come to him in the furtive moment that his mind had wrested free of the voice of the philistine.

Were these two inexplicable sudden deaths indeed the only ones that had occurred at 11 p.m. on September 5th?

If not—that is, if there had been other, similar, incidents—then the chances of them being a coincidence were practically nil. Asakawa decided to take a look at the newspapers from early September. Part of his job was reading the newspaper meticulously. But in his case, he usually read only the headlines in the local news section, so there was more than just a chance that there was something he'd missed. He had a feeling there had been. He had the feeling that about a month ago, in the corner of a page in the local news section, he'd seen an odd headline. It had been a small article, on the lower left-hand page.... All he remembered was where it had appeared. He remembered reading the headline and thinking, *hey*, but then someone from the desk had called to him, and he'd gotten so distracted by work that he never actually read the article.

With the buoyance of a child on a treasure hunt, Asakawa began his search with the morning edition from September 6th. He was certain he'd find a clue. Reading month-old newspapers in the gloomy archives was giving him a sort of psychological uplift he never got from interviewing a philistine. Asakawa was much more cut out for this kind of thing than for running around on the beat dealing with people of all sorts.

The September 7th evening edition—that's where the article was, in just the position he'd remembered it being. Squeezed into a corner by news of a shipwreck that had claimed 34 lives, the article took up even less space than he'd recalled. No wonder he had overlooked it. Asakawa took off his silver-rimmed glasses, buried his face in the newspaper, and pored over the article.

YOUNG COUPLE DEAD OF UNNATURAL CAUSES IN RENTAL CAR

At 6:15 am on the 7th, a young man and woman were found dead in the front seats of a car on a vacant lot in Ashina, Yokosuka, along a prefectural road. The bodies were discovered by a truck driver who happened to pass by and who then reported the case to the Yokosuka police precinct.

From the car registration they were identified as a preparatory school student from Shibuya, Tokyo (age 19), and a private girls' high school student from Isogo, Yokohama (age 17). The car had been rented from an agency in Shibuya two evenings previously by the preparatory school student.

At the time of discovery, the car was locked with the key in the ignition. The estimated time of death was sometime between late night on the 5th and the predawn hours of the 6th. Since the windows were rolled up, it is thought that the couple fell asleep and asphyxiated, but the possibility that they had taken an overdose of drugs in order to commit a love suicide has not been ruled out. The exact cause of death has not been determined. As of yet there is no suspicion of homicide.

This was all there was to the article, but Asakawa felt like he'd gotten a bite. First of all, the girl who died was seventeen and attended a private girls' school in Yokohama, just like his niece Tomoko. The guy who rented the car was nineteen and a prep school student, just like the kid who died in front of Shinagawa Station. The estimated time of death was virtually identical. Cause of death unknown, too.

There had to be some connection among these four deaths. It couldn't take too long to establish definitive commonalities. After all, Asakawa was on the inside of a major news-gathering organization—he wasn't lacking for sources of information. He made a copy of the article and headed back to the editorial office. He felt like he'd just struck gold, and his pace quickened of its own accord. He could barely wait for the elevator.

The Yokosuka City Hall press club. Yoshino was sitting at his desk, his pen scurrying across a sheet of manuscript paper. As long as the expressway wasn't crowded, you could make it here from the main office in Tokyo in an hour. Asakawa came up behind Yoshino and called his name.

"Hey, Yoshino."

He hadn't seen Yoshino in a year and a half.

"Huh? Hey, Asakawa. What brings you down to Yokosuka? Here, have a seat."

Yoshino pulled up a chair toward the desk and urged Asakawa to sit. Yoshino hadn't shaved, and it gave him a seedy look, but he could be surprisingly considerate toward others.

"You keeping busy?"

"You could say that."

Yoshino and Asakawa had known each other when Asakawa was still in the local-news department, which Yoshino had entered three years ahead of him. Yoshino was thirty-five now.

"I called the Yokosuka office. That's how I learned you were here."

"Why? You need me for something?"

Asakawa handed him the copy he'd made of the article. Yoshino stared at it for an extraordinarily long time. Since he'd written the article himself, he should have been able to remember what it said just by looking at it. As it was, he sat there concentrating all his nerves on it, hand frozen halfway through the motion of putting a peanut in his mouth. It was as if he were chewing it: recalling what he'd written and digesting it.

"What about it?" Yoshino had assumed a serious expression.

"Nothing special. I just wanted to find out more details."

Yoshino stood up. "All right. Let's go next door and talk over a cup of tea or something."

"Do you have time for this right now? Are you sure I'm not interrupting?"

"Not a problem. This is more interesting than what I was doing."

There was a little cafe right next to City Hall where you could get coffee for two hundred yen a cup. Yoshino sat down and immediately turned to the counter and called out, "Two coffees." Then, turning back to Asakawa, he hunched over, leaning close. "Okay, look, I've been on the local beat for 12 years now. I've seen a lot of things. But. Never have I come across anything as downright odd as this."

Yoshino paused for a sip of water, then continued. "Now, Asakawa. This has got to be a fair trade of information. Why is someone from the main office looking into this?"

Asakawa wasn't ready to tip his hand. He wanted to keep the scoop for himself. If an expert like Yoshino caught wind of it, in a heartbeat he'd chase and nab the prize for himself. Asakawa promptly came up with a lie.

"No special reason. My niece was a friend of the dead girl, and she keeps badgering me for information—you know, about the incident. So as long as I was down here...."

It was a poor lie. He thought he saw Yoshino's eyes flash with suspicion, and he shrank back, unnerved.

"Really?"

"Yeah, well, she's a high school student, right? It's bad enough that her friend's dead, but then there are the circumstances. She just keeps bugging me about it. I'm begging you. Give me details."

"So, what do you want to know?"

"Did they ever decide on the cause of death?"

Yoshino shook his head. "Basically, they're saying their hearts just stopped all of a sudden. They have no idea why."

"How about the murder angle? Strangulation, for example."

"Impossible. No bruise marks on the neck."

"Drugs?"

"No traces in the autopsy."

"In other words, the case hasn't been solved."

"Shit, no. No solving to be done. It isn't a murder—it's not even an incident, really. They died of some illness, or from some kind of accident, and that's all there is to it. Period. There's not even an investigation."

It was a blunt way of putting it. Yoshino leaned back in his chair.

"So why haven't they released the names of the deceased?"

"They're minors. Plus, there's the suspicion that it was a love suicide."

At this point Yoshino suddenly smiled, as if he'd just remembered something, and he leaned forward again.

"You know, the guy? He had his jeans and his briefs down around his knees. The girl, too—her panties were pulled down to her knees."

"So, you mean it was *coitus interruptus*?"

"I didn't say they were doing it. They were just getting ready to do it. They were just getting ready to have a little fun and, bam! That's when it happened," Yoshino clapped his hands together for effect.

"When what happened?"

Yoshino was telling his story for maximum effect.

"Okay, Asakawa, level with me. You've got something. I mean, something that connects with this case. Right?"

Asakawa didn't reply.

"I can keep a secret. I won't steal your scoop, either. It's just that I'm interested in this."

Asakawa still remained silent.

"Are you gonna keep me hanging here in suspense?"

Should I tell?... But I can't. I mustn't say anything yet. But lies aren't working....

"Sorry, Yoshino. Could you wait just a little longer? I can't tell you quite yet. But I will in two or three days. I promise."

Disappointment clouded Yoshino's face. "If you say so, pal...."

Asakawa gave him a pleading look, urging him to continue his story.

"Well, we've got to assume that something happened. A guy and a gal suffocate just when they're getting ready to do it? That's not even funny. I guess it's possible that they'd taken poison earlier and it had only taken effect just then, but there were no traces. Sure, there are poisons that leave no trace, but you can't figure on a couple of students getting their hands on something like that."

Yoshino thought of the place where the car had been found. He'd actually gone there himself and still had a clear impression. The car was parked on an overgrown piece of vacant land in a little ravine just off the unpaved prefectural road that led from Ashina to Mt. Okusu. Cars coming up the road could just catch the reflection of its taillights as they passed. It wasn't hard to imagine why the prep school kid, who'd been driving, had chosen this place to park in. After nightfall hardly any cars used this road, and with the thick growth of trees providing cover, it made for a perfect hideaway for a penniless young couple.

"Then, you've got the guy with his head jammed up against the steering wheel and the side window. Meanwhile, the girl's got her head buried between the passenger seat and the door. That's how they died. I saw them being taken out of the car, with my own eyes. Each body came tumbling out the moment the doors were opened. It's like at the moment of death some sort of force had been pushing them from the inside, didn't stop when they died but kept pushing for thirty hours or so until the investigators opened the doors, and then burst out. Now, are you with me here? This car was a two-door, one of those where you can't lock the doors with the key still inside. And the key was in the ignition, but the doors...well, you catch my drift. The car was completely sealed. It's hard to imagine that any force from the outside could have affected them. And what kind of expression do you suppose they had on their dead faces? They were both scared shitless. Faces contorted with terror."

Yoshino paused to catch his breath. There was a loud gulping sound. It wasn't clear which of them had swallowed his saliva.

"Think about it. Suppose, just for the hell of it, that some fearsome beast had come out of the woods. They'd have been scared, and they would have huddled close to each other. Even if he hadn't, the girl would absolutely have clung to him. After all, they were lovers. But instead, their backs were pressed up against the doors, as if they were trying to get as far away from each other as they could."

Yoshino threw up his hands in a gesture of surrender. "Beats the hell out of me."

If it hadn't been for the shipwreck in the waters off Yokosuka, the article might have been given more space. And if it had, there would have been a lot of readers who would have enjoyed trying to solve the puzzle, playing detective. But... But. A consensus had spread, an atmosphere, among the investigators and everybody else who had been at the scene. They all thought more or less the same thing, and all of them were on the verge of blurting it out, but nobody actually did. That kind of consensus. Even though it was completely impossible for two young people to die of heart attacks at exactly the same moment, even though none of them really believed it, everybody told themselves the medical lie that it had happened just like that. It wasn't that people refrained from saying anything out of fear of being laughed at for being unscientific. It was that they felt they'd be drawing unto themselves some unimaginable horror by admitting it. It was more convenient to indulge in the scientific explanation, no matter how unconvincing it was.

A chill ran up Asakawa's spine and Yoshino's simultaneously. Unsurprisingly, they were both thinking the same thing. The silence only confirmed the premonition which was welling up in each man's breast. *It's not over—it's only just started.* No matter how much scientific knowledge they fill themselves with, on a very basic level, people believe in the existence of something that the laws of science can't explain.

"When they were discovered...where were their hands?" Asakawa suddenly asked.

"On their heads. Or, well, it was more like they were covering their faces with their hands."

"Were they by any chance pulling at their hair, like this?" Asakawa tugged at his own hair to demonstrate.

"Eh?"

"In other words, were they tearing at their heads, or pulling out their hair, or anything like that?"

"No. I don't think so."

"I see. Could I get their names and addresses, Yoshino?"

"Sure. But don't forget your promise."

Asakawa smiled and nodded, and Yoshino got up. As he stood the table swayed and their coffee spilled into their saucers. Yoshino hadn't even touched his.

5

Asakawa kept investigating the four victims' backgrounds whenever he had a free minute, but had so much work to do that he wasn't getting as far as he'd hoped. Before he knew it a week had passed, it was a new month, and both August's rain-soaked humidity and September's summery heat became distant memories pushed aside by the signs of deepening autumn. Nothing happened for a while. Ever since then he'd made a point of reading every inch of the local-news pages, but without coming across anything remotely similar. Or was it just that something horrible was advancing, slowly but surely, where Asakawa couldn't see? But the more time elapsed, the more inclined he was to think that the four deaths were just coincidences, unconnected in any way. He hadn't seen Yoshino since then, either. He had probably forgotten the whole thing, too. If he hadn't, he would have contacted Asakawa by now.

Whenever his passion for the case showed signs of waning, Asakawa would take four cards out from his pocket and be reminded once again that it couldn't have been a coincidence. On the cards he'd written the deceased's names, addresses, and other pertinent information, and on the remaining space he planned to record their activities during the months of August and September, their upbringing, and anything else his research turned up.

CARD 1:

TOMOKO OISHI

Date of birth: 10/21/72

Keisei School for Girls, senior, age 17

Address: 1-7 Motomachi, Honmoku, Naka Ward, Yokohama

Approx. 11 pm, Sept. 5: dies in kitchen on first floor of home, parents away. Cause of death sudden heart failure.

CARD 2:

SHUICHI IWATA

Date of birth: 5/26/71

Eishin Preparatory Academy, first year, age 19

Address: 1-5-23 Nishi Nakanobu, Shinagawa Ward, Tokyo

10:54 pm, Sept. 5: falls over and dies at intersection in front of Shinagawa Sta. Cause of death cardiac infarction.

CARD 3:

HARUKO TSUJI

Date of birth: 1/12/73

Keisei School for Girls, senior, age 17

Address: 5-19 Mori, Isogo Ward, Yokohama

Late night, Sept. 5 (or early next morning): dies in car off pref. road at foot of Mt. Okusu. Cause of death sudden heart failure.

CARD 4:

TAKEHIKO NOMI

Date of birth: 12/4/70

Eishin Preparatory Academy, second year, age 19

Address: 1-10-4 Uehara, Shibuya Ward, Tokyo

Late night, Sept. 5 (or early next morning): dies w/Haruko Tsuji in car at foot of Mt. Okusu. Cause of death sudden heart failure.

Tomoko Oishi and Haruko Tsuji went to the same high school and were friends; Shuichi Iwata and Takehiko Nomi studied at the same prep school and were friends: this much had been clear prior to legwork, which indeed confirmed it. And from the simple fact that Tsuji and Nomi had gone for a drive together on Mt. Okusu in Yokosuka on the night of September 5th, it was obvious that they were, if not quite lovers, at least fooling around. When he'd asked her friends, he'd heard the rumor that Tsuji had been dating a prep school guy from Tokyo. However, Asakawa still didn't know when or how they'd met. Naturally, he suspected that Oishi and Iwata were going out, too, but he couldn't find anything to back this up. It was equally possible that Oishi and Iwata had never even seen each other. In which case, what was there to link these four? They seemed far too closely related for this unknown being to have picked them totally at random. Maybe there was some secret that only the four of them knew, and they'd been killed for it.... Asakawa tried out a more scientific explanation with himself: perhaps the four of them had been in the same place at the same time, and all four had been infected with a virus that attacks the heart.

Hey, now. Asakawa shook his head as he walked. *A virus that causes sudden heart failure? Come on.*

He climbed the stairs, muttering to himself, *a virus, a virus.* Indeed, he should start out with attempts at scientific explanation. Well, suppose there *was* a virus that caused heart attacks. At least it was a little more realistic than imagining that something supernatural was behind it all; it seemed less likely to get him laughed at. Even if such a virus hadn't yet been discovered on earth, maybe it had just recently fallen to earth inside a meteor. Or maybe it had been developed as a biological weapon and had somehow escaped. You couldn't rule out the possibility. Sure. He'd try thinking of it as a kind of virus for a while. Not that this would satisfy all his doubts. Why had they all died with looks of astonishment on their faces? Why had Tsuji and Nomi died on opposite sides of that small car, as if they were trying to get away from each other? Why hadn't the autopsies revealed anything? The possibility of an escaped germ weapon could at least answer the third question. There would have been a gag order.

If he were to pursue this hypothesis further, he could deduce that the fact that there hadn't been any other victims yet meant that the virus was not airborne. It was either blood-borne, like AIDS, or was fairly noncontagious. But more importantly, where had these four picked it up? He'd have to go back and sift through their activities in August and September again and look for places and times they had in common. Since the participants' mouths had been shut permanently, it wouldn't be easy. If their meeting had been a secret among the four of them, something neither parents nor friends knew about, then how was he to ferret it out? But he was sure that these four kids had some time, some place, some *thing* in common.

Sitting down at his word processor Asakawa chased the unknown virus from his thoughts. He needed to get out the notes he'd just taken, to sum up the contents of the cassette he'd made. He had to get this article finished today. Tomorrow, Sunday, he and his wife Shizu were going to visit her sister, Yoshimi Oishi. He wanted to see with his own eyes the spot where Tomoko had died, to feel on his own flesh whatever air still lingered. His wife had agreed to go to Honmoku to console her bereaved older sister; she had no inkling of her husband's true motives.

Asakawa started pounding the keys of the word processor before he'd come up with a decent outline.

6

Shizu was seeing her parents for the first time in a month. Ever since their granddaughter Tomoko had died, they came to Tokyo from their home in Ashikaga whenever they could, not only to console their daughter but to be consoled in turn. Shizu only understood this today. Her heart ached when she saw her aged parents' thin, grief-stricken faces. They had once had three grandchildren: their oldest daughter Yoshimi's daughter Tomoko, their second daughter Kazuko's son Kenichi, and Shizu's daughter Yoko. One grandchild from each of their three daughters—not all that common. Tomoko had been their first grandchild, and their faces had crinkled up every time they had seen her; they had enjoyed spoiling her. Now they were so depressed that it was impossible to say whose grief was deeper, the parents' or the grandparents'.

I guess grandchildren really mean a lot.

Shizu had just turned thirty this year. It was all she could do to imagine what her sister must be feeling, putting herself in her sister's place, imagining how she'd feel if she lost her child. But really, there was no comparison to be made between her daughter Yoko, only a year and a half old, and Tomoko, who had died at seventeen. She couldn't fathom how every passing year would deepen her love for her child.

Sometime after three in the afternoon, her parents began to get ready to go home to Ashikaga.

Shizu could hardly contain her surprise. Why had her husband, who always protested that he was too busy, suggested this visit to her sister's house? This was the same husband who'd skipped the poor girl's funeral, pleading that he had a deadline to meet. And now here it was almost dinnertime, and he wasn't showing the slightest inclination of leaving. He'd only met Tomoko a few times, and had probably never talked with her for very long. Surely he wasn't feeling detained by memories of the deceased.

Shizu tapped Asakawa lightly on the knee and whispered in his ear, "Dear, it's probably about time...."

"Look at Yoko. She's sleepy. Maybe we ought to see if we could let her take a nap here."

They had brought their daughter. Normally, this was nap time. Sure enough, Yoko had started blinking like she did when she was sleepy. But if they let her sleep here, they'd have to stay in this house for at least two more hours. What would they find to talk about with her grieving sister and her husband for two more hours?

"She can sleep on the train, don't you think?" said Shizu, dropping her voice.

"Last time we tried that she got fussy, and it was awful all the way home. No, thanks."

Whenever Yoko got sleepy in a crowd, she got unbelievably fussy. She'd flail her little arms and legs, wail at the top of her lungs, and just generally make life difficult for her parents. Scolding her only made it worse—there was no way to calm her down except to try to get her to sleep. At times like that Asakawa became intensely conscious of the looks of people around him, and he'd start sulking himself, as though he were the prime victim of his daughter's shrieking. The accusing stares of the other passengers always made him feel like he was choking.

Shizu preferred not to see her husband in that state, with his cheeks twitching nervously and all. "All right, then, if you say so."

"Great. Let's see if she'll take a nap upstairs."

Yoko lay in her mother's lap, eyes half closed.

"I'll go put her down," he said, caressing his daughter's cheek with the back of his hand. The words sounded strange coming from Asakawa, who hardly ever helped with the baby. Maybe he'd had a change of heart, now that he'd witnessed the sorrow of parents who'd lost a child.

"What's come over you today? It's spooky."

"Don't worry. She looks like she'll go right down. Leave it to me."

Shizu handed the child over. "Thanks. I just wish you were like this all the time."

As she was transferred from her mother's bosom to her father's, Yoko began to scrunch up her face, but before she had time to follow through she had fallen asleep. Asakawa climbed the stairs, cradling his daughter. The second floor consisted of two Japanese-style rooms and the Western-style room which had been Tomoko's. He laid Yoko on the futon in the Japanese-style room that faced south. He didn't even need to stay with her as she fell asleep. She was already out, her breathing regular.

Asakawa slipped out of the room and listened to see what was going on downstairs, and then entered Tomoko's bedroom. He felt a little guilty about invading a dead girl's privacy. Wasn't this the kind of thing he abhorred? But it was for a good cause—defeating evil. There was nothing but to do it. But even as he thought this, he hated the way he was always willing to seize on any reason, no matter how specious, in order to rationalize his actions. But, he protested, it wasn't like he was writing an article about it: he was just trying to figure out when and where the four had been together. *Sorry.*

He opened her desk drawers. Just the normal assortment of stationery supplies, like any high school girl would have, rather neatly arranged. Three snapshots, a junk box, letters, a notepad, a sewing kit. Had her parents gone through here after she died? It didn't look like it. Probably she was just naturally neat. He was hoping to find a diary—it would save him a lot of time. *Today I got together with Haruko Tsuji, Takehiko Nomi, and Shuichi Iwata, and we....* If he could just find an entry like that. He took a notebook from her bookshelf and flipped through it. He actually came across a very girlish diary in the back of a drawer, but there were only a few desultory entries on the first few pages, all of them dated long ago.

On the shelf beside the desk there were no books, only a red flowered makeup stand. He opened the drawer. A bunch of cheap accessories. A lot of mismatched earrings—it seemed she had a habit of losing one of every pair she owned. A pocket comb with several slender black strands of hair still wrapped around it.

Opening the built-in wardrobe, his nose was assailed by the scent of high school girls. It was packed tight with colorful dresses and skirts on hangers. His sister-in-law and her husband had obviously not figured out what to do with these clothes, which still carried their daughter's fragrance. Asakawa pricked up his ears at what was going on downstairs. He wasn't sure what they'd think if they caught him in here. There was no sound. His wife and her sister must still be talking about something. Asakawa searched the pockets of the clothes in the wardrobe one by one. Handkerchiefs, movie ticket stubs, gum wrappers, napkins, commuter pass case. He examined it: a pass for the stretch between Yamate and Tsurumi, a student ID card, and a card. There was a name written on the card: Something-or-other Nonoyama. He wasn't sure how to pronounce the characters for the first name—Yuki, maybe? From the characters alone he couldn't tell if it was a man or a woman. Why did she have someone else's card in her pass case? He heard footsteps coming up the stairs. He slipped the card into his pocket, put the case back where he'd found it, and shut the wardrobe. He stepped into the hall just as his sister-in-law reached the top of the stairs.

"Sorry, is there a bathroom up here?" He made a show of acting antsy.

"It's there at the end of the hall." She didn't seem to suspect anything. "Is Yoko sleeping like a good girl?"

"Yes, thanks. Sorry to put you to such trouble."

"Oh no, not at all." The sister-in-law bowed slightly, then stepped into the Japanese-style room, hand on her kimono sash.

In the bathroom, Asakawa took out the card. "Pacific Resorts Club Member's Card," it read. Underneath this was Nonoyama's name and membership number and the expiration date. He flipped it over. Five membership conditions, in fine print, plus the name of the company and its address. Pacific Resorts Club, Inc., 3-5 Kojimachi, Chiyoda Ward, Tokyo. Phone no. (03) 261-4922. If it wasn't something she'd found or swiped, Tomoko must have borrowed this card from this Nonoyama person. Why? To use Pacific Resorts facilities, of course. Which one, and when?

He couldn't call from the house. Saying he was going to go buy cigarettes, he ran to a pay phone. He dialed the number.

"Hello, Pacific Resorts, may I help you?" A young woman's voice.

"I'd like to know what facilities I can use with a membership card."

The voice didn't respond right away. Maybe they had so many facilities available that she couldn't just list them all.

"That is...I mean...for example, like on an overnight trip from Tokyo," he added. It would have stood out if the four of them had gone away for two or three nights together. The fact that he hadn't turned anything up so far meant that they had probably gone for no longer than a single night. She could easily get away for a single night by lying to her parents that she was staying at a friend's house.

"We have a full range of facilities at our Pacific Land in South Hakone," she said, in her businesslike manner.

"Specifically, what sorts of leisure activities do you have there?"

"Certainly, sir. We have provisions for golf, tennis, and field sports, as well as a swimming pool."

"And you have lodging there?"

"Yes, sir. In addition to a hotel, Pacific Land features the Villa Log Cabin community of rental cottages. Shall I send you our brochure?"

"Yes. Please." He pretended to be a prospective customer, hoping it would make it easier to extract information from her. "The hotel and the cabins, are they open to the general public?"

"Certainly, at non-member rates."

"I see. Can you give me the phone number? Maybe I'll go have a look."

"I can take care of reservations right now, if you wish...."

"No, I, ah, may be going for a drive down there sometime and just decide to have a look... So could I just have the phone number?"

"One moment, please."

As he waited, Asakawa took out a memo pad and pen.

"Are you ready?" The woman returned and dictated two eleven-digit phone numbers. The area codes were long—they were way out in the sticks. Asakawa scribbled them down.

"Just for future reference, where are your other facilities located?"

"We have the same sort of full-service resorts at Lake Hamana and at Hamajima in Mie Prefecture."

Much too far! Students wouldn't have that kind of war chest.

"I see. Sounds like they're all on the Pacific, just like the name says."

Then the woman began to detail all the fabulous advantages of becoming a Pacific Resorts Club member; Asakawa listened politely for a while before cutting her off. "Great. The rest I'm sure I can find out from the pamphlet. I'll give you my address so you can send it." He told her his address and hung up. Listening to her sales pitch, he'd begun to think it actually wouldn't be a bad idea to join, if he could afford it.

It had been over an hour since Yoko had gone to sleep, and Shizu's parents had already returned to Ashikaga. Shizu herself was in the kitchen doing the dishes for her sister, who was still prone to break down at the slightest provocation. Asakawa briskly helped carry dishes in from the living room.

"What's gotten into you today? You're acting weird," said Shizu, without interrupting her dishwashing. "You put Yoko down, you're helping in the kitchen. Are you turning over a new leaf? If so, I hope it sticks."

Asakawa was lost in thought, and didn't want to be bothered. He wished his wife would act like her name, which meant "quiet." The best way to seal a woman's mouth was not to reply.

"Oh, by the way, did you put a disposable on her before putting her to bed? We wouldn't want her to leak at someone else's house."

Asakawa showed no interest, but just looked around at the kitchen walls. Tomoko had died here. There had been shards of glass and a pool of coke next to her when she was found. She must have been attacked by the virus right when she was going to have a drink of coke from the fridge. Asakawa opened the refrigerator, mimicking Tomoko's movements. He imagined holding a glass, and pretended to drink.

"What in the world are you doing?" Shizu was staring at him, mouth wide open. Asakawa kept going: still pretending to drink, he looked behind him. When he turned around, there was a glass door right in front of him, separating the living room from the kitchen. It reflected the fluorescent light above the sink. Maybe because it was still bright outside and the living room was filled with light, it only reflected the fluorescent light, and not the expressions of the people on this side. If the other side of the glass was dark, and this side light, like it would have been that night when Tomoko was standing here.... That glass door would have been a mirror reflecting the scene in the kitchen. It would have reflected Tomoko's face, contorted with terror. Asakawa could almost start to think of the pane of glass as a witness to everything that had happened. Glass could be transparent or reflective, depending on the interplay of light and darkness. Asakawa was bringing his face nearer the glass, as if drawn there, when his wife tapped him on the back. Just at that moment, they heard Yoko crying upstairs. She was awake.

"Yoko's up." Shizu wiped her wet hands on a towel. Their daughter usually didn't cry so hard upon waking up. Shizu rushed up to the second floor.

As she was going out, Yoshimi came in. Asakawa handed her the card he'd found. "This had fallen under the piano." He spoke casually and waited for a reaction.

Yoshimi took the card and turned it over. "This is strange. What was this doing there?" She cocked her head, puzzled.

"Could Tomoko have borrowed it from a friend, do you suppose?"

"But I've never heard of this person. I don't think she had a friend by that name." Yoshimi looked at Asakawa with exaggerated worry. "Darn it. This looks important. I swear, that girl...." Her voice choked up. Even the slightest thing would set the wheels of grief in motion for her. Asakawa hesitated to ask, but did.

"Did, ah...did Tomoko and her friends by any chance go to this resort during summer vacation?"

Yoshimi shook her head. She trusted her daughter. Tomoko hadn't been the kind of child to lie about staying over at her friends'. Plus, she had been studying for exams. Asakawa could understand how Yoshimi felt. He decided not to ask about Tomoko any further. No high school student with exams looming in front of her was going to tell her parents that she was renting a cottage with her boyfriend. She would have lied and said she was studying at a friend's house. Her parents would never know.

"I'll find the owner and return it."

Yoshimi bowed her head in silence, and then her husband called from the living room and she hurried out of the kitchen. The bereaved father was seated in front of a newly-installed Buddhist altar, speaking to his daughter's photograph. His voice was shockingly cheerful, and Asakawa became depressed. He was obviously living in denial. Asakawa could only pray that he'd be able to get through.

Asakawa had found out one thing. If this Nonoyama had in fact lent Tomoko the membership card, he or she would have contacted Tomoko's parents to ask for the card back upon learning of her death. But Tomoko's mother knew nothing about the card. Nonoyama couldn't have forgotten about the card. Even if the card were part of a family membership deal, dues were expensive enough that Nonoyama wouldn't just allow the card to stay lost. So what did this mean? This was how Asakawa figured it: Nonoyama had lent the card to one of the other three, either Iwata, Tsuji, or Nomi. Somehow it passed into Tomoko's possession, and that's how things had ended. Nonoyama would have contacted the parents of the person he or she had lent it to. The parents would have searched their child's belongings. They wouldn't have found the card. The card was here. If Asakawa contacted the families of the other three victims, he might be able to unearth Nonoyama's address. He should call right away, tonight. If he couldn't dig up a clue this way, then it would be unlikely that the card would provide a means for finding when and where the four had been together. At any rate, he wanted to meet Nonoyama and hear what he or she had to say. If he had to, he could always find some way to track down Nonoyama's address based on the membership number. Asking Pacific Resorts directly probably wouldn't get him anywhere, but he was sure that his newspaper connections could come up with something.

Someone was calling him. A distant voice. "Dear... dear...."

His wife's flustered voice mingled with the baby's crying.

"Dear, could you come here for a minute?"

Asakawa came to himself again. Suddenly he wasn't even sure what he'd been thinking about all this time. There was something strange about the way his daughter was crying. That feeling became stronger as he mounted the stairs.

Asakawa snapped out of his reverie forgetting all about what he had been thinking. He suddenly realized there was something unusual about the sound of his daughter's crying. He raced up the stairs fearing that something was wrong.

"What's wrong?" he asked his wife, accusingly.

"Something's not right with Yoko. I think something's happened to her. The way she's crying—it's different from how it usually sounds. Do you think she's sick?"

Asakawa placed his hand on Yoko's forehead. She didn't have a fever. But her little hands were trembling. The trembling spread to her whole body, and sometimes her back shook. Her face was beet red, her eyes clenched shut.

"How long has she been like this?"

"It's 'cause she woke up and there was no one here with her."

The baby often cried if her mother wasn't there when she woke up. But she always calmed down when her mother ran to her and held her. When a baby cried it was trying to ask for something, but what.... The baby was trying to tell them something. She wasn't just being bratty. Her two tiny hands were clasped tightly over her face...cowering. That was it. The child was wailing out of fear. Yoko turned her face away, and then opened her fists slightly: she seemed to be trying to point forward. Asakawa looked in that direction. There was a pillar. He raised his eyes. Hanging about thirty centimeters from the ceiling was a fist-sized mask, of a *han-*

nya—a female demon. Was the child afraid of the mask?

"Hey, look," said Asakawa, pointing with his chin. They looked at the mask simultaneously, then slowly turned their gazes to each other.

"No way...she's frightened of a demon?"

Asakawa got to his feet. He took down the demon mask from where it hung on the beam and laid it face down on top of the dresser. Yoko couldn't see it there. She abruptly stopped crying.

"What's the matter, Yoko? Did that nasty demon scare you?" Shizu seemed relieved now that she understood, and she happily rubbed her cheek against the child's. Asakawa wasn't so easily satisfied; for some reason, he didn't want to be in this room any longer.

"Hey. Let's go home," he urged his wife.

That evening, as soon as he got home from the Oishis', he called the Tsujis, the Nomis, and the Iwatas, in that order. He asked each family whether they hadn't been contacted by one of their child's acquaintances regarding a membership card for a resort club. The last person he spoke to, Iwata's mother, gave him a long, rambling answer: "There was a call, from someone who said he'd gone to the same high school as my son, an older boy, saying he'd lent my son his resort membership card, and could he get it back.... But I searched every corner of my son's room and never could find it. I've been worried about it ever since." He quickly asked for Nonoyama's phone number, and immediately called it.

Nonoyama had run into Iwata in Shibuya on the last Sunday in August, and lent him his card, just as Asakawa had suspected. Iwata had told him he was going away with this high school girl he'd been hitting on. *Summer vacation's almost over, y'know. I want to really live it up once before it's over, or else I won't be able to buckle down and study for the exams.*

Nonoyama had laughed when he heard this. *You idiot, prep school students aren't supposed to have summer vacations.*

The last Sunday in August had been the 26th: if they'd gone anywhere for the night, it would have to have been the 27th, 28th, 29th, or 30th. Asakawa didn't know about the college prep school, but for the high school girls at least, fall semester began on the first of September.

Maybe it was because she was tired from being so long in unfamiliar surroundings: Yoko soon fell asleep right next to her mother. When he put his ear to the bedroom door, he could hear both of them breathing regularly, fast asleep. Nine in the evening...this was Asakawa's time to relax. Until his wife and child were asleep, there was no room in this tiny condo for him to settle down to work.

Asakawa got a beer from the fridge and poured it into a glass. It tasted special tonight. He'd made definite progress, finding that membership card. There was a good chance that sometime between the 27th and the 30th of August, Shuichi Iwata and the other three had stayed at facilities belonging to Pacific Resorts. The most likely place was Villa Log Cabin at Pacific Land in South Hakone. South Hakone was the only Pacific Resorts property close enough to be a viable candidate, and he couldn't imagine a group of poor students going all out and staying at a hotel. They would probably have used the membership to rent one of the cottages on the cheap. They were only five thousand yen a night for members, which came to a little over a thousand apiece.

He had the phone number for Villa Log Cabin at hand. He put

his memos on the table. The quickest thing would be to simply call the front desk and ask if a party of four had stayed there under the name Nonoyama. But they'd never tell him over the phone. Naturally, anybody who had risen within the firm to the position of rental cottage manager would have been well trained to consider it his duty to protect guests' privacy. Even if he revealed his position as a reporter for a major newspaper and clearly stated his reasons for inquiring, the manager would never tell him over the phone. Asakawa considered contacting the local bureau and getting them to use a lawyer with whom they had connections to ask for a look at the guest register. The only people a manager was legally bound to show the register to were the police and attorneys. Asakawa could try to pose as one or the other, but he'd probably be spotted immediately, and that would mean trouble for the newspaper. It was safer and more effective to go through channels.

But that would take at least three or four days, and he hated to wait that long. He wanted to know *now*. His passion for the case was such that he couldn't bear to wait three days. What in the world was going to come of this? If indeed the four of them had stayed the night at Villa Log Cabin at Pacific Land in South Hakone at the end of August, and if indeed that clue allowed him to unravel the riddle of their deaths—well, what could it have been anyway? *Virus, virus*. He was all too aware that the only reason he was calling it a virus was to keep himself from being overawed by the thought of some mysterious *thing* being behind it all. It made sense—to a degree—to marshal the power of science in facing down supernatural power. He wasn't going to get anywhere fighting a thing he didn't understand with words he didn't understand. He had to translate the thing he didn't understand into words he did.

Asakawa recalled Yoko's cries. Why was she so frightened when she saw the demon mask this afternoon? On the way home on the train, he'd asked his wife, "Hey, have you been teaching Yoko about demons?"

"What?"

"You know, with picture books or something like that. Have you been teaching her to be afraid of demons?"

"No way. Why would I?"

The conversation had ended there. Shizu was unconcerned, but Asakawa worried. That kind of fear only existed on a deep, spiritual level. It was different from fearing something because you had been taught to fear it. Ever since he'd come down out of the trees, man had lived in fear of something or other. Thunder, typhoons, wild beasts, volcanic eruptions, the dark... The first time a child experiences thunder and lightning, he or she feels an instinctive fear—that was understandable. To begin with, thunder was real. It really existed. But what about demons? The dictionary would tell you that demons were imaginary monsters, or the spirits of dead people. If Yoko was going to be afraid of the demon because it looked scary, then she should also have been afraid of models of Godzilla—after all, they were made to look fearsome, too. She'd seen one, once, in a department store show window: a cunningly-made Godzilla replica. Far from being frightened, she had stared at it intently, eyes glowing with curiosity. How did you explain that? The only thing he knew for sure was that Godzilla, no matter how you looked at it, was an imaginary monster. *So what about demons...? And are demons unique to Japan? No, other cultures have the same type of thing. Devils...* The second beer wasn't tasting as good as the first one. *Is there anything else Yoko's afraid of? That's right, there is. Darkness. She's terribly afraid of the dark. She absolutely never goes into an unlit room alone. "Yo-ko," sun-child.* But darkness, too, really existed, as light's opposite pole. Even now, Yoko was asleep in her mother's embrace, in a dark room.

PART TWO *Highlands*

1

October 11—Thursday

The rain was coming down harder now, and Asakawa turned his wipers on high. The weather at Hakone was liable to change at any moment. The skies had been clear down in Odawara, but the higher he climbed, the moister the air, and as he neared the pass he'd encountered several pockets of wind and rain. If it had been daytime, he would have been able to guess at the weather on the mountains from the appearance of the clouds over Mt. Hakone. But it was night, and his attention was fixed on whatever came into the beams of his headlights. It wasn't until he had stopped the car and looked up at the sky that he'd realized the stars had disappeared. When he'd gotten on the Kodama bullet-train at Tokyo Station, the city had still been wrapped in twilight. When he'd rented the car at Atami Station, the moon was still intermittently peeking out from gaps in the clouds. But now the fine water droplets drifting across his headlight beams were growing into a full-fledged downpour, pounding on his windshield.

The digital clock over the speedometer said 7:32. Asakawa quickly calculated how long it had taken him to come this far. He'd taken the 5:16 down from Tokyo, arriving in Atami at 6:07. By the time he'd left the gates and finished the paperwork at the rent-a-car place it had been 6:30. He'd stopped at a market and bought two packs of cup o' noodles and a small bottle of whiskey; it had been seven by the time he'd found his way through the maze of one-way streets and out of town.

A tunnel loomed in front of him, its entrance outlined in brilliant orange light. On the other side, just after he entered the Atami-Kannami Highway, he should start to see signs for South Hakone Pacific Land. The long tunnel would take him through the Tanna Ridge. As he entered it the sound of the wind changed. At the same time, his flesh, the passenger seat, and everything else in the car was bathed in orange light. He could feel his calm slipping away, he could feel his hackles rise. There were no cars coming from the opposite direction. The wipers squeaked as they rubbed against the now-dry windshield. He turned them off. He should reach his destination by eight. He didn't feel quite like flooring it, although the road was empty. Unconsciously, Asakawa was dreading the place he was heading to.

At 4:20 this afternoon, Asakawa had watched as a fax had crawled out of the machine at the office. It was a reply from the Atami bureau, and he had expected it to contain a copy of the Villa Log Cabin's guest register for August 27th through the 30th. When he saw it he did a little dance. His hunch was right. There were four names he recognized: Nonoyama, Tomoko Oishi, Haruko Tsuji, and Takehiko Nomi. The four of them had spent the night of the 29th in cabin B-4. Obviously, Shuichi Iwata had used Nonoyama's name. With this he knew when and where the four had been together: on Wednesday, August 29th, at South Hakone Pacific Land, Villa Log Cabin, No. B-4. It was exactly a week prior to their mysterious deaths.

There and then he'd picked up the receiver and dialed the number for Villa Log Cabin to make a reservation for tonight for cabin B-4. All he had tomorrow was a staff meeting at eleven. He could spend the night down in Hakone and easily be back in time.

...Well, that's it. I'm going. The actual place.

He was eager. Never in his wildest dreams could he imagine what awaited him there.

There was a tollbooth just as he came out of the tunnel, and as he handed over three hundred-yen coins he asked the attendant, "Is South Hakone Pacific Land up ahead?"

He knew full well it was. He'd checked his map any number of times. He just felt like it had been a long time since he'd seen another human being, and something within him wanted to talk.

"There's a sign just up ahead. Make a left there."

He took his receipt. With so little traffic, it hardly seemed worth having someone stationed here. How long was this guy planning to stand there in his booth? Asakawa made no move to drive off, and the man began to give him a suspicious look. Asakawa forced a smile and pulled away slowly.

The joy he'd felt a few hours ago at establishing a common time and place for the four victims had withered and died. Their faces flickered behind his eyelids. They'd died exactly one week after staying in Villa Log Cabin. *Now's the time to turn back*, they seemed to be telling him, leering. But he couldn't turn back now. First of all, his instincts as a reporter had kicked into gear. On the other hand, there was no denying that he was scared to be going alone. If he'd called Yoshino, chances were he would have come running, but he didn't think having a colleague along was such a good idea. Asakawa had already written up his progress so far and saved it on a floppy disk. What he wanted was someone who wouldn't run around getting in his way, but simply help him pursue this.... It wasn't like he didn't have someone in mind. He did know one man who would tag along out of pure curiosity. He was a part-time lecturer at a university, so he had plenty of free time. He was just the guy. But he was...idiosyncratic. Asakawa wasn't sure how long he could take his personality.

There, on the mountainside, was the sign for South Hakone Pacific Land. There was no neon, just a white panel with black lettering. If he'd happened to be looking away when his headlights hit it, he would have missed it completely. Asakawa turned off the highway and began climbing a mountain road between terraced fields. The road seemed awfully narrow for the entrance to a resort, and he had lonely visions of it dead-ending in the middle of nowhere. He had to shift down to negotiate the road's steep, dark curves. He hoped he didn't encounter anybody coming from the opposite direction: there was no room for two cars to pass.

The rain had let up at some point, although Asakawa had just noticed it. The weather patterns seemed different east and west of the Tanna Ridge.

At any rate, the road didn't dead-end, but kept climbing higher and higher. After a while he started to see summer homes scattered here and there on the sides of the road. And the road suddenly widened to two lanes, the surface improved drastically, and elegant streetlights graced the shoulders. Asakawa was amazed at the change. The minute he entered the grounds of Pacific Land he was confronted with lavish accoutrements. So what was with the garden path that led here? The corn and weeds hanging over the road had narrowed it even further, heightening his nervousness over what lay around the next hairpin curve.

The three-story building on the other side of the spacious parking lot doubled as an information center and a restaurant. Without thinking twice, Asakawa parked in front of the lobby and walked toward the hall. He looked at his watch: eight on the nose. Right on schedule. From somewhere he heard the sound of balls bouncing. There were four tennis courts below the center, with several couples giving it their all under the yellowish lights. Surprisingly, all four courts were occupied. Asakawa couldn't fathom what made people come all the way up here at eight on a Thursday night in the middle of October, just to play tennis. Far below the tennis courts he could see the distant lights of the cities of Mishima and Numazu, glittering in the darkness. The emptiness beyond, black as tar, was Tago Bay.

Entering the information center, the restaurant was directly in front of him. Its outer wall was glass, so he could see inside. Here Asakawa got another surprise. The restaurant closed at eight, but it was still half full of families and young women in groups. What was going on here? He cocked his head in puzzlement. Where had everybody come from? He couldn't believe all these people came here on the same road that had brought him here. Maybe what he had used was the back entrance. There must be a brighter, wider road somewhere else. But that was how the girl he'd spoken to on the phone had told him to get here.

Go about halfway down the Atami-Kannami road and turn left. Drive up the mountain from there. Asakawa had done just that. It was inconceivable that there was another way out of here.

Nodding as he was told that it was past time for last orders, he went into the restaurant. Below its wide windows, a carefully groomed lawn sloped gently through the night toward the cities. The inside lights were kept intentionally low, probably to better allow customers to enjoy the view of the distant lights. Asakawa stopped a passing waiter and asked where he could find Villa Log

Cabin. The waiter pointed back toward the entry hall Asakawa had just come through.

"Follow that road to the right about two hundred meters. You'll see the office."

"Is there a parking lot?"

"You can park in front of the office."

That was all there was to it. If he had just kept going instead of stopping in here, he would have found it on his own. Asakawa could more or less analyze why he'd been drawn to this modern building, to the point of barging into the restaurant. He found it somehow comforting. All the way here he had been imagining dark, utterly primitive log cabins—the perfect backdrop for a *Friday the 13th* scenario—and there was nothing of that in this building. Faced with this proof that the power of modern science functioned here, too, he felt somewhat reassured, strengthened. The only things that bothered him were the bad road that led here from the world below, and the fact that in spite of it there were so many people playing tennis and enjoying their dinner here in the world above. He wasn't sure exactly why this bothered him. It was just that, somehow, nobody here seemed quite...lifelike.

Since the tennis courts and restaurant were crowded, he should have been able to hear the cheerful voices of people from the log cabins. That's what he expected. But standing at the edge of the parking lot, looking down over the valley, he could discern only about six of the ten cabins built among the trees scattered over the gentle slope. Everything below was immersed in the darkness of the forest, beyond the pale of the street lamps, unrelieved by any light coming from inside the cabins. B-4, where Asakawa would be spending the night, seemed to stand on the border between the darkness and the lighted area—all he could see was the top of the door.

Asakawa walked around front, opened the office door, and stepped inside. He could hear a television, but there was no sign of anyone. The manager was in a Japanese-style room in the back, off to the left, and hadn't noticed Asakawa. Asakawa's view was blocked by the counter and he couldn't see into the room. The manager seemed to be watching an American movie on video, not a TV program. He could hear English dialogue as he watched the flickering light from the screen reflected in the glass of a cabinet out front. The built-in cabinet was full of videotapes, neatly lined up in their cases. Asakawa placed his hands on the counter and spoke up. Immediately, a small man in his sixties stuck his head out and bowed, saying, "Oh, welcome." He must be the same man who had so cheerfully showed the guest register to the guy from the Atami bureau and the lawyer, thought Asakawa, smiling back at him pleasantly.

"I have a reservation, name of Asakawa."

The man opened his notebook and confirmed the reservation. "You're in B-4. Can I get you to write your name and address here?"

Asakawa wrote his real name. He'd just sent Nonoyama's membership card back to him, so he couldn't use it.

"Just you, then?" The manager looked up at Asakawa, suspiciously. He'd never had anybody stay here alone. At nonmember rates, it was more economical for one person to stay at the hotel. The manager handed over a set of sheets and turned to the cabinet.

"If you'd like you're free to borrow one. We have most of the popular titles."

"Oh, you rent videos?" Asakawa ran his gaze casually over the titles of the videos covering the wall. *Raiders of the Lost Ark, Star*

Wars, Back to the Future, Friday the 13th. All popular American films, mostly science fiction. A lot of new releases, too. Probably the cabins were mostly used by groups of young people. There was nothing that grabbed him. Besides, Asakawa had ostensibly come here to work.

"I'm afraid I've brought work with me." Asakawa picked up his portable word processor from where he'd placed it on the floor and showed the manager. Seeing it, the manager seemed to understand why he was staying here alone.

"So, there are dishes and everything?" Asakawa said, just to make sure.

"Yes. Use anything you like."

The only thing Asakawa needed to use, though, was a kettle to boil water for his cup o' noodles. He took the sheets and his room key from the manager, who told him how to find B-4 and then said, with odd formality, "Please, make yourself at home."

Before touching the knob Asakawa put on his rubber gloves. He'd brought them to give him peace of mind, as a charm to ward off the unknown virus.

He opened the door and flipped on the light switch in the entry hall. A hundred-watt bulb lit a spacious living room. Papered walls, carpet, four-person sofa, television, dinette set: everything was new, everything was functionally arranged. Asakawa took off his shoes and went in. There was a balcony on one edge of the living room and small Japanese-style rooms on the first and second floor. It was a little luxurious for a single guest, after all. He drew the lace curtains and opened the sliding glass door to allow the night air in. The room was perfectly clean, as if to betray his expectations. It suddenly occurred to him that he might go home clueless.

He went into the Japanese-style room off the living room and checked the closet. Nothing. He took off his shirt and slacks and changed into a sweatshirt and sweatpants, hanging his street clothes in the closet. Next he went upstairs and turned on the light in the Japanese-style room. I'm acting like a child, he thought wryly. Before he'd realized it he'd turned on every single light in the place.

With everything sufficiently illuminated, he now opened the bathroom door, gently. He checked inside first, and left the door slightly ajar while he was inside. It reminded him of his fear-rituals as a child, when he was too scared to go to the bathroom alone on summer nights. He used to leave the door open a crack and have his dad stand watch outside. A neat shower room stood behind a pane of frosted glass. There wasn't even a hint of steam, and the area outside the tub and the tub itself were both dry as a bone. It must have been some time since anybody had stayed here. He went to take off his rubber gloves; they stuck to his sweaty hands. The cool highlands breeze blew into the room, disturbing the curtains.

Asakawa filled a glass with ice from the freezer and poured it half full of the whiskey he had bought. He was about to top it off with tap water, but then hesitated. Turning off the tap he persuaded himself that he'd really rather have it straight, on the rocks. He didn't have the courage to put anything from this room into his mouth. He'd been careless enough to use ice cubes from the freezer, but he was under the impression that micro-organisms didn't like extreme heat or cold.

He sank back deep into the sofa and turned on the TV. Singing filled the room: some new pop idol. A Tokyo station was showing the same program right about now. He changed channels. He didn't really intend to watch anything, though, so he adjusted the volume to a suitable level and then opened his bag. He took out a video camera and placed it on the table. If anything strange happened, he wanted to catch it all on tape. He sipped a mouthful of whiskey. It was only a little, but it plucked up his courage. Asakawa went over in his head again everything he knew. If he couldn't find a clue here tonight then the article he was trying to write would be dead in the water. But on the other hand, maybe it was better that way. If not finding a clue meant not picking up the virus, well...after all, he had a wife and child to think about. He didn't want to die, not in some weird way. He propped his feet up on the table.

So, what are you waiting for? he asked himself. *Aren't you afraid? Hey—shouldn't you be afraid? The angel of death might be coming to get you.*

His gaze darted around the room nervously. Asakawa couldn't fix his eyes on any one point on the wall. He had the feeling that if he did so, his fears would begin to take physical form while he watched.

A chill wind blew in from outside, stronger than before. He closed the window and as he went to draw the curtains he happened to glance at the darkness outside. The roof of B-5 was directly in front of him, and in its shadow the darkness was even deeper. There had been lots of people on the tennis courts and in the restaurant. But here Asakawa was alone. He shut the curtains and looked at his watch. 8:56. He hadn't even been in this room for thirty minutes. It easily could have been an hour or more, he felt. But just being here wasn't dangerous in and of itself. He tried to believe that, to calm himself down. After all, how many people must have stayed in B-4 in the six months since these cabins were built? It wasn't like all of them had died under mysterious circumstances. Only those four, according to his research. Maybe if he dug deeper he'd find more, but at the moment that appeared to be all. Thus, simply being here wasn't the problem. The problem was what they'd done here.

So, what did they do here?

Asakawa then subtly rephrased the question. *What* could *they have done here?*

He'd found nothing resembling a clue—not in the bathroom, not in the bath, not in the closet, not in the fridge. Even assuming there had been something, the manager would have disposed of it when he cleaned the place. Which meant that, instead of sitting here drinking whiskey, he should be talking to the manager. That would be quicker.

He'd drained his first glass; he made his second a little smaller. He couldn't afford to get drunk. He put a lot of ice in it, and this time he cut it with tap water. His sense of danger must have been numbed a little. He suddenly felt foolish: stealing time from work, coming all the way up here. He took off his glasses, washed his face, then looked at his reflection in the mirror. It was the face of a sick man. Maybe he'd already caught the virus. He gulped down the whiskey-and-water he'd just made and fixed himself another.

Returning from the dining room, Asakawa noticed a notebook on the shelf beneath the telephone stand. The cover said *Memories*. He leafed through a few pages.

Saturday, April 7

Nonko will never forget this day. Why? That's a s-e-c-r-e-t.

Yuichi is wonderful. Hee-hee! ❤

NONKO

Inns, B&B's, and the like often had notebooks like this in the rooms, so that guests could write down their memories and impressions. On the next page was a crude drawing of mommy and daddy. Must have been a family trip. It was dated April 14th—also a Saturday, naturally.

Daddys fat,
Mommys fat,
So Im fat too.
Aprul 14nth

Asakawa kept turning pages. He could feel some sort of force urging him to open the pages at the end of the book, but he kept going through them in order. He was afraid that if he messed up the chronology he might miss something.

He couldn't say for sure, since there were probably a lot of guests who didn't write anything, but it seemed like there were only people here on Saturdays until summer started. After that the time between each entry shrank. By the end of August there was a steady stream of entries lamenting the end of summer.

Sunday, August 20
Another summer vacation come and gone. And it sucked. Somebody help me! Rescue poor little me! I have a motorbike, 400cc. I'm pretty good-looking. A bargain!

A.Y.

This guy looked like he'd decided the guest book was a means to advertise himself, maybe find a pen-pal. It looked like a lot of people had the same ideas about the place. When couples stayed here, their entries showed it, while when single people stayed, they wrote about how much they wanted a companion.

Still, it made for interesting reading. Presently his watch showed nine o'clock.

Then he turned the page:

Thursday, August 30
Ulp! Consider yourself warned: you'd better not see it unless you've got the guts. You'll be sorry you did. (Evil laughter.)
S. I.

That was all there was to the message. August 30th was the morning after the four had stayed here. The initials "S.I." would stand for "Shuichi Iwata." His entry was different from all the rest. What did it mean? *You'd better not see it.* What in the world was *it*? Asakawa closed the guest book and looked at it from the side. There was a slight gap where it didn't close tightly. He put his finger there and opened it to that page. *Ulp! Consider yourself warned: you'd better not see it unless you've got the guts. You'll be sorry you did. (Evil laughter.) S.I.* The words jumped out at him. Why did the book want to open to this exact page? He thought for a moment. Perhaps the four had opened the book here and set something heavy on top of it. The weight had created this force that remained even now, trying to open to this page. And maybe whatever they'd placed on top of the page was the "it" that he'd "better not see." That must be it.

Asakawa looked around anxiously, searching every corner of

the shelf beneath the telephone stand. Nothing. Not even a pencil.

He sat back down on the sofa and continued reading. The next entry was dated Saturday, September 1st. But it said only the usual things. It didn't say if the group of students who had stayed here had seen *it*. None of the remaining pages mentioned it, either.

Asakawa closed the guest book and lit a cigarette. *...you'd better not see it unless you've got the guts*. He imagined that *it* must be something frightening. He opened the notebook at random and pressed down on the page lightly. Whatever it was must have been heavy enough to overcome the pages' tendency to close. One or two photos of ghosts, for example, wouldn't have done the trick. Maybe a weekly, or a hardcover book... Anyway, something you look at. Maybe he'd ask the manager if he remembered finding anything strange left in the cabin after the guests had checked out on August 30th. He wasn't sure if the manager would even remember, but he figured that if it had been strange enough he would. Asakawa began to get to his feet when the VCR in front of him caught his eye. The TV was still on, showing a famous actress chasing her husband around with a vacuum. A home appliance commercial.

...Yeah, a VHS tape would be heavy enough to keep the notebook open, and they might have had one handy, too.

Still in a crouch, Asakawa ground out his cigarette. He recalled the video collection he had seen in the manager's office. Maybe they'd happened to watch a particularly interesting horror flick, and thought they'd recommend it to the next guests—*hey, this one's cool, check it out*. If that's all it was... But wait. If that was it, why hadn't Shuichi Iwata used the name? If he wanted to tell somebody that, say, *Friday the 13th* was a great movie, wouldn't it have been easier just to say *Friday the 13th* was a great movie? He didn't need to go to all the trouble of actually leaving it on top of the notebook. So maybe *it* was something that didn't have a name, something they could only indicate with the word *it*.

...Well? Worth checking out?

Well, he certainly didn't have anything to lose, not with no other clues presenting themselves. Besides, sitting around here thinking wasn't getting him anywhere. Asakawa left the cabin, climbed the stone steps and pushed open the office door.

Just as before, there was no sign of the manager at the counter, only the sound of the television coming from the back room. The guy had retired from his job in the city and decided to live out his years surrounded by Mother Nature, so he'd taken a job as a manager at a resort, but the work turned out to be utterly boring, and now all he did every day was watch videos. That's how Asakawa interpreted the manager's situation. Before he had a chance to call the guy, though, he crawled to the doorway and stuck his head out. Asakawa spoke somewhat apologetically.

"I thought I'd maybe borrow a video after all."

The manager grinned happily. "Go right ahead, whichever you'd like. They're three hundred yen each."

Asakawa scanned the titles for scary-looking movies. *The Legend of Hell House, The Exorcist, The Omen*. He had seen them all in his student days. *Nothing else?* There had to be some he hadn't seen. He searched from one end of the shelves to the other, and saw nothing that looked likely. He started over, reading the titles of every one of the two hundred or so videos. And then, on the very bottom shelf, way over in the corner, he noticed a video without a case, fallen over on its side. All the other tapes were encased in jackets with photos and imposing logos, but this one lacked even a label.

"What's that there?" After he'd asked the question, Asakawa realized that he'd used a pronoun, *that*, as he pointed to the tape. If it didn't have a name, what else was he supposed to call it?

The manager gave a bothered frown and replied, none too brightly, "Huh?" Then he picked up the tape. "This? This isn't anything."

...Hey, I wonder if this guy even knows what's on that tape.

"Have you seen it? That one," asked Asakawa.

"Let me see." The manager cocked his head repeatedly, as if he couldn't figure out what something like this was doing here.

"If you don't mind, could I borrow that tape?"

Instead of replying, the manager slapped his knee. "Ah, I remember now. It was kicking around in one of the rooms. I just figured it was one of ours and brought it here, but..."

"This wouldn't have happened to be in B-4, I don't suppose?" Asakawa asked slowly, pressing the point home. The manager laughed and shook his head.

"I haven't the foggiest. It was a couple of months ago."

Asakawa asked once more, "Have you...seen...this video?"

The manager just shook his head. The smile disappeared from his face. "No."

"Well, let me rent it."

"You going to record something on the TV?"

"Yeah, well, I, ah..."

The manager glanced at the video. "The tab is broken. See? You can't record on it."

Maybe it was the alcohol, but Asakawa was getting irritated. *I'm telling you to rent it to me, you idiot, just hand it over*, he griped to himself. But no matter how drunk he was, Asakawa was never able to come on very strong with other people.

"Please. I'll bring it right back."

He bowed. The manager couldn't figure out why his guest was showing so much interest in this old thing. Maybe there was something *interesting* on it, something somebody had forgotten to erase.... Now he wished he'd watched it when he found it. He felt the sudden temptation to watch it right now, but he couldn't very well refuse now that a guest had asked for it. The manager handed over the tape. Asakawa reached for his wallet, but the manager stopped him with his hand.

"That's alright, you don't need to pay. I can't charge you for this, now, can I?"

"Thanks a lot. I'll bring it right back."

"If it turns out to be interesting, then please do!" The manager's curiosity had been piqued. He'd already seen every video here at least once, and most of them had ceased to interest him. How did I miss that one anyway? *It would have killed a few hours. Aw, but it probably only has some stupid TV show recorded on it anyway.*

The manager was sure the video would come back right away.

2

The tape had been rewound. It was an ordinary 120 minute tape, the sort you could get anywhere, and, as the manager had pointed out, the anti-erasure tabs had been broken off. Asakawa turned on the VCR and pushed the tape into the slot. He sat down cross-legged right in front of the screen and pushed play. He heard the capstans start to turn. He had high hopes that the key to unlock the riddle of four people's deaths was hidden on this tape. He'd pushed play fully intending to be satisfied with just a clue, any clue. There can't be any danger, he was thinking. What harm could come from just watching a videotape?

Random sounds and distorted images flickered on the screen, but once he had selected the right channel, the picture steadied. Then the screen went black as ink. This was the video's first scene. There was no sound. Wondering if it had broken, he brought his face close to the screen. *Consider yourself warned: you'd better not see it. You'll be sorry you did.* Shuichi Iwata's words came back to him. Why should he be sorry? Asakawa was used to things like this. He'd covered the local news. No matter what sort of horrific images he might be shown, he felt confident he wouldn't regret watching.

In the middle of the black screen he thought he saw a pinpoint of light begin to flicker. It gradually expanded, jumping around to the left and right, before finally coming to rest on the left-hand side. Then it branched out, becoming a frayed bundle of lights, crawling around like worms, which finally formed themselves into words. Not the kind of captions one normally saw on film, though. These were poorly-written, as if scrawled by a white brush on jet-black paper. Somehow, though, he managed to make out what they said: *WATCH UNTIL THE END*. A command. These words disappeared, and the next floated up into view. *YOU WILL BE EATEN BY THE LOST...* The last word didn't make much sense, but being eaten didn't sound too pleasant. It seemed that there must have been an "or else" implied there. Don't turn off the video halfway through, or else something awful will happen: it was a threat.

YOU WILL BE EATEN BY THE LOST... The words grew larger and chased all the black from the screen. It was a flat change, from black to milk-white. It was a patchy, unnatural color, and it began to resemble a series of concepts painted on a canvas, one over another. The unconscious, squirming, worrying, finding an exit, spurting out—or maybe it was the throb of life. Thought had energy, bestially satiating itself on darkness. Strangely, he felt no desire to push stop. Not because he was unafraid of whatever wanted to eat him, but because this intense outpouring of energy felt good.

Something red burst onto the monochrome screen. At the same time he heard the ground rumble, from an indefinable direction. The sound seemed to come from everywhere, such that he began to imagine that the whole cabin was shaking. It didn't feel like the sound was coming from those little speakers. The sluggish red fluid exploded and flew about, sometimes occupying the whole screen. From black to white, and now red... It was nothing but a violent succession of colors, he hadn't seen any natural scenery yet. Just concepts in the abstract, etched vividly into his brain by the brilliantly shifting colors. It was tiring, actually. And then, as if it had read the viewer's mind, the red retreated from the screen, and a mountain vista stretched out on-screen. At one glance he could tell it was a volcano, with a gentle peak. The volcano was sending up white puffs of smoke against a clear blue sky. The camera seemed to be situated somewhere at the foot of the mountain, where the ground was covered with rugged blackish-brown lava.

Again the screen was swathed in darkness. The clear blue sky was instantaneously painted black, and then, a few seconds later, a scarlet liquid spurted out from the center of the screen, flowing downward. A second explosion. The spray thrown up by it burned red, and as a result he could begin to make out, faintly, the outline of the mountain. The images were now concrete where they had previously been abstract. This was clearly a volcanic eruption, a natural phenomenon, a scene that could be explained. The molten lava flowing from the mouth of the volcano threaded its way down through ravines and headed this way. Where was the camera positioned? Unless it was an aerial shot, it looked like the camera was about to be swallowed up. The rumblings of the earth increased until the whole screen seemed about to be engulfed in molten rock, and then the scene abruptly changed. There was no continuity from one scene to the next, only sudden shifts.

Thick, black letters floated into view against a white background. Their edges were blurred, but he somehow managed to make out the character for "mountain." It was surrounded by black splatters, as if it had been written sloppily by a brush dripping with ink. The character was motionless, the screen was calm.

Another sudden shift. A pair of dice, tumbling around in the rounded bottom of a lead bowl. The background was white, the bottom of the bowl was black, and the one on the dice was red. The same three colors he'd seen so often already. The dice rolled around soundlessly, finally coming to rest: a one and a five. The single red dot and the five black ones arranged on the white faces of the dice... What did it mean?

In the next scene people appeared for the first time. An old woman, face lined with wrinkles, sat perched on a pair of tatami mats on a wooden floor. Her hands rested on her knees and her left shoulder was thrust slightly forward. She was speaking, slowly, looking straight ahead. Her eyes were different sizes—when she blinked, it looked like she was winking instead.

She was speaking in an unfamiliar dialect, and he could only catch every other word or so:

...your health...since...spend all your time...bound to get you. Understand? Be careful of...you're going to...you listen to granny now because...there's no need to....

The old expressionless woman made her statement, then vanished. There were a lot of words he didn't understand. But he had the impression he'd just been lectured to. She was telling him to be careful of something, warning him. Who was this old lady talking to—and about?

The face of a newborn baby filled the screen. From somewhere he could hear a baby's first cry. This time, too, he was sure it didn't come from the television speakers. It came from very near, beneath his face. It was very like a real voice. On-screen, he could now see hands holding the baby. The left hand was under its head, and the right was behind its back, holding it carefully. They were beautiful hands. Totally absorbed by the image, Asakawa found himself holding his own hands in the same position. He heard the birth cry directly below his own chin. Startled, he pulled back his hands. He had felt something. Something warm and wet—like amniotic fluid, or blood—and the weight of flesh. Asakawa jerked his hands apart, as if casting something aside, and brought his palms close to his face. A smell lingered. The faint smell of blood—had it come from the womb, or...? His hands felt wet. But in reality, they weren't even damp. He restored his gaze to the screen. It still showed the baby's face. In spite of the crying its face was swathed in a peaceful expression, and the shaking of its body had spread to its groin, even wiggling its little thing.

The next scene: a hundred human faces. Each one displayed hatred and animosity; he couldn't see any distinguishing features other than that. The myriad faces, looking as if they had been painted on a flat surface, gradually receded into the depths of the screen. And as each face diminished in size, the total number increased, until they had swollen to a great multitude. It was a strange multitude, though—existing only from the neck up—but the sounds welling up from them befit a crowd. Their mouths were shouting something, even as they shrank and multiplied. He couldn't quite make out what they were saying. It sounded like the commotion of a great gathering, but the voices were tinged with criticism, abuse. The voices were clearly not welcoming or cheering. Finally he made out a word: *"Liar!"* And another: *"Fraud!"* By now there were perhaps a thousand faces: they had become nothing but black particles, filling the screen until it looked like the television had been turned off, but the voices continued. It was more than Asakawa could bear. All that criticism, directed right at him. That's how it felt.

When the next scene appeared, it showed a television on a wooden stand. It was an old-fashioned nineteen-inch set with a round channel selector, and a rabbit-ear antenna sat on its wooden cabinet. Not a play within a play, but a TV within a TV. The television within had nothing on its screen yet. But it seemed to be on: the red light by the channel knob was lit. Then the screen-within-the-screen wavered. It stabilized and then wavered again, over and over, with increasing frequency. Then a single character appeared, hazily: *sada*. The word faded in and out of focus, distorted, and began to look like another before disappearing altogether, like chalk on a blackboard wiped with a wet rag.

As he watched, Asakawa began to find it hard to breathe. He could hear his heart beat, feel the pressure of the blood flowing in his veins. A smell, a touch, a sour-sweet taste stabbing his tongue. Strange—something was stimulating his five senses, some medium besides the sounds and visions that appeared as if he were suddenly recalling them.

Then the face of a man appeared. Unlike the previous images, this man was definitely alive—he had a pulsating vitality. As he watched, Asakawa began to feel hatred toward him. He had no idea why he should hate this man. He wasn't particularly ugly. His forehead sloped a bit, but other than that he was actually rather well-formed. But there was something dangerous in his eyes. They were the eyes of a beast closing in on its prey. The man's face was sweaty. His breathing was ragged, his gaze was turned upward, and his body was moving rhythmically. Behind the man grew scattered trees, the afternoon sunlight shone between their branches. The man brought his eyes down and looked straight ahead again, and his gaze locked with the viewer's. Asakawa and the man stared at each other for a while. The stifling sensation grew, and he suddenly wanted to tear his gaze away. The man was drooling; his eyes were bloodshot. His neck muscles began to fill the screen in a close-up, then disappeared off the left side of the screen. For a while only the black shade of the trees could be seen. A scream began to well up from deep down inside. At the same time, the man's shoulder came back into view, then his neck, and finally his face again. His shoulders were bare, and the right one carried a deep, bloody gash several centimeters long. Drops of blood seemed to be sucked toward the camera, growing larger and larger until they hit the lens and clouded over the view. The screen cut to black once, twice, almost like blinking, and when the light returned everything was red. There was a murderous look in the man's eyes. His face drew closer, along with his shoulder, the bone peeking out white where the flesh had been gouged out. Asakawa felt a violent pressure on his chest. He saw trees again. The sky was spinning. The color of the sky fading into sunset, the rustling of dry grass. He saw dirt, then weeds, and then sky again. Somewhere he heard a baby crying. He wasn't sure if it was the little infant from before. Finally, the edge of the screen turned black, darkness gradually encroaching in a ring on the center. Dark and light were clearly defined now. At the center of the screen, a small round moon of light floated in the middle of the darkness. There was a man's face in the moon. A fist-sized clump of something fell from the moon, making a dull thud. Another, and then another. With each sound, the image jumped and swayed. The sound of flesh being smashed, and then true darkness. Even then, a pulse remained. Blood still circulated, throbbing. The scene went on and on. A darkness that seemed as if it would never end. Then, just as at the beginning, words faded into view. The writing in the first scene had been crude, like that of a child just learning to write, but this was somewhat better. White letters, drifting into view and then fading, read:

Those who have viewed these images are fated to die at this exact hour one week from now. If you do not wish to die, you must follow these instructions exactly....

Asakawa gulped and stared wide-eyed at the television. But then the scene changed yet again. A complete and utter change. A commercial came on, a perfectly ordinary, common television commercial. A romantic old neighborhood on a summer's evening, an actress in a light cotton robe sitting on her verandah, fireworks lighting up the night sky. A commercial for mosquito-repelling coils. After about thirty seconds the commercial ended, and just as another scene was about to start, the screen returned to its previous state. Darkness, with the last afterglow of faded words. Then the sound of static as the tape ended.

Bug-eyed, Asakawa rewound the tape and replayed the last scene. The same sequence repeated itself: a commercial interrupted at the most important point. Asakawa stopped the video and turned off the television. But he kept staring at the screen. His throat was parched.

"What the hell?"

There was nothing else to say. One unintelligible scene after another, and the only thing he'd comprehended was that anybody who watched would die in exactly a week. And the part which told how to avoid this fate had been taped over with a commercial.

...Who erased it? Those four?

Asakawa's jaw quivered. If he didn't know that the four young people had died simultaneously, he could have laughed this off as sheer nonsense. But he knew. They had died, mysteriously, as predicted.

At that moment the phone rang. Asakawa's heart nearly

jumped out of his chest at the sound. He picked up the receiver. He felt as though *something* were concealing itself, watching him from the darkness.

"Hello," he finally managed to croak. There was no reply. Something was swirling around in a dark, cramped place. There was a deep rumble, as if the earth were resounding, and the damp smell of earth. There was a chill at his ear, and the hairs on the nape of his neck stood up. The pressure on his chest increased, and bugs from the bowels of the earth were crawling on his ankles and his spine, clinging to him. Unspeakable thoughts and long-ripened hatred almost reached him through the receiver. Asakawa slammed down the receiver. Covering his mouth, he ran to the bathroom. Chills ran up and down his backbone, waves of nausea swept over him: the thing on the other end of the line hadn't said anything, but Asakawa knew what it wanted. It was a confirmation call.

You've seen it now, you know what that means. Do like it said. Or else...

Asakawa vomited over the toilet. He didn't have much to throw up. The whiskey he'd drunk earlier flowed out of him now, mixed with bile. The bitterness seeped into his eyes, squeezing out tears; it hurt his nose. But he felt that if he threw up everything now, here, maybe the images he'd just watched would go flowing out of him, too.

"If I don't, what? I *don't* know! What do you want me to do? Huh? What am I supposed to do?"

He sat on the bathroom floor and yelled, trying not to give in to his fear. "Look, those four erased it, the important part.... I don't understand it! Help me out here!"

All he could do was make excuses. Asakawa jumped back from

the toilet, not even realizing how awful he looked, and looked around the room in every direction, bowing his head in supplication to whatever might be there. He didn't realize that he was trying to look pathetic, to draw sympathy. Asakawa stood up and rinsed his mouth at the sink, swallowing some water. He felt a breeze. He looked at the living room window. The curtains were trembling.

Hey, I thought I shut that.

He was certain that before drawing the curtains he'd shut the sliding glass door tightly. He remembered doing it. He couldn't stop trembling. For no reason at all, the image of skyscrapers at night flashed across his brain, the way the lighted and unlighted windows formed a checkerboard pattern, sometimes even forming characters. If you saw the buildings as huge, oblong tombstones, then the lights were epitaphs. The image disappeared, but the white lace curtains still danced in the breeze.

In a frenzy, Asakawa grabbed his bag from the closet and threw his things inside. He couldn't stay here one second longer.

I don't care what anybody says. If I stay here I won't last the night, forget about the week.

Still in his sweats, he stepped down into the entryway. He tried to think rationally before going outside. *Don't just run away in fear, try to figure out some way to save yourself!* An instantaneous survival instinct: he went back into the living room and pushed the eject button. He wrapped the videotape tightly in a bath towel and stowed it in his bag. The tape was his only clue, he couldn't afford to leave it behind. Maybe if he figured out the riddle as to how the scenes were connected he'd find a way to save himself. No matter what, he only had a week left. He looked at his watch: 10:18. He was sure he'd finished watching at 10:04.

Suddenly, the time seemed quite important to him. Asakawa left the key on the table and went out, leaving all the lights on. He ran to his car, not even stopping by the office first, and jammed his key in the ignition.

"I can't do this alone. *I'll have to ask him to help.*" Talking to himself, Asakawa put the car in motion, but he couldn't help glancing in the rear-view mirror. No matter how he floored it, he couldn't seem to get up any speed. It was like being chased in a dream, running in slow-motion. Over and over he looked at the mirror. But the black shadow chasing him was nowhere to be seen.

PART THREE *Gusts*

1

October 12—Friday

"First let's have a look at this video."

Ryuji Takayama grinned as he spoke. They sat on the second floor of a coffee shop near Roppongi Crossing. Friday, October 12th, 7:20 p.m. Almost twenty-four hours had passed since Asakawa had watched the video. He'd chosen to have this meeting on a Friday night in Roppongi, the city's premier entertainment district, in the hopes that, surrounded by the gay voices of girls, his dread would dissipate. It didn't seem to be working. The more he talked about it, the more vividly the events of the previous night replayed themselves in his mind. The terror only increased. He even thought he sensed, fleetingly, a shadow lurking somewhere within his body that possessed him.

Ryuji's dress shirt was buttoned all the way up to the top, and his tie seemed rather tight, but he made no move to loosen it. As a result, the skin of his neck above his collar was slightly swollen—just looking at it was uncomfortable. Then there were his angular features. Even his smile would have struck your average person as being somehow nasty.

Ryuji took an ice cube from his glass and popped it into his mouth.

"Weren't you listening to what I just said?" hissed Asakawa. "I told you, it's dangerous."

"Then what did you bring this to me for? You want my help, don't you?" Still smiling, he crunched the ice cube loudly between his teeth.

"There're still ways for you to help without watching it."

Ryuji hung his head sulkily, but a faint grin still played over his features.

Asakawa was suddenly seized with anger and raised his voice hysterically. "You don't believe me, do you? You don't believe a thing I've been telling you!" There was no other way for him to interpret Ryuji's expression.

For Asakawa himself, watching the video had been like unsuspectingly opening a letter-bomb. It was the first time in his life he'd experienced such terror. And it wasn't over. Six more days. Fear tightened softly around his neck like a silken noose. Death awaited him. And this joker actually *wanted* to watch the video.

"You don't have to make a scene. So I'm not scared—do you have a problem with that? Listen, Asakawa, I've told you before: I'm the kind of guy who'd get front-row seats for the end of the world if he could. I want to know how the world is put together, its beginning and its end, all its riddles, great and small. If someone offered to explain them all to me, I'd gladly trade my life for the knowledge. You even immortalized me in print. I'm sure you recall."

Of course Asakawa remembered it. That's exactly why he'd opened up to Ryuji and told him everything.

It had been Asakawa who first dreamed up the feature. Two years ago, when he was thirty, he had begun to wonder what other young Japanese people his age were really thinking—what dreams they had in life. The idea was to pick out several thirty-year-olds, people active in all walks of life—from a MITI bureaucrat and a Tokyo city councilman to a guy working for a top trading firm to regular, average Joes—and summarize each one, from the sort of general data every reader would want to know to their more unique aspects. By doing this regularly, in a carefully limited area of newsprint, he would try to analyze what it meant to be thirty in contemporary Japan. And just by chance, among the ten to twenty names that had surfaced as candidates for this kind of treatment, Asakawa encountered an old high school classmate, Ryuji Takayama. His official position was listed as Adjunct Lecturer in Philosophy at Fukuzawa University, one of the nation's top private schools. Asakawa found this puzzling, as he recalled Ryuji going on to medical school. Asakawa himself had done the groundwork, and had listed scholar as one of the vocations to be included in his survey, but Ryuji was far too much of an individual to be a fair representative of thirty-year-old budding scholars as a whole. His personality had been hard to get a handle on in high school, and with the added polishing of the intervening years it seemed it had only gotten more slippery. Upon finishing medical school, he had enrolled in a graduate philosophy program, completing his Ph.D. the year of the survey. He undoubtedly would have been snapped up for the first available assistant professorship if it weren't for the unfortunate fact that there were older students in the pipeline ahead of him, and positions were awarded strictly on the basis of seniority. So he took the part-time lecturer's job and ended up teaching two classes a week on logic at his alma mater.

These days, philosophy as a field of inquiry had drawn ever closer to science. No longer did it mean amusing oneself with silly questions such as how man should live. Specializing in philosophy meant, basically, doing math without the numbers. In ancient

Greece, too, philosophers doubled as mathematicians. Ryuji was like that: the philosophy department signed his paychecks, but his brain was wired like a scientist's. On the other hand, in addition to his specialized professional knowledge, he also knew an extraordinary amount about paranormal psychology. Asakawa saw this as a contradiction. He considered paranormal psychology, the study of the supernatural and the occult, to be in direct opposition to science. Ryuji's answer: *Au contraire. Paranormal psychology is one of the keys to unlocking the structure of the universe.* It had been a hot day in the middle of summer, but just like today he'd been wearing a striped long-sleeved dress shirt with the top button buttoned tightly. *I want to be there when humanity is wiped out,* Ryuji had said, sweat gleaming on his overheated face. *All those idiots who prattle on about world peace and the survival of humanity make me puke.*

Asakawa's survey had included questions like this:

Tell me about your dreams for the future.

Calmly, Ryuji had replied: "While viewing the extinction of the human race from the top of a hill, I would dig a hole in the earth and ejaculate into it over and over."

Asakawa had pressed him: "Hey, are you sure it's okay for me to write that down?"

Ryuji had just smiled faintly, just like he was doing now, and nodded.

"Like I said, I'm not afraid of anything." After saying this, Ryuji leaned over and brought his face close to Asakawa's.

"I did another one last night."

Again?

This made the third victim Asakawa knew about. He'd learned of the first one in their junior year in high school. Both of them had lived in Tama Ward in Kawasaki, an industrial city wedged between Tokyo and Yokohama, and commuted to a prefectural high school. Asakawa used to get to school an hour before classes started every morning and preview the day's lessons in the crisp dawn. Aside from the janitors, he was always the first one there. By contrast, Ryuji hardly ever made it to first period. He was what was known as habitually tardy. But one morning right after the end of summer vacation, Asakawa went to school early as usual and found Ryuji there, sitting on top of his desk as if in a daze. Asakawa spoke to him. "Hey, what's up? Didn't think I'd see you here this early." "Yeah, well," was the curt reply: Ryuji was staring out the window at the schoolyard, as if his mind were somewhere else. His eyes were bloodshot. His cheeks were red, too, and there was alcohol on his breath. They weren't that close, though, so that was as far as the conversation went. Asakawa opened his schoolbook and began to study. "Hey, listen, I want to ask you a favor..." said Ryuji, slapping him on the shoulder. Ryuji was highly individualistic, got good grades, and was a track star as well. Everybody at school kept one eye on him. Asakawa, meanwhile, was thoroughly unremarkable. Having someone like Ryuji ask him a favor didn't feel bad at all.

"Actually, I want you to call my house for me," said Ryuji, laying his arm on Asakawa's shoulders in an overly familiar manner.

"Sure. But why?"

"All you have to do is call. Call and ask for me."

Asakawa frowned. "For you? But you're right here."

"Never mind that, just do it, okay?"

So he did as he was told and dialed the number, and when Ryuji's mother answered he said, "Is Ryuji there?" while looking at Ryuji, who stood right in front of him.

"I'm sorry, Ryuji has already left for school," his mother said calmly.

"Oh, I see," Asakawa said, and hung up the phone. "There, is that good enough?" he said to Ryuji. Asakawa still didn't quite get the meaning of all this.

"Did it sound like there was anything wrong?" asked Ryuji. "Did Mom sound nervous or anything?"

"No, not particularly." Asakawa had never heard Ryuji's mother's voice before, but he didn't think she sounded especially nervous.

"No excited voices in the background or anything?"

"No. Nothing special. Nothing like that. Just, like, breakfast table sounds."

"Well, okay, then. Thanks."

"Hey, what's going on? Why did you ask me to do that?"

Ryuji looked vaguely relieved. He put his arm around Asakawa's shoulders and pulled Asakawa's face close. He put his mouth to Asakawa's ear and said, "You seem like you can keep a secret, like I can trust you. So I'll tell you. As a matter of fact, at five o'clock this morning, I raped a woman."

Asakawa was shocked speechless. The story was that at dawn that morning, around five, Ryuji had sneaked into the apartment of a college girl living alone and attacked her. As he left he threatened her that if she called the cops he wouldn't take it lying down, and then he came straight to school. As a result he was worried that the police might be at his house right about now, and so he'd asked Asakawa to call for him to check.

After that, Asakawa and Ryuji began to talk fairly often. Naturally, Asakawa never told anyone about Ryuji's crime. The following year Ryuji had come in third in the shot-put in the area high-school track and field meet, and the year after that he'd entered the medical program at Fukuzawa University. Asakawa spent that year studying to retake the entrance exam for the school of his choice, having failed the first time. The second time he succeeded, and was accepted into the literature department of a well-known university.

Asakawa knew what he really wanted. In truth, he wanted Ryuji to watch the video. Ryuji's knowledge and experience wouldn't be of much use to Asakawa if they were based only on what Asakawa was able to verbalize about the video. On the other hand, he saw that it was ethically wrong to get someone else wrapped up in this just to save his own skin. He was conflicted, but he knew if he had to weigh the two options which way the scale would tip. He wanted to maximize his own chances of survival, no question. But, still... He suddenly found himself wondering, like he always did, just why he was friends with this guy. His ten years of reporting for the newspaper company had allowed him to meet countless people. But he and Ryuji could just call each other up anytime to go have a drink—Ryuji was the only one Asakawa had that kind of relationship with. Was it because they happened to have been classmates? No, he had plenty of other classmates. There was something in the depths of his heart that resonated with Ryuji's eccentricity. At that thought, Asakawa began to feel like he didn't really understand himself.

"Hey, hey. Let's get a move on. You've only got six days left, right?" Ryuji grabbed Asakawa's upper arm and squeezed it. His grip was strong. "Hurry up and show me that video. Think how lonely I'll be if you bite the dust because we dawdled."

Rhythmically squeezing Asakawa's arm with one hand, Ryuji jabbed his fork into his untouched cheesecake, shoveled it into his mouth and began to chew noisily. Ryuji had the habit of chewing with his mouth open. Asakawa felt himself beginning to get sick at the sight of the food mixing with saliva and dissolving before his eyes. His angular features, his squat build, his bad habits. Now, while still munching away on his cheesecake, he fished more ice out of the glass with his hand and started crunching it, making even more noise.

That's when Asakawa realized that he had no one else he could rely on but this guy.

It's an evil spirit I'm dealing with, an unknown quantity. Nobody normal could deal with it. There's probably nobody but Ryuji who could watch that video and not bat an eye. Set a thief to catch a thief. There's no way around it. What do I care if Ryuji ends up dead? Someone who says he wants to watch the extinction of mankind doesn't deserve to live a long life.

That was how Asakawa rationalized getting someone else wrapped up in this.

2

The two men headed for Asakawa's place in a taxi. If the streets weren't crowded it took less than twenty minutes to get from Roppongi to Kita Shinagawa. All they could see in the mirror was the driver's forehead. He maintained a resolute silence, one hand on the wheel, and didn't try to start up a conversation with his passengers. Come to think of it, this whole thing had started with a talkative cabby. If he hadn't caught a taxi that time he wouldn't have gotten caught up in this whole horrific mess, Asakawa thought as he recalled the events of half a month ago. He regretted not having bought a subway ticket and made all those transfers anyway, no matter how much of a pain in the neck they were.

"Can we make a copy of the video at your place?" asked Ryuji. Asakawa had two video decks because of his work. One was a machine he'd bought when they had first started to catch on, and it wasn't functioning as well as it could, but it did at least make copies with no problem.

"Yeah, sure."

"Okay, in that case I want you to make me a copy as soon as possible. I want to take my time and study it at my place."

He's got the guts, thought Asakawa. And in his present state of mind, Asakawa found his words encouraging.

They decided to get out of the cab at Gotenzan Hills and walk from there. It was 8:50. There was still the possibility that his wife and kid would be awake at this hour. Shizu always gave Yoko a bath at a little before nine, and then put her to bed. She'd lie down beside the baby to help her get to sleep, and in the process would fall asleep herself. And once she went to sleep, nothing was going to get Shizu out of bed. In an effort to maximize time talking alone with her husband, Shizu used to leave messages on the table saying "wake me up." So when he got home from work, Asakawa would follow her instructions, thinking she really meant to get up, and try to shake his wife awake. But she wouldn't wake up. He would try harder, but she would just wave her hands around her head like she was shooing a fly, frowning and making annoyed sounds. She was half awake, but the will to go back to sleep was much stronger than Asakawa was, and he eventually had to cut his losses and retreat. Eventually, note or no, Asakawa stopped trying to wake her up, and then she stopped leaving notes. By now, nine o'clock had become Shizu 'n' Yoko's inviolate sleepytime. On a night like this, though, it was actually more convenient that way.

Shizu hated Ryuji. Asakawa thought this was an eminently reasonable attitude, so he never even asked her why. *I'm begging you, don't bring him into our home anymore.* Asakawa still remembered the repugnance on his wife's face when she said that. But most of all, he couldn't play this video in front of Shizu and Yoko.

The house was dark and still, and the fragrance of hot bath water and soap wafted even out to the entry hall. Evidently mommy and baby had just now gone to bed, towels under their wet hair. Asakawa put his ear to the bedroom door to make sure they were asleep, and then showed Ryuji into the dining room.

"So the baby's gone night-night?" Ryuji asked with an air of disappointment.

"Shhh," said Asakawa, putting a finger to his lips. Shizu wasn't going to wake up from something like that, but then again he couldn't swear she wouldn't sense that something was different from usual and come out after all.

Asakawa connected the output jacks of one of the video decks to the input jacks of the other, and then inserted the video. Before pressing play, he looked at Ryuji as if to say, do you really want to do this?

"What's wrong? Hurry up and play it," urged Ryuji, without taking his eyes off the screen. Asakawa pressed the remote into Ryuji's hand and then stood up and went to the window. He didn't feel like watching. In reality he should watch it over and over, analyzing it cool-headedly, but he couldn't seem to find the will to chase this thing any further. He just wanted to run away. Nothing more. Asakawa went out onto the balcony and smoked a cigarette. He'd promised his wife when Yoko was born that he wouldn't smoke inside the apartment, and he'd never broken that promise. Although they'd been married for a full three years, he and his wife had a relatively good relationship. He couldn't go against his wife's wishes, not after she'd given him darling Yoko.

Standing on the balcony, he peered into the room: through the frosted glass, the image on the screen was flickering. The fear quotient was different watching it here, tentatively surrounded by three people on the sixth floor of a downtown apartment building, compared to watching it alone at Villa Log Cabin. But even if Ryuji watched it under the same conditions, he probably wouldn't lose his head and start crying or anything. Asakawa was counting on him to laugh and fling abuse as he watched, even turning a menacing gaze toward what he saw on the screen.

Asakawa finished his cigarette and went to go back inside. Just at that moment, the door separating the dining room from the hall opened, and Shizu appeared in her pajamas. Flustered, Asakawa grabbed the remote and stopped the video.

"I thought you were asleep." There was a note of reproach in Asakawa's voice.

"I heard noises." As she said this Shizu looked back and forth between the TV screen, with its distorted images and staticky sound, and Ryuji and Asakawa. Her face clouded over with suspicion.

"Go back to bed!" said Asakawa in a tone of voice that allowed for no questions.

"I think we ought to let the missus join us, if she'd like to. It's quite interesting." Ryuji, still seated cross-legged on the floor, looked up. Asakawa wanted to yell at him. But instead of speaking, he balled all his thoughts up into his fist and slammed it down onto the table. Startled by the sound, Shizu quickly put her hand on the doorknob, then narrowed her eyes and bowed ever-so-slightly and said to Ryuji, "Please make yourself at home." With that she turned on her heel and disappeared back behind the door. Two guys alone at night, turning videos on and off... Asakawa knew just what his wife was imagining. He didn't miss the look of disdain in her narrowed eyes—disdain not so much for Ryuji as for male instincts in general. Asakawa felt bad that he couldn't explain.

Just as Asakawa had expected, Ryuji was still utterly calm after he'd finished watching. He hummed as he rewound the tape, then set about checking it point by point, alternately fast-forwarding and pausing it.

"Well, it looks like yours truly is mixed up in it now. You've got six days left, I've got seven," said Ryuji happily, as if he'd been allowed to join in a game.

"So what do you think?" asked Asakawa.

"It's child's play."

"Huh?"

"Didn't you use to do this sort of thing when you were a kid? Scare your friends by showing them a spooky picture or something and saying that whoever looked at it would come to harm? Chain letters, that sort of thing."

Of course Asakawa had experienced that kind of thing, too. The same sort of thing had come up in the ghost stories they'd told each other on summer nights.

"So what are you getting at?"

"Nothing, I guess. Just, that's how it felt to me."

"Was there anything else you noticed? Tell me."

"Hmm. Well, the images themselves aren't especially frightening. It seems like a combination of realistic images and abstract ones. If it wasn't for the fact that four people had died exactly as dictated in the video, we could just snort and pass it off as an oddity. Right?"

Asakawa nodded. Knowing that the words on the video were no lie was what made the whole thing so troublesome.

"The first question is, why did those poor fools die? What's the reason? I can think of two possibilities. The last scene on the video is the statement, 'he who watches this is fated to die,' and then immediately thereafter, there was...well, for lack of a better word, let's call it a charm. A way to escape that fate. So the four erased the part that explained the charm, and because of that they were killed. Or, perhaps they simply failed to make use of the charm, and that's why they were killed. I suppose even before that, though, we have to determine if it was really those four who erased the charm. It's possible that the charm had already been erased when they watched the video."

"How are we going to determine that? We can't just ask them, you know."

Asakawa got a beer from the refrigerator, poured a glassful, and set it in front of Ryuji.

"Just you watch." Ryuji replayed the end of the video, watching closely for the exact moment when the charm-erasing mosquito coil commercial ended. He paused the tape and began to advance it slowly, frame by frame. He'd go past it, rewind it, pause it, advance it again frame by frame.... Then, finally, just for a split second, the screen showed a scene of three people sitting around a table. For just the briefest second, the program which had been interrupted by the commercial was resuming. It was a late-night talk show broadcast nightly at eleven on one of the national networks. The gray-haired gent was a best-selling author, and he was joined by a lovely young woman and a young man whom they recognized as a traditional storyteller from the Osaka region. Asakawa brought his face close to the screen.

"I'm sure you recognize this show," said Ryuji.

"It's *The Night Show* on NBS."

"Right. The writer is the host, the girl is his foil, and the storyteller is today's guest. Therefore, if we know what day the storyteller was a guest on the show, we know whether or not our four kids erased the charm."

"I get it."

The Night Show was on every weeknight at eleven. If this particular episode turned out to have been broadcast on August 29th, then it had to be those four who erased it, that night at Villa Log

Cabin.

"NBS is affiliated with your publisher, isn't it? This ought to be an easy one."

"Gotcha. I'll look into it."

"Yes, please do. Our lives may depend on it. Let's make sure of everything, no matter what. Right, my brother-in-arms?"

Ryuji slapped Asakawa on the shoulder. They were both facing their deaths now. Brothers in arms.

"Aren't you scared?"

"Scared? Au contraire, my friend. It's kind of exciting to have a deadline, isn't it? The penalty is death. Fantastic. It's no fun playing if you're not willing to bet your life on the outcome."

For a while now Ryuji had been acting pleased about the whole thing, but Asakawa had worried it was just bravado, a cover for his fear. Now that he peered into his friend's eyes, though, he couldn't find the smallest fragment of fear there.

"Next: we figure out who made this video, when, and to what end. You say Villa Log Cabin is only six months old, so we contact everybody who's stayed in B-4 and ferret out whoever brought in a videotape. I suppose it wouldn't hurt to limit the search to late August. Chances are it was somebody who stayed there right before our four victims."

"That's mine, too?"

Ryuji downed his beer in one swig and thought for a moment. "Of course. We've got a deadline. Don't you have a buddy you can rely on? If so, get him to help."

"Well, there is one reporter who's got an interest in this case. But this is a matter of life and death. I can't just..." Asakawa was thinking about Yoshino.

"Not to worry, not to worry. Get him involved. Show him the

video—that'll light a fire under his ass. He'll be happy to help out, trust me."

"Not everybody's like you, you know."

"So tell him it's black-market porn. Force him to watch it. Whatever."

It was no use reasoning with Ryuji. He couldn't show it to anybody without figuring out the charm first. Asakawa felt he was in a logical cul-de-sac. To crack the secrets of this video would require a well-organized search, but because of the nature of the video it would be next to impossible to enlist anybody. People like Ryuji, willing to play dice with death at the drop of hat, were few and far between. How would Yoshino react? He had a wife and kids himself—Asakawa doubted he'd be willing to risk his life just to satisfy his curiosity. But he might be able to help even without watching the video. Maybe Asakawa should tell him everything that had happened, just in case.

"Yeah. I'll give it a try."

Ryuji sat at the dining room table holding the remote.

"Right, then. Now, this falls into two broad categories: abstract scenes and real scenes." Saying this, he pulled up the volcanic eruption and paused the tape on it. "There, take that volcano. No matter how you look at it, that's real. We have to figure out what mountain that is. And then there's the eruption. Once we know the name of the mountain, we should be able to find out when it erupted, meaning we'll be able to ascertain when and where this scene was shot."

Ryuji unpaused the tape again. The old woman came on and started saying God knew what. Several of the words sounded like some sort of regional dialect.

"What dialect is that? There's a specialist in dialects at my university. I'll ask him about it. That'll give us some idea of where this old woman is from."

Ryuji fast-forwarded to the scene near the end with the man with the distinctive features. Sweat poured down his face, he was panting while rocking his body rhythmically. Ryuji paused just before the part where his shoulder was gouged. It was the closest view of the man's face. It was quite a clear shot of his features, from the set of his eyes to the shape of his nose and ears. His hairline was receding, but he looked to be around thirty.

"Do you recognize this man?" Ryuji asked.

"Don't be stupid."

"Looks faintly sinister."

"If you think so, then he must be pretty evil indeed. I'll defer to your opinion."

"As well you should. There aren't many faces that make this kind of an impact. I wonder if we can locate him? You're a reporter, you must be a pro at this sort of thing."

"Don't be funny. You might be able to identify criminals or celebrities by their faces alone, but ordinary people can't be located by face alone. There are over a hundred million people in Japan."

"So start with criminals. Or maybe porn actors."

Instead of answering, Asakawa took out a memo pad. When he had a lot of things to do he tended to make lists.

Ryuji stopped the video. He helped himself to another beer from the refrigerator and poured some into each of their glasses.

"Let's drink a toast."

Asakawa couldn't think of a single good reason to pick up his glass.

"I have a premonition," said Ryuji, his dirt-colored cheeks flushing slightly.

"There's a certain universal evil clinging to this incident. I can smell it—the impulse I felt then.... I told you about it, right? The first woman I raped."

"I haven't forgotten."

"It's already been fifteen years since then. Then, too, I felt a strange premonition tickling my heart. I was seventeen. It was September of my junior year in high school. I studied math until three in the morning, then did an hour of German to give my brain some rest. I always did that. I found language study was perfect for loosening up tired brain cells. At four, as always, I had a couple of beers and then went out for my daily walk. When I set out there was already something unusual budding in my brain. Have you ever walked around a residential neighborhood late at night? It feels really good. The dogs are all asleep. Just like your baby is now. I found myself in front of a certain apartment building. It was an elegant wood-framed two-story affair, and I knew that inside it lived a certain well-groomed college girl that I sometimes saw on the street. I didn't know which apartment was hers. I let my gaze roam over the windows of all eight apartments in turn. At this point, as I looked, I didn't have anything definite in mind. Just...you know. When my eyes came to rest on the southern end of the second floor, I heard something crack open in the depths of my heart, and I felt like the darkness that had sent forth its shoots in my mind was growing gradually larger. Once more I looked at all the windows in turn. Once again, in the same place, the darkness began to whirlpool. And I knew. I knew that the door wouldn't be locked. I don't know if she just forgot, or what. Guided by the darkness that was living in my heart I climbed the apartment stairs and stood in front of that door. The nameplate was in Roman letters, in Western order, given name first: YUKARI

MAKITA. I grasped the doorknob firmly with my right hand. I held onto it for a while, and then forcefully turned it to the left. It wouldn't turn. What the hell? I thought, and then suddenly, there was a click and the door opened. Are you with me? She hadn't forgotten to lock it at all: it unlocked itself at that very moment. Some energy was being exerted on it. The girl had spread her bedding beside her desk and gone to sleep. I had totally expected to find her in a bed, but she wasn't. One of her legs poked out from under the covers...."

Here Ryuji interrupted his story. He seemed to be replaying the ensuing events agilely in the back of his mind, staring down distant memories with a mixture of tenderness and cruelty. Asakawa had never seen Ryuji look so conflicted.

"...then, two days later, on my way home from school, I passed in front of that apartment building. A two-ton truck was parked in front of it, and guys were hauling furniture and stuff out of the building. And the person moving was Yukari. She was standing around aimlessly, leaning on a wall, accompanied by a guy who looked like he must be her dad, just staring at her furniture as it was being carried away. I'm sure her dad didn't know the real reason his daughter was moving so suddenly. And so Yukari disappeared from my life. I don't know if she moved back in with her parents or got another apartment somewhere and kept going to the same college.... But she just couldn't live in that apartment a second longer. Heh, heh, poor thing. She must've been awfully scared."

Asakawa found it hard to breathe as he listened. He felt disgusted even to be sitting here drinking beer with this man.

"Don't you feel the least bit guilty?"

"I'm used to it. Try slamming your fist into a brick wall every day. Eventually you won't even feel the pain anymore."

Is that why you go on doing it? Asakawa made a silent vow never to bring this man into his home again. At any rate, to keep him away from his wife and daughter.

"Don't worry—I'd never do anything like that to your babykins."

Asakawa had been seen through. Flustered, he changed the subject.

"You said you have a premonition. What is it?"

"You know, just a bad feeling. Only some fantastically evil energy could come up with such an involved bit of mischief."

Ryuji got to his feet. Even standing, he wasn't much taller than Asakawa was when sitting down. He wasn't even five-three, but he had broad, sculpted shoulders—it wasn't hard to believe he'd medalled in shot-put in high school.

"Well, I'm off. Do your homework. In the morning, you'll be down to five days left." Ryuji extended the fingers of one hand.

"I know."

"Somewhere, there's this vortex of evil energy. I know. It makes me feel...nostalgic." As if for emphasis, Ryuji clutched his copy of the tape to his breast as he headed for the entry hall.

"Let's have the next strategy session at your place." Asakawa spoke quietly but distinctly.

"Alright, alright." Ryuji's eyes were smiling.

The moment Ryuji left, Asakawa looked at the wall clock in the dining room. A wedding gift from a friend, its butterfly-shaped red pendulum was swinging. 11:21. How many times had he checked the time today? He was becoming obsessed with the passage of time. Just like Ryuji said, in the morning he'd only have five days left. He wasn't at all sure if he'd be able to unlock the riddle of the erased part of the tape in time. He felt like a cancer patient facing a surgery with a success rate of almost nil. There was debate over whether cancer patients should be told they had cancer or not; until now Asakawa had always thought they deserved to be allowed to know. But if this was how it would feel, then he preferred not knowing. There were some people who, when facing death, would burn brightly with what life they had left. Asakawa couldn't manage that feat. He was still alright for the moment. But as the clock chipped away at his remaining days, hours, minutes, he wasn't confident he'd be able to keep his wits about him. He felt like he understood, now, why he was attracted to Ryuji even while being disgusted by him. Ryuji had a psychological strength he just couldn't match. Asakawa lived his life tentatively, always worried about what people around him thought. Ryuji, meanwhile, kept a god—or a devil—chained up inside him that allowed him to live with complete freedom and abandon. The only time Asakawa felt his desire to live chase away his fear was when he thought of how his wife and daughter would feel after his death. Now he suddenly worried about them, and softly opened the bedroom door to check on them. Their faces in sleep were soft and unsuspecting. He had no time to shrink in terror. He decided to call Yoshino and explain the situation and ask for his help. If he put off until tomorrow what he could do today, he was bound to regret it.

3

October 13—Saturday

Asakawa had thought of taking the week off work, but then decided that using the company's information system to the full would give him a better chance of clearing up the mysteries of the videotape than holing up in his apartment pointlessly cowering. As a result, he went in to work, even though it was a Saturday. "Went in to work," but he knew full well that he wouldn't get any actual work done. He figured the best policy would be to confess everything to his editor and ask that he be temporarily taken off his assignments. Nothing would help more than enlisting his editor's cooperation. The problem was whether or not his editor would believe his story. He'd probably bring up the previous incident yet again and snort. Even though he had the video as proof, if Oguri started out by denying everything, he'd have all sorts of other arguments arrayed to support his view. He'd skewer all sorts of things his way to convince himself he was right. *Still...it would be interesting,* Asakawa thought. He'd brought the video in his briefcase, just in case. How would Oguri react if he showed it to him? More to the point, though, would he even give it a glance? Last night he'd stayed up late explaining the whole sequence of events to Yoshino, and he'd believed. And then, as if to prove it, he'd said he absolutely didn't want to see the video—please don't show it to him. In exchange, he'd try to cooperate however he could. Of course, in Yoshino's case, there was a firm foundation for that belief. When Haruko Tsuji and Takehiko Nomi's corpses had been discovered in a car by a prefectural road in Ashina, Yoshino had rushed to the scene and felt the atmosphere there, the stifling atmosphere that had the investigators convinced that only something monstrous could have done this, but that kept them from saying so. If Yoshino hadn't actually been there himself, he probably wouldn't have accepted Asakawa's story quite so easily.

In any case, what Asakawa had on his hands was a bomb. If he flashed it in front of Oguri's eyes threateningly, it ought to have some effect. Asakawa was tempted to use it out of curiosity, if for nothing else.

Oguri's customary mocking smile had been wiped from his face. Both elbows were planted on his desk, and his eyes moved restlessly as he went over Asakawa's story once again with a fine-toothed comb.

Four young people almost certainly watched a particular video together at Villa Log Cabin on the night of August 29th, and exactly a week later, just as the video had predicted, they died under mysterious circumstances. Subsequently, the video had caught the eye of the cabin manager, who had brought it into the office where it calmly waited until Asakawa discovered it. Asakawa had then watched the damned thing. And now he was going to die in five days? Was he supposed to believe that? And yet those four deaths were an indisputable fact. How could he explain them? What was the logical thread to connect all this?

Asakawa's expression, as he stood looking down at Oguri, had an air of superiority that was rare for him. He knew from experience just what Oguri was thinking right about now. Asakawa waited until he thought Oguri's thought process would have reached a dead end, and then extracted the videotape from his briefcase. He did it with exaggerated dignity, theatrically, as if laying down a royal flush.

"Would you like to take a look at it? You're quite welcome to." Asakawa indicated with his eyes the TV by the sofa under the window, flashing a composed, provocative smile. He could hear Oguri swallow loudly. Oguri didn't even glance in the direction of the window; his eyes were fixed on the jet-black videotape that had been placed on his desk. He was honestly trying to decide what to do.

If you want to watch it, you could just press play. It's that easy. C'mon, you can do it. Just laugh like you always do and say how stupid it is, and shove it in the video deck. Do it, give it a shot. Oguri's mind was trying to issue the command to his body. *Stop being such an idiot and watch it. If you watch it, doesn't it show that you don't believe Asakawa? Which means, right, think about it now, it means if you refuse to watch it, you must believe this cock-and-bull story. So watch it already. You believe in modern science, don't you? You're not a kid afraid of ghosts.*

In fact, Oguri was 99% sure that he didn't believe Asakawa. But still, way back in a corner of his mind, there was that *what if*. What if it were true? Maybe there were some niches in this world that modern science couldn't reach yet. And as long as there was that risk, no matter how hard his mind worked, his body was going to refuse. So Oguri sat in his chair and didn't move. He *couldn't* move. It didn't matter what his mind understood: his body wasn't listening to his mind. As long as there was the possibility of danger, his body would keep loyally activating his instincts for self-preservation. Oguri raised his head and said, in a parched voice:

"So, what is it you want from me?"

Asakawa knew he had won. "I'd like you to relieve me of my assignments. I want to make a thorough investigation of this video. Please. I think you realize my life is on the line here."

Oguri shut his eyes tightly. "Are you going to get an article out of it?"

"Well, regardless of how I may appear to you, I'm still a reporter. I'll write down my findings so everything isn't buried with Ryuji Takayama and myself. Of course, whether or not to print them is something I'll leave up to you."

Oguri gave two decisive nods. "Well, it can't hurt. I guess I'll have a cub take your feature interview."

Asakawa bowed slightly. He went to return the video to his briefcase, but couldn't resist the temptation to have a little more fun. He proffered the tape to Oguri once again, saying, "You believe me, don't you?"

Oguri gave a long sigh and shook his head. It wasn't that he believed or disbelieved; he just felt a tinge of uneasiness. Yeah, that was it.

"I feel the same way," were Asakawa's parting words. Oguri watched him walk out and told himself that if Asakawa was still alive after October 18th, then he'd watch that video with his own eyes. But even then, maybe his body wouldn't let him. That *what if* didn't feel like it was ever going to go away.

In the reference room Asakawa stacked three thick volumes on a table. *Volcanoes of Japan, Volcanic Archipelago*, and *Active Volcanoes of the World*. Figuring that the volcano in the video was probably in Japan, he started with *Volcanoes of Japan*. He looked at the color photos at the beginning of the book. Mountains belching white smoke and steam rose gallantly into the sky, sides covered with brownish-black lava rock; bright red molten rock spewed into the night sky from craters whose black edges melted into the darkness; he thought of the Big Bang. He turned the pages, comparing these scenes to the one seared into his brain. Mt. Aso, Mt. Asama, Showa Shinzan, Sakurajima... It didn't take as long to locate as he'd feared. After all, Mt. Mihara on Izu Oshima Island, part of the same chain of volcanoes that included Mt. Fuji, is one of Japan's more famous active volcanoes.

"Mount Mihara?" muttered Asakawa. The two-page spread for Mt. Mihara had two aerial shots and one photo taken from a nearby hilltop. Asakawa recalled the image on the video and tried to imagine it from various angles, comparing it to these photos. There was a definite similarity. From a perspective at the foot of the mountain, the peak seemed gently sloped. But from the air one could see a circular rim surrounding a caldera, in the center of which was a mound which was the mouth of the volcano. The photo taken from a nearby hilltop especially resembled the scene in the video. The color and contours of the mountainside were almost the same. But he needed to confirm it, instead of just relying on his memory. Asakawa made a copy of the photos of Mt. Mihara, along with two or three other candidates.

Asakawa spent the afternoon on the phone. He called people who had used cabin B-4 in the last six months. He would have been better off meeting them face to face and gauging their reactions, but he simply didn't have that kind of time. It was tough to spot a lie just from a voice on a telephone. Asakawa pricked up his ears, determined to catch the slightest crack. There were sixteen parties he needed to check out. The low number was due to the fact that the cabins hadn't been equipped with individual video decks when Villa Log Cabin opened in April. A major regional hotel was torn down over the summer, and it was decided to transfer the large number of VCRs it no longer needed to Villa Log Cabin. That was in mid-July. The decks had been installed and the tape library assembled by the end of that month, just in time for the summer vacation season. As a result, the brochure didn't mention that each room had its own video equipment. Most guests had been surprised to see the VCR when they arrived, and thought of it as nothing more than a way to kill time on a rainy day; almost nobody had expressly brought a tape for the purpose of recording something. Of course, that was *if* he believed the voices on the phone. So who had brought the tape in question? Who had made it? Asakawa was desperate not to overlook anything. He chipped away at people's responses time and again, but not once did anybody seem like they were hiding something. Of the sixteen guests he called, three had come to play golf and hadn't even noticed the VCR. Seven had noticed it but hadn't touched it. Five had come to play tennis but had been rained out, and with nothing else to do had watched videos: classic films, mostly. Probably old favorites. The last group, a family of four named Kaneko, from Yokohama, had brought a tape so they could record something on another channel while watching a historical miniseries.

Asakawa put down the receiver and cast an eye over the data he had collected concerning the sixteen groups of guests. Only one looked pertinent. Mr. and Mrs. Kaneko and their two grade-school-aged kids. They'd stayed in B-4 twice last summer. The first time had been the night of Friday, August 10th, and the second time they had stayed two nights, Saturday and Sunday, August 25th and 26th. The second time was three days before the four victims had been there. Nobody had stayed there on the Monday or Tuesday following the Kanekos' stay: the four teenagers were the very next people to use the room. Not only that, the Kanekos' sixth-grade son had brought a tape from home to record a show. The boy was a faithful fan of a certain comedy series broadcast every Sunday at eight, but his parents, of course, controlled the TV, and every Sunday at eight they made a habit of watching the annual historical miniseries on NHK, the public television network. There was only one television in the cabin, but knowing it had a VCR, the boy had brought a tape, thinking to record his show and watch it later. But while he was recording, a friend came over to tell him that the rain had let up. He and his younger sister ran off to play tennis. His parents finished their program and turned off the television, forgetting that the VCR was still recording. The children ran around on the courts until almost ten, then came home all tuckered out and went straight to bed. They, too, had completely forgotten about the tape. The next day, when they were almost home, the kid suddenly remembered he'd left the tape in the VCR and shouted to his father, who was driving, to go back. This turned into quite an argument, but eventually the boy gave up. He was still whimpering when they got home.

Asakawa took out the videotape and stood it on his desk. Where the label would have been stuck the words *Fujitex VHS T120 Super AV* glinted in silver. Asakawa redialed the Kanekos' number.

"Hi, sorry to keep calling you like this. It's Asakawa again, from the *Daily News*."

There was a pause, then the same voice he had spoken to

before said, "Yes?" It was Mrs. Kaneko.

"You mentioned that your son left behind a videotape. Do you happen to know what brand it was?"

"Well, now, let me see," she replied, trying not to laugh. He heard noises in the background. "My son's just gotten home. I'll ask him."

Asakawa waited. There was no way the kid'd remember.

"He says he doesn't know. But we only use cheap brands, the kind you buy in packs of three."

He wasn't surprised. Who really paid attention to what brand of tape they used every time they wanted to record something? Then Asakawa had an idea. *Hold on, where's the case for this tape? Videotapes are always sold in cardboard cases. Nobody just throws them away.* At least, Asakawa himself had never thrown away a tape case, neither for an audio cassette or a video tape.

"Does your family store your videotapes in their cases?"

"Yes, of course."

"Look, I'm very sorry, but could you please check to see if you have an empty case lying around?"

"Huh?" she asked vacantly. Even if she understood his question, she couldn't guess what he was getting at, and it made her slow on the uptake.

"Please. Someone's life may depend on it." Housewives were susceptible to the "matter of life and death" ploy. Whenever he needed to save time and get one moving, he found that the phrase had just the right impact. But this time, he wasn't lying.

"Just a moment, please."

Just as he'd expected, her tone changed. There was quite a long pause after she set down the receiver. If the case had been left at Villa Log Cabin along with the tape, then it must have been thrown away by the manager. But if not, then there was a good chance the Kanekos still had it. The voice returned.

"An empty case, right?"

"That's right."

"I found two."

"Alright. Now, the manufacturer's name and the type of tape should be printed on the case...."

"Let's see. One says Panavision T120. The other is a...Fujitex VHS T120 Super AV."

The exact same name as on the videotape he held in his hand. Since Fujitex had sold countless numbers of these tapes, this was hardly definitive proof, but at least he'd taken a step forward. That much was certain. This demon tape had originally been brought there by a sixth-grade boy, it was probably safe to conclude. Asakawa thanked the woman politely and hung up the phone.

Starting at eight o'clock on the night of Sunday, August 26th, the video deck in cabin B-4 is left recording. The Kaneko family forgets the tape and goes home. Then come the four young people in question. It's rainy that day, too. Thinking to watch a movie, they go to use the video deck, only to find a tape already inside. Innocently they watch it. They see incomprehensible, eerie things. Then, the threat at the end. Cursing the evil weather, they think up a cruel bit of mischief. Erasing the section that tells how to escape certain death, they leave the video there to frighten the next guests. Of course, they hadn't believed what they'd seen. If they had, they wouldn't have been able to carry out their prank. He wondered if they remembered the tape at the moment of their deaths. Maybe there hadn't been any time for that before the angel of death carried them off. Asakawa shivered—it wasn't just them. Unless he could find a way to avoid dying in five days, he'd end up just like them. Then he'd know exactly how they felt when they died.

But if the boy had been recording a TV show, then where had those images come from? All along Asakawa had thought that someone had shot them with a video camera and then brought the tape there. But the tape had been set to record from the television, meaning that somehow these incredible scenes had infiltrated over the airwaves. He would never have dreamed it.

The airwaves had been hijacked.

Asakawa recalled what had happened last year at election time, when, after NHK had signed off for the night, an illicit broadcast had appeared on the same channel, slandering one of the candidates.

The airwaves had been hijacked. That was the only thing that fit. He was faced with the possibility that on the evening of August 26th, these images had been riding the airwaves in the South Hakone region, and that this tape had picked them up, purely by chance. If that was true, then there must be a record of it. Asakawa realized he needed to contact the local bureau and find out some facts.

4

It was ten when Asakawa got home. As soon as he entered the apartment, he softly opened the bedroom door and checked the sleeping faces of his wife and daughter. No matter how tired he was when he got home, he always did this.

There was a note on the dining room table. *Mr. Takayama called.* Asakawa had been trying to call Ryuji all day long, but he hadn't been able to catch him home. He was probably out and about on his own investigations. *Maybe he has something,* thought Asakawa as he dialed. He let it ring ten times. No answer. Ryuji lived alone in his East Nakano apartment. He wasn't home yet.

Asakawa took a quick shower, opened a beer, and tried calling again. Still not home. He switched to whiskey on the rocks. He'd never be able to get a good night's sleep without alcohol. Tall and slender, Asakawa had never in his life had an illness worth the name. To think that this was how he was sentenced to die. Part of him still felt it was a dream, that he'd reach ten o'clock on October 18th without having understood the video or figured out the charm, but in the end nothing would happen and the days would stretch out before him as they always had. Oguri would wear a mocking expression and expound on the foolishness of believing in superstitions, while Ryuji would laugh and say, "We just don't understand how the world works." And his wife and daughter would greet their daddy with these same sleeping faces. Even a passenger on an airplane falling from the sky can't shake the hope that he'll be the one to survive.

He drained his third glass of whiskey and dialed Ryuji's number a third time. If he didn't answer this time, Asakawa was going to give up for the night. He heard seven rings, then a *click* as someone picked up the receiver.

"What the hell have you been up to all this time?" he shouted, without even checking to see who he was talking to. Thinking he was addressing Ryuji, he allowed his anger full vent. Which only served to emphasize the strangeness of their relationship. Even with his friends, Asakawa always maintained a certain distance and carefully controlled his attitude. But he had no qualms about calling Ryuji every name in the book. And yet, he'd never once thought of Ryuji as a truly close friend.

But surprisingly, the voice that answered wasn't Ryuji's.

"Hello? Excuse me..."

It was a woman, startled from having been yelled at out of nowhere.

"Oh, sorry. Wrong number." Asakawa started to hang up.

"Are you calling for Professor Takayama?"

"Well, ah, yes, as a matter of fact I am."

"He's not back yet."

Asakawa couldn't help but wonder who this young, attractive voice belonged to. He figured it was a safe bet she wasn't a relative, since she'd called him "Professor." A lover? Couldn't be. What girl in her right mind would fall for Ryuji?

"I see. My name is Asakawa."

"When Professor Takayama returns, I'll have him call you. That's Mr. Asakawa, right?"

Even after he had replaced the receiver, the woman's soft voice continued to ring pleasantly in his ears.

Futons were usually only used in Japanese-style rooms, with tatami-mat floors. Their bedroom was carpeted, and had originally had a Western-style bed in it, but when Yoko was born they took it out. They couldn't have a baby sleeping on a bed, but the room was too small for a crib and a bed. So they were forced to get rid of their double bed and switch to futons, rolling them up every morning and spreading them out again every night. They laid two futons side-by-side and the three of them slept together. Now Asakawa crawled into the open space on the futons. When the three of them went to bed at the same time, they always slept in the same positions. But Shizu and Yoko were restless sleepers, so when they went to bed before Asakawa, it was less than an hour before they had rolled around and sprawled all over. As a result, Asakawa ended up having to fit himself into whatever space was left. If he was gone, how long would it take for that space to be filled, Asakawa wondered. It wasn't that he was worried about Shizu remarrying, necessarily. It was just that some people were never able to fill the space left behind by the loss of a spouse. Three years? Three years would be about right. Shizu would move back home and let her parents take care of the baby while she went to work. Asakawa forced himself to imagine her face, shining with as much vitality as could be expected. He wanted her to be strong. He couldn't stand to imagine the kind of hell his wife and child would have to live through with him gone.

Asakawa had met Shizu five years ago. He had just been transferred back to the main Tokyo office from the Chiba bureau; she was working in a travel agency connected with the *Daily News* conglomerate. She worked on the third floor, he worked on the seventh, and they sometimes saw each other on the elevator, but that was the extent of it until one day when he'd gone to the travel agency to pick up some tickets. He was traveling for a story, and as the person handling his arrangements wasn't in Shizu had taken care of him. She was just twenty-five and loved to travel, and her gaze told how much she envied Asakawa being able to go all over the country on assignments. In that gaze, he also saw a reflection of the first girl he'd ever loved. Now that they knew each other's names, they started to make small talk when they ran into each other on the elevator, and their relationship rapidly deepened. Two years later they married, after an easy courtship with no objections from either set of parents. About six months before their wedding they had bought the three-room condo in Kita Shinagawa—their parents had helped with the down payment. It wasn't that they'd anticipated the spike in land value and had therefore rushed to buy even before the wedding. It was simply that they wanted to get the mortgage paid off as quickly as possible. But if they hadn't bought when they did, they might never have been able to afford to live in the city like this. Within a year, their condo had tripled in value. And their monthly mortgage payments were less than half of what they would have been paying to rent. They were constantly complaining that the place was too small, but in truth it constituted quite an asset for the couple. Now Asakawa was glad he had something to leave them. If Shizu used his life insurance to pay off the mortgage, then the condo would belong to her and Yoko free and clear.

I think my policy pays twenty million yen, but I'd better check, just to be sure.

His mind was clouded, but he mentally divided up the money

in different ways, telling himself that he must write down any financial advice that might occur to him. He wondered how they'd rule his death. Death by illness? Accident? Homicide?

In any case, I'd better reread my insurance policy.

Every night for the past three days he had gone to bed in a pessimistic mood. He pondered how to influence a world he would have disappeared from, and thought about leaving a sort of last testament.

October 14—Sunday

The next morning, Sunday, Asakawa dialed Ryuji's number as soon as he woke up.

"Yeah?" answered Ryuji, sounding for all the world like he'd just woken up. Asakawa immediately remembered his frustration of the night before, and barked into the receiver.

"Where were you last night?"

"Huh? Oh. Asakawa?"

"You were supposed to call, weren't you?"

"Oh, yeah. I was drunk. College girls these days sure can drink. Sure can do other stuff, too, if you know what I mean. Whoo-whee. I'm exhausted."

Asakawa was momentarily at a loss: it was like the past three days were just a dream. He felt foolish for having taken everything so seriously.

"Well, I'm on my way over. Wait for me," said Asakawa, hanging up the phone.

To get to Ryuji's place Asakawa rode the train to East Nakano and then walked for ten minutes in the direction of Kami Ochiai.

As he walked Asakawa reflected hopefully that even though Ryuji had been out drinking the night before, he was still Ryuji. Surely he'd found something. Maybe he'd even solved the riddle, and he'd gone out drinking and carousing to celebrate. The closer he drew to Ryuji's apartment the more upbeat he became, and he began to walk faster. Asakawa's emotions were wearing him out, bouncing back and forth between fear and hope, pessimism and optimism.

Ryuji opened the door in his pajamas. Unkempt and unshaven, he'd obviously just gotten out of bed. Asakawa couldn't take his shoes off fast enough; he was still in the entryway when he asked, "Have you learned anything?"

"No, not really. But come in," said Ryuji, scratching his head vigorously. His eyes were unfocused and Asakawa knew at a glance that his brain cells weren't awake yet.

"Come on, wake up. Drink some coffee or something." Feeling like his hopes had been betrayed, Asakawa put the kettle on the stove with a loud clatter. Suddenly he was obsessed with the time.

The two men sat cross-legged on the floor in the front room. Books were stacked all along one wall.

"So tell me what you've turned up," said Ryuji, jiggling his knee. There was no time to waste. Asakawa collected everything he'd learned the day before and laid it out chronologically. First he informed Ryuji that the video had been recorded from the television in the cabin beginning at 8 p.m. on August 26th.

"Really?" Ryuji looked surprised. He, too, had assumed it had been made on a video camera and then brought in later.

"Now, that's interesting. But if the airwaves were hijacked as you say, there should be others who saw the same thing...."

"Well, I called our bureaus in Atami and Mishima and asked about that. But they say they haven't received any reports of suspicious transmissions flying around South Hakone on the night of August 26th."

"I see, I see...." Ryuji folded his arms and thought for a while. "Two possibilities come to mind. First, everybody who saw the transmission is dead. But hold on—when it was broadcast, the charm should have been intact. So... And, anyway, the local papers haven't picked up on anything, right?"

"Right. I've already checked that out. You mean whether or not there were any other victims, right? There weren't. None at all. If it was broadcast, then other people should have seen it, but there haven't been any other victims. Not even any rumors."

"But remember when AIDS started to appear in the civilized world? At first doctors in America had no idea what was going on. All they knew was that they were seeing people die from symptoms they'd never encountered before. All they had was a suspicion of some strange disease. They only started calling it AIDS two years after it had appeared. That kind of thing happens."

The mountainous valleys west of the Tanna Ridge only contained a few scattered farmhouses, on the lower reaches of the Atami-Kannami Highway. If you gazed south, all you could see was South Hakone Pacific Land, isolated in its dreamy alpine meadows. Was something invisible at work in that land? Maybe lots of people were dying suddenly, but it just hadn't made it into the news yet. It wasn't just AIDS: Kawasaki Disease, first discovered in Japan, had been around for ten years before it was officially recognized as a new disease. It was still only a month and a half since the phantom broadcast had been accidentally caught on videotape. It was quite possible that the syndrome hadn't yet been recognized. If Asakawa hadn't discovered the common factor in four deaths—if his niece hadn't been among them—this "illness" would probably still be sleeping underground. That was even scarier. It usually took hundreds, thousands, of deaths before something was officially recognized as a "disease."

"But we don't have time to go door-to-door down there talking to residents. But, Ryuji, you mentioned a second possibility."

"Right. Second, the only people who saw it are us and the four young people. Hey, do you think the grade-school brat who recorded this knew that broadcast frequencies are different from region to region? What they're showing on Channel 4 in Tokyo might be broadcast on a completely different channel out in the country. A dumb kid wouldn't know that—maybe he set it to record according to the channel he watches in Tokyo."

"What are you getting at?"

"Think about it. Do people like us, who live in Tokyo, ever turn to Channel 2? It's not used here."

Ah-ha. So the boy had set the VCR to a channel a local would never have used. Since they were recording while watching something else, he hadn't actually seen what was being recorded. In any event, with the population so sparse in those mountains, there couldn't be too many viewers in the first place.

"Either way, the real question is, where did the broadcast originate from?" It sounded so simple when Ryuji said it. But only an organized, scientific investigation would be able to determine the transmission's point of origin.

"W-wait a minute. We're not even sure your basic premise is right. It's only a guess that the boy accidentally recorded phantom airwaves."

"I know that. But if we wait for hundred-percent proof before proceeding, we'll never get anywhere. This is our only lead."

Airwaves. Asakawa's knowledge of science was paltry. He didn't even really know what airwaves were: he'd have to start his investigation there. There was nothing to do but check it out. The broadcast's point of origin. That meant he'd have to go back *there*. And after today, there were only four days left.

The next question was: who had erased the charm? If they allowed that the tape had been recorded on-site, it couldn't have been anybody but the four victims. Asakawa had checked with the TV network and found out when the young storyteller, Shinraku Sanyutei, had been a guest on *The Night Show*. They'd been right. The answer that came back was August 29th. It was almost certain that the four young people had erased the charm.

Asakawa took several photocopies from his briefcase. They were photographs of Mt. Mihara, on Izu Oshima Island. "What do you think?" he asked, showing them to Ryuji.

"Mt. Mihara, eh? I'd say this is definitely the one."

"How can you be sure?"

"Yesterday afternoon, I asked an ethnologist at the university about Granny's dialect. He said it wasn't used much anymore, but that it was probably one found on Izu Oshima. In fact, it contained features traceable to the Sashikiji region on the southern tip of the island. He's pretty cautious, so he wouldn't swear that that was it, but combined with this photo I think we're safe in assuming that the dialect is Izu Oshima's, and the mountain is Mt. Mihara. By the way, did you do any research into Mt. Mihara's eruptions?"

"Of course. Since the war—and I think we're probably okay in limiting ourselves to eruptions since the war..." Considering developments in film technology, this seemed a safe assumption.

"Right."

"Now, are you with me? Since the war, Mount Mihara has erupted four times. The first time was in 1950-1951. The second was in '57, and the third was in '74. The fourth time I'm sure we both remember well: the autumn of 1986. The '57 eruption produced a new crater; one person died and fifty-three were injured."

"Considering when video cameras came out, I'd guess we're looking at the '86 eruption, but I don't think we can be sure yet."

At this point Ryuji seemed to remember something, and started rummaging around in his bag. He pulled out a slip of paper. "Oh, yes. Evidently this is what she's saying. The gentleman kindly translated it into standard Japanese for me."

Asakawa looked at the scrap of paper, on which was written:

How has your health been since then? If you spend all your time playing in the water, monsters are bound to get you. Understand? Be careful of strangers. Next year you're going to give birth to a child. You listen to granny now, because you're just a girl. There's no need to worry about local people.

Asakawa read through it twice, carefully, and then looked up.

"What is this? What does it mean?"

"How should I know? That's what you're going to have to find out."

"We've only got four days left!"

Asakawa had too many things to do. He didn't know where to start. His nerves were on edge and he'd begun to lash out.

"Look. I've got one more day to spare than you. You're the point man on this. Act like it. Give it your all."

Suddenly misgivings began to well up in Asakawa's heart. Ryuji could abuse his extra day. If, for example, he came up with two guesses as to the nature of the charm, he could tell Asakawa about one, and wait for Asakawa's survival or death to tell him which one was right. That single day could turn into a powerful weapon.

"It doesn't really matter to you if I live or die, does it, Ryuji? Sitting there calmly like that, laughing..." Asakawa wailed, knowing as he did that he was becoming shamefully hysterical.

"You're talking like a woman now. If you've got time to bitch and whine like that you ought to use your head a bit more."

Asakawa still glared at him resentfully.

"I mean, how would you prefer I put it? You're my best friend. I don't want you to die. I'm doing my best. I want you to do your best, too. We both have to do our best, for each other. Happy now?" Midway through his speech Ryuji's tone suddenly became childish, and he finished with an obscene laugh.

As he laughed, the front door opened. Startled, Asakawa leaned over and peered through the kitchen at the entry hall. A young woman was bending over to remove a pair of white pumps. Her hair was cut short, brushing the tops of her ears, and earrings gleamed white. She took her shoes off and raised her gaze, her eyes meeting Asakawa's.

"Oh, pardon me. I thought the Professor was alone," said the woman, covering her mouth with her hand. Her elegant body language and her pure white outfit clashed utterly with the apartment. Her legs below her skirt were slim and willowy, her face slender and intelligent; she looked like a certain female novelist who appeared in TV commercials.

"Come in." Ryuji's tone had changed. The vulgarity was concealed beneath a newfound dignity. "Allow me to introduce you. This is Miss Mai Takano from the philosophy department at Fukuzawa University. She's one of the department's star pupils, and always pays close attention in my classes. She's probably the only one who really understands my lectures. This is Kazuyuki Asakawa, from the *Daily News*. He's my...best friend."

Mai Takano looked at Asakawa with some surprise. At this point he still didn't know why she should be surprised. "Pleased to meet you," said Mai, with a thrilling little smile and bow. The kind of smile that made any onlooker feel refreshed. Asakawa had never met such a beautiful woman. The fine texture of her skin, the way her eyes glowed, the perfect balance of her figure—not to mention the intelligence, class, and kindness she radiated from within. There was literally nothing to find fault with in this woman. Asakawa shrank back like a frog from a snake. Words failed him.

"Hey, say something." Ryuji elbowed him in the ribs.

"Hello," he said finally, awkwardly, but his gaze was still transfixed.

"Professor, were you out last night?" asked Mai, gracefully sliding her stockinged feet two or three steps closer.

"Actually, Takabayashi and Yagi invited me out with them, so..."

Now that they were standing next to each other, Asakawa could see that Mai was a good ten centimeters taller than Ryuji. She probably only weighed half as much as he did, though.

"I wish you'd tell me if you're not coming home. I waited up for you."

Asakawa suddenly returned to his senses. This was the voice he'd spoken to last night. This was the woman who'd answered the phone when he'd called.

Meanwhile, Ryuji was hanging his head like a boy scolded by his mother.

"Well, never mind. I'll forgive you this time. Here, I brought you something." She held out a paper bag. "I washed your underwear for you. I was going to straighten up here, too, but you get angry when I move your books."

From this exchange Asakawa couldn't help but guess the nature of their relationship. It was obvious that they were more than just teacher and student, but lovers as well. On top of that, she'd waited here alone for him last night! Were they that close? He felt the kind of annoyance he sometimes felt when he saw a badly mismatched couple, but this went far beyond that. Everything to do with Ryuji was crazy. Then there was the love in Ryuji's eyes as he gazed at Mai. He was like a chameleon, changing his expression, even his speech patterns. For an instant, Asakawa was mad enough to want to open Mai's eyes by exposing Ryuji's crimes.

"It's nearly lunchtime, Professor. Shall I fix something? Mr. Asakawa, you'll be staying too, won't you? Have you any requests?"

Asakawa looked at Ryuji, uncertain how to respond.

"Don't be shy. Mai's quite the chef."

"I'll leave it up to you," Asakawa finally managed to say.

Mai immediately left for a nearby market to buy ingredients for lunch. Even after she had gone, Asakawa stared dreamily toward the door.

"Man, you look like a deer caught in the headlights of a car," said Ryuji with an amused leer.

"Oh, sorry."

"Look, we don't have time for you to space out like this." Ryuji slapped Asakawa lightly on the cheek. "We have things to talk about while she's gone."

"You haven't shown Mai the video."

"What do you think I am?"

"Okay, then. Let's get through it. I'll go after we eat."

"Right, now the first thing you have to find is the antenna."

"The antenna?"

"You know, the spot where the broadcast originated."

He couldn't afford to relax, then. On the way home he'd have to stop by the library and read up on airwaves. Part of him wanted to rush down to South Hakone now, but he knew it would be quicker in the long run to do some background reading first, to get an idea of what he was looking for. The more he knew about the characteristics of airwaves, and about how to track down pirate broadcasts, the more options he'd be able to give himself.

There was a mountain of things to be done. But now Asakawa felt distracted, his thoughts somewhere else. He couldn't get her face, her body, out of his mind. Why was Mai with a guy like Ryuji? He felt both puzzled and angry.

"Hey, are you listening to me?" Ryuji's voice brought Asakawa back down to earth. "There was a scene in the video with a baby boy, remember?"

"Yes." He chased Mai's image from his mind momentarily and recalled the vision of the newborn, covered in slippery amniotic fluid. But the transition didn't go well; he ended up imagining Mai wet and naked.

"When I saw that scene I got a strange sensation in my own hands. Almost as if I were holding that boy myself."

Sensation. Holding someone. In the arms of his imagination he was holding first Mai and then the baby boy, in blinding succession. Then, finally, he had it—the feeling he'd had watching the video, of holding the infant and then throwing both hands up in the air. Ryuji had felt the exact same sensation. This had to be significant.

"I felt it too. I definitely felt something wet and slippery."

"You too, huh? So what does it mean?"

Ryuji got down on all fours, bringing his face up close to the television screen as he replayed that scene. It lasted about two minutes, the baby boy giving his birth-cry all the while. They could see a pair of graceful hands beneath the child's head and bottom.

"Wait a minute, what's this?" Ryuji paused the video and began to advance it a frame at a time. Just for a second the screen went dark. Watching it at normal speed it was so brief as to be hardly noticeable. But watching it over and over, frame by frame, it was possible to pick out moments of total blackness.

"There it is again," cried Ryuji. For a time he arched his back like a cat and stared at the screen intently, and then he moved his head back and his eyes darted around the room. He was thinking furiously—Asakawa could tell by the movements of his eyes. But he had no idea what Ryuji was thinking. In all, the screen went dark thirty-three times during the course of the two-minute scene.

"So what? Are you telling me you've been able to figure something out just from this? It's just a glitch in the filming. The video camera was defective."

Ryuji ignored Asakawa's comment and began to search through other scenes. They heard footsteps on the outside stairs. Ryuji hurriedly pushed the stop button.

Finally the front door opened and Mai appeared, saying, "I'm back." The room was once again wrapped in her fragrance.

It was Sunday afternoon, and families with children were playing on the lawn in front of the city library. Some fathers were playing catch with their boys; others were lying on the grass, letting their kids play. It was a beautiful clear Sunday afternoon in mid-October, and the world seemed blanketed in peace.

Faced with the scene, Asakawa suddenly wanted nothing more than to rush home. He'd spent some time on the fourth floor in the natural sciences section, boning up on airwaves, and now he was just staring out the window, looking at nothing in particular. All day he'd found himself drifting off like this. All sorts of thoughts would come to him, without rhyme or reason; he couldn't concentrate. Probably it was because he was impatient. He stood up. He wanted to see the faces of his wife and child, now. He was overcome with the thought. *Now.* He didn't have much time left. Time to play with his daughter on the lawn like that....

Asakawa got home just before five. Shizu was making dinner. He could read her bad mood as he stood behind her and watched her slice vegetables. He knew the reason, too—all too well. He finally had a day off, but he'd left her early that morning, saying only, "I'm going to Ryuji's place." If he didn't look after Yoko once in a while, at least when he had a day off, Shizu tended to feel swamped by the stresses of raising a child. And to top it off, he'd been with Ryuji. That was the problem. He could have just lied to her, but then she wouldn't have been able to contact him in an emergency.

"There was a call from a realtor," said Shizu, not missing a beat with the knife.

"What about?"

"He asked if we were thinking about selling."

Asakawa had sat Yoko on his knee and was reading her a picture book. She most likely didn't understand, but they were hoping that if they exposed her to a lot of words now, maybe they'd accumulate in her head and then come flowing out like a burst dam when she got to be two or so.

"Did he make a good offer?"

Ever since land prices had begun to skyrocket, realtors had been trying to get them to sell.

"Seventy million yen."

That was less than before. Still, it was enough to leave quite a bit for Shizu and Yoko, even after they paid off the mortgage.

"So what did you tell him?"

Wiping her hands on a towel, Shizu finally turned around. "I told him my husband wasn't home."

That's how it always went. *My husband's not at home*, she'd say, or *I'd have to talk it over with my husband first*. Shizu never decided anything on her own. He was afraid she'd have to start soon.

"What do you think? Maybe it's about time we considered it. We'd have enough to buy a house in the suburbs, with a yard. The realtor said so, too."

It was the family's modest dream: to sell the condo they were living in now and build a big house in the suburbs. Without capital, a dream was all it would ever be. But they did have this one powerful asset: a condo in the heart of the city. They had the means to make that dream come true, and every time they spoke of it now it was with excitement. It was right there—all they had to do was reach out their hands....

"And then, you know, we could have another baby, too." It was perfectly clear to Asakawa just what Shizu was seeing in her mind's eye. A spacious suburban residence, with a separate study room for each of their two or three kids, and a living room large enough that she needn't be embarrassed no matter how many guests dropped in. Yoko, on his knee, started to act up. She'd noticed that her daddy's eyes had strayed from the picture book, that his attention was focussed on something besides herself, and she was registering her objections. Asakawa looked at the picture book once more.

"Long, long ago Marshyland was called Marshybeach, because the reed-thick marshes stretched all the way down to the seashore."

As he read aloud, Asakawa felt tears well up in his eyes. He wanted to make his wife's dream come true. He really did. But he only had four days left. Would his wife be able to cope when he died of unknown causes? She didn't yet know how fragile her dream was, how soon it would come crashing down.

9 p.m. Shizu and Yoko were asleep as usual. Asakawa was preoccupied by the last thing Ryuji had brought up. *Why did he keep replaying the scene with the baby? And what about that old woman's words—"Next year you're going to have a child."* Was there a connection between the baby boy and the child the old woman mentioned? And what about the moments of total blackness? Thirty-odd times they occurred, at varying intervals.

Asakawa thought he'd watch the video again, to try and confirm this. Ryuji had been looking for something specific, no matter how capricious it had seemed at the time. Ryuji had great powers of logic, of course, but he also had a finely-tuned sense of intuition. Asakawa, on the other hand, specialized in the work of dragging out the truth through painstaking investigation.

Asakawa opened the cabinet and picked up the videotape. He went to insert it into the video deck, but just at that moment, he noticed something that stayed his hand. *Wait a minute, something's not right.* He wasn't sure what it was, but his sixth sense was telling him something was out of the ordinary. More and more he was sure that it wasn't just his imagination. He really had felt something was funny when he touched the tape. Something had changed, ever so slightly.

What is it? What's different? His heart was pounding. *This is bad. Nothing about this is getting any better. Think, man, try to remember. The last time I watched this...I rewound it. And now the tape's in the middle. About a third of the way through. That's right about where the images end, and it hasn't been rewound. Somebody watched it while I was away.*

Asakawa ran to the bedroom. Shizu and Yoko were asleep, all tangled up together. Asakawa rolled his wife over and shook her by the shoulder.

"Wake up. Shizu! Wake up!" He kept his voice low, trying not to awaken Yoko. Shizu twisted her face into a scowl and tried to squirm away.

"I said, wake up!" His voice sounded different from usual.

"...what...what's wrong?"

"We have to talk. Come on."

Asakawa dragged his wife out of bed and pulled her into the dining room. Then he held the tape out to her. "Did you watch this?"

Taken aback by the ferocity of his tone, Shizu could only look back and forth from the tape to her husband's face. Finally, she said, "Was I not supposed to?"

What're you so mad about? she thought. *Here it is Sunday, and you're off somewhere, and I'm bored. And then there was that tape you and Ryuji were whispering over, so I pulled it out. But it wasn't even interesting. Probably just something the boys in the office cooked up anyway.* Shizu remained silent, only talking back in her mind. *There's no call for you to get so upset about it.*

For the first time in his married life, Asakawa felt a desire to hit his wife. "You...idiot!" But somehow he managed to resist the urge and just stood there, fist clenched. *Calm down and think. It's your own fault. You shouldn't have left it where she could see it.* Shizu never even opened mail addressed to him; he'd figured it was safe just leaving the tape in the cabinet. *Why didn't I hide it? After all, she came in the room while Ryuji and I were watching it. Of course she'd be curious about it. I was wrong not to hide it.*

"I'm sorry," Shizu mumbled, discontentedly.

"When did you watch it?" Asakawa's voice shook.

"This morning."

"Really?"

Shizu had no way of knowing how important it was to know exactly when she watched it. She just nodded, curtly.

"What time?"

"Why do you ask?"

"Just tell me!" Asakawa's hand started to move again.

"Around ten-thirty, maybe. It was right after *Masked Rider* ended."

Masked Rider? That was a children's show. Yoko was the only one in the family who'd have any interest in that. Asakawa fought desperately to keep from collapsing.

"Now, this is very important, so listen to me. While you were watching this video, where was Yoko?"

Shizu looked like she was about to burst into tears.

"On my lap."

"Yoko, too? You're saying both of you...watched...this video?"

"She was just watching the screen flicker—she didn't understand it."

"Shut up! That doesn't matter!"

This was no longer just a matter of destroying his wife's dreams of a house in the suburbs. The entire family was threatened now—they could all perish. They'd all die an utterly meaningless death.

As she observed her husband's anger, fear, and despair, Shizu began to realize the seriousness of the situation. "Hey...that was just a...a joke, right?"

She recalled the words at the end of the video. At the time she'd dismissed them as just a tasteless prank. They couldn't be real. But what about the way her husband was acting?

"It's not for real, right? Right?"

Asakawa couldn't respond. He merely shook his head. Then he was filled with tenderness for the ones who now shared his fate.

5

October 15—Monday

Every morning when he woke up now, Asakawa found himself wishing that it had all been a dream. He called a rent-a-car place in the neighborhood and told them that he'd be in on schedule to pick up the car he'd reserved. They had his reservation on file, no mistake. Reality marched on without a break.

He needed a way to get around if he was going to go try to find out where that broadcast had originated. It would be too hard to break in on TV frequencies with an off-the-shelf wireless transmitter; he figured that it had to have been done with an expertly modified unit. And the image on the tape was clear, with no interference. That meant that the signal had to have been strong, and close. With more information he might have been able to establish the area in which the broadcast was receivable, and thus to pinpoint the point of origin. But all he had to go on was the fact that the television in Villa Log Cabin B-4 had picked up the transmission. All he could do was go there, check out the lay of the land, and then start going over the area with a fine-toothed comb. He had no idea how long it would take. He packed enough clothes for three days. He certainly wouldn't need any more than that.

They looked at each other, but Shizu didn't say anything about the video. Asakawa hadn't been able to think of a good lie, and so he'd let her go to bed with only the vaguest of excuses about the threat of death in a week. For her part, Shizu seemed to fear finding out anything specific, and seemed happy to let things remain ambiguous and unexplained. Rather than questioning him like she usually would, she seemed to guess at something on her own that made her keep an eerie silence. Asakawa didn't know exactly how she was interpreting things, but it didn't seem to assuage her uneasiness. As she watched her usual morning soap opera on TV she seemed extraordinarily sensitive to noises from outside, starting from her seat any number of times.

"Let's just not talk about this, okay? I don't have any answers for you. Just let me handle it." This was all Asakawa could think to say to calm his wife's anxieties. He couldn't allow himself to appear weak to his wife.

Just as he was stepping out of the house, as if on cue, the phone rang. It was Ryuji.

"I've made a fascinating discovery. I want you to tell me what you think." There was a hint of excitement in Ryuji's voice.

"Can't you tell me about it over the phone? I'm supposed to go pick up a rental car."

"A rental car?"

"You're the one who told me to find out where the broadcast originated from."

"Right, right. Listen, put that on the back burner for a while and get over here. Maybe you don't have to go looking for an antenna after all. Maybe that whole premise will just crumble away."

Asakawa decided to pick the car up first anyway, so that if he still needed to go to South Hakone Pacific Land, he could leave straight from Ryuji's place.

Asakawa parked the car with two wheels up on the sidewalk and banged on Ryuji's door.

"Enter! It's unlocked."

Asakawa jerked the door open and deliberately stomped through the kitchen. "So what's this big discovery?" he asked, forcefully.

"What's eating you?" Ryuji glanced over from where he sat, cross-legged on the floor.

"Just hurry up and tell me what you've found!"

"Relax!"

"How am I supposed to relax? Just tell me, already!"

Ryuji held his tongue for a moment. Then, gently, he asked, "What's wrong? Did something happen?"

Asakawa plopped himself down in the middle of the floor, clenching his hands on his knees. "My wife and...my wife and daughter watched that piece of shit."

"Well, that's a hell of a thing. I'm sorry to hear that." Ryuji watched until Asakawa began to regain his composure. The latter sneezed once and blew his nose loudly.

"Well, you want to save them too, don't you?"

Asakawa nodded his head like a little boy.

"Well then, all the more reason to keep a cool head. So I won't tell you my conclusions. I'll just lay out the evidence. I want to see what the evidence suggests to you first. That's why I couldn't have you excited like that, see."

"I understand," Asakawa said, meekly.

"Now go wash your face or something. Pull yourself together."

Asakawa could cry in front of Ryuji. Ryuji was the outlet for all the emotions he couldn't break down and show his wife.

He came back into the room, wiping his face with a towel, and Ryuji held out a piece of paper. On it was a simple chart:

1) Intro	83 seconds	[0]	abstract
2) Red fluid	49 "	[0]	abstract
3) Mt. Mihara	55 "	[11]	real
4) Mt. Mihara erupting	32 "	[6]	real
5) The word 'mountain'	56 "	[0]	abstract
6) Dice	103 "	[0]	abstract
7) Old woman	111 "	[0]	abstract
8) Infant	125 "	[33]	real
9) Faces	117 "	[0]	abstract
10) Old TV	141 "	[35]	real
11) Man's face	186 "	[44]	real
12) Ending	132 "	[0]	abstract

Some things were clear at a glance. Ryuji had broken down the video into separate scenes.

"Last night I suddenly got the idea for this. You see what it is, right? The video consists of twelve scenes. I've given each one a number and a name. The number after the name is the length of the scene in seconds. The next number, in brackets, is—are you with me?—the number of times the screen goes dark during that scene."

Asakawa's expression was full of doubt.

"After you left yesterday I started to examine other scenes besides the one with the infant. To see if they had any of these instants of darkness, too. And, lo and behold, there were, in scenes

3, 4, 8, 10, and 11."

"The next column says 'real' or 'abstract.' What's that?"

"Broadly speaking, we can divide the twelve scenes into these two categories. The abstract scenes, the ones like images in the mind, what I suppose we could almost call mental landscapes. And the real ones, scenes of things that really exist, that you could actually look at with your eyes. That's how I divided them up."

Here Ryuji paused for a second.

"Now, look at the chart. Notice anything?"

"Well, your black curtain only comes down on the 'real' scenes."

"Right. That's absolutely right. Keep that in mind."

"Ryuji, this is getting annoying. Hurry up and tell me what you're driving at. What does this mean?"

"Now, now, hold your horses. Sometimes when one is given the answers up front it dulls one's intuition. My intuition has already led me to a conclusion. And now that I have that in mind, I'll twist any phenomenon to rationalize holding onto that conclusion. It's like that in criminal investigations, too, isn't it? Once you get the notion that *he's the guy*, it suddenly seems like all the evidence agrees with you. See, we can't afford to wander off the track here. I need you to back up my conclusion. That is, I want to see, once you've taken a look at the evidence, if your intuition tells you the same thing mine told me."

"Okay, okay. Get on with it."

"Alright: the black curtain only appears when the screen is showing real landscapes. We've established that. Now, cast your mind back on the sensations you felt the first time you saw these images. We discussed the scene with the infant yesterday. Anything besides that? What about the scene with all the faces?"

Ryuji used the remote to find the scene. "Take a good, long look at those faces."

The wall of dozens of faces slowly retreated, the number swelling into the hundreds, the thousands. When he looked closely at them, each one seemed different, just like real faces.

"How does this make you feel?" Ryuji asked.

"Like somehow I'm the one being reproached. Like they're calling me a liar, a fraud."

"Right. As it happens, I felt the same thing—or, at least, what I felt was very similar to the sensation you're describing."

Asakawa tried to concentrate his nerves on where this fact led. Ryuji was awaiting a clear response.

"Well?" asked Ryuji again.

Asakawa shook his head. "It's no good. I've got nothing."

"Well, if you had the leisure to spend more time thinking about it, you might notice the same thing I did. See, both of us have been thinking that these images were captured by a TV camera, in other words by a machine with a lens. No?"

"They weren't?"

"Well, what's this black curtain that momentarily covers the screen?"

Ryuji advanced the film frame by frame until the screen went black. It stayed black for three or four frames. If you calculated one frame at a thirtieth of a second, then the darkness lasted for about a tenth of a second.

"Why does this happen in the real scenes and not the imagined ones? Look closer at the screen. It's not completely black."

Asakawa brought his face closer to the screen. Indeed, it wasn't totally dark. Something like a faint white haze hung suspended within the darkness.

"A blurred shadow. What we have here is the persistence of vision. And as you watch, don't you get an incredible sense of immediacy, as if you're actually a participant in the scene?"

Ryuji looked Asakawa full in the face and blinked once, slowly. The black curtain.

"Eh?" murmured Asakawa, "Is this...the blink of an eye?"

"Exactly. Am I wrong? If you think about it, it's consistent. There are things we see with our eyes, but there are also scenes we conjure up in our minds. And since these don't pass through the retina, there's no blinking involved. But when we actually look with our eyes, the images are formed according to the strength of the light that hits the retina. And to keep the retina from drying out, we blink, unconsciously. The black curtain is the instant when the eyes shut."

Once again, Asakawa was filled with nausea. The first time he'd finished watching the video he'd run to the toilet, but this time the evil chill was even worse. He couldn't shake the feeling that something had climbed into his body. This video hadn't been recorded by a machine. A human being's eyes, ears, nose, tongue, skin—all five senses had been used to make this video. These chills, this shivering, were from somebody's shadow sneaking into him through his sense organs. Asakawa had been watching the video from the same perspective as this *thing* within him.

He mopped his brow again and again, but still it was damp with cold sweat.

"Did you know—hey, are you listening? Individual differences aside, the average man blinks twenty times a minute, and the average woman fifteen times. That means that it might have been a woman who recorded these images."

Asakawa couldn't hear him.

"Heh, heh, heh. What's the matter? You look like you're dead already, you're so pale," Ryuji laughed. "Look on the bright side. We're one step closer to a solution now. If these images were collected by the sense organs of a particular person, then the charm must have something to do with that person's will. In other words: maybe she wants us do something."

Asakawa had temporarily lost his faculty of reason. Ryuji's words vibrated in his ears, but their meaning didn't make it to his brain.

"At any rate, we now know what we have to do. We have to find out who this person is. Or was. I think he or she is probably no longer with us. And then we have to find out what this person desired while he or she was still alive. And that'll be the charm that will allow us to go on living."

Ryuji winked at Asakawa, as if to say, *how'm I doin'*?

Asakawa had left the No. 3 Tokyo-Yokohama Freeway and was now heading south on the Yokohama-Yokosuka road. Ryuji had reclined the passenger seat and was sleeping a perfect, stressless sleep. It was almost two in the afternoon, but Asakawa wasn't the least bit hungry.

Asakawa reached out a hand to wake Ryuji, but then pulled it back. They weren't at their destination yet. Asakawa didn't even really know what their destination was. All Ryuji had done was tell him to drive to Kamakura. He didn't know where they were going or why they were going there. It made him a nervous, irritable driver. Ryuji had packed in a hurry, saying he'd explain where they were going once they were in the car. But once underway, he'd said, "I didn't sleep last night—don't wake me till Kamakura," and then he'd promptly gone to sleep.

He exited the Yokohama-Yokosuka road at Asahina and then took the Kanazawa road five kilometers until they reached Kamakura Station. Ryuji had been asleep for a good two hours.

"Hey, we're here," said Asakawa, shaking him. Ryuji stretched his body like a cat, rubbed his eyes with the backs of his hands, and shook his head rapidly from side to side, lips flapping.

"Ahh, I was having such a pleasant dream...."

"What do we do now?"

Ryuji sat up and looked out the window to see where he was. "Just go straight on this road, and then when you reach the Outer Gate to the Hachiman Shrine turn left and stop." Then Ryuji went to lie down again, saying, "Maybe I can still catch the tail-end of that dream, if you don't mind."

"Look, we'll be there in five minutes. If you've got time to sleep, you've got time to explain to me what we're doing here."

"You'll see once we get there," said Ryuji, jamming his knees up against the dashboard and going back to sleep.

Asakawa made the left and stopped. Dead ahead was an old two-story house with a small sign reading "Tetsuzo Miura Memorial Hall."

"Pull into that parking lot." Ryuji had apparently opened his eyes slightly. He wore a satisfied look and his nostrils were flared like he was sniffing perfume. "Thanks to you I was able to finish my dream."

"What was it about?" asked Asakawa, as he turned the steering wheel.

"What do you think? I was flying. I love dreams where I'm flying." Ryuji snorted happily and licked his lips.

The Tetsuzo Miura Memorial Hall looked deserted. A large open space on the ground floor featured photographs and documents in frames on the wall or in cases under glass, and an outline of this Miura fellow's achievements was plastered onto the center wall. Reading it, Asakawa finally figured out who the man was.

"Excuse me. Is there anyone here?" called Ryuji into the depths of the building. There was no reply.

Tetsuzo Miura had died two years ago at the age of 72, after retiring from a professorship at Yokodai University. He'd specialized in theoretical physics, concentrating on theories of matter and statistical dynamics. But the Memorial Hall, modest as it was, didn't result from his achievements as a physicist, but from his scientific investigations of paranormal phenomena. The resume on the wall claimed that the Professor's theories had attracted worldwide interest, although undoubtedly only a limited number of people had actually paid any attention. After all, Asakawa had never even heard of the guy. And what exactly were this man's theories? To find the answer, Asakawa began to examine the items on the walls and in the display cases. *Thoughts have energy, and that energy...* Asakawa had read this far when he heard, echoing from another room, the sound of someone hurrying down stairs. A door opened and a fortyish man with a mustache poked his head in. Ryuji approached the man, holding out one of his business cards. Asakawa decided to follow his example and took his own cardholder from his breast pocket.

"My name is Takayama. I'm at Fukuzawa University." He spoke smoothly and affably; Asakawa was amused at how different he sounded. Asakawa held out his own card. Faced with the credentials of an academic and a reporter, the man looked rather dismayed. It was Asakawa's card he was frowning at.

"If it's alright, there's something we'd like to consult with you about."

"What would that be?" The man eyed them cautiously.

"As a matter of fact, I once had the pleasure of meeting the late Professor Miura."

For some reason the man seemed relieved to hear this, and relaxed his expression. He brought out three folding chairs and arranged them to face each other.

"Is that so? Please, have a seat."

"It must have been about three years ago…yes, that's right, it was the year before he died. My *alma mater* was sounding me out about possibly giving a lecture on the scientific method, and I thought I might take the opportunity to hear what the Professor had to say…."

"Was it here, in this house?"

"Yes. Professor Takatsuka introduced us."

Hearing this name, the man at last smiled. He realized he had something in common with his visitors. *These two must be on our side. They're not here to attack us after all.*

"I see. I'm sorry about all that. My name is Tetsuaki Miura. Sorry, I'm fresh out of business cards."

"So you must be the Professor's…?"

"Yes, I'm his only son. Hardly worthy of the name, though."

"Is that right? Well, I had no idea the Professor had such an outstanding son."

It was all Asakawa could do to keep from laughing at the sight of Ryuji addressing a man ten years older than himself and calling him an "outstanding son."

Tetsuaki Miura showed them around briefly. Some of his late father's students had gotten together after his death to open the house to the public, and to put in order the materials he'd collected over the years. As for Tetsuaki himself, he said, somewhat self-deprecatingly, that he hadn't been able to become a researcher like his father had wanted, but instead had built an inn on the same lot as the Hall, and devoted himself to managing it.

"So here I am exploiting both his land and his reputation. Like I say, I'm hardly a worthy son." Tetsuaki gave a chagrined laugh. His inn was used largely for high-school excursions—mostly physics and biology clubs, but he also mentioned a group devoted to parapsychological research. High-school clubs needed to have a reason to go on trips. Basically, the Memorial Hall was bait to bring in student groups.

"By the way…" Ryuji sat up straight and tried to guide the conversation to the heart of the matter.

"Oh, I'm sorry. I'm afraid I've been boring you, babbling on like this. So tell me, what brings you here?"

It was apparent that Tetsuaki didn't have much in the way of talent for science. He was nothing but a merchant who adjusted his attitude to suit the situation—Asakawa could tell that Ryuji thought little of the man.

"To tell you the truth, we're looking for someone."

"Who?"

"Actually, we don't know the name. That's why we're here."

"I'm afraid I don't follow you." Tetsuaki looked troubled, as if to urge his visitors to make a little more sense.

"We can't even say for sure if this person is still alive, or has already died. What's clear is that this person had powers that ordinary people don't."

Ryuji paused to watch Tetsuaki, who seemed to understand immediately what he meant.

"Your father was probably Japan's greatest collector of this sort of information. He told me that, using a network of connections he himself had forged, he had assembled a list of people all over the country with paranormal powers. He said he was storing the information."

Tetsuaki's face clouded over. Surely they weren't going to ask him to search through all those records for a single name. "Yes, of course the files have been preserved. But there are so many of them. And many of those people are frauds anyway." Tetsuaki blanched at the thought of looking through all those files again. It had taken a dozen of his father's students several months to organize them. Following the wishes of the deceased, they'd included even uncertain cases, swelling the number of files even further.

"We certainly don't intend to put you to any trouble. With your permission, we'll search through them ourselves, just the two of us."

"They're in the archives upstairs. Perhaps you'd like to take a look at them first?" Tetsuaki stood up. They could only talk like that because they had no idea how much there was. Once they had a look at all those shelves, he had a feeling they wouldn't feel like tackling them. He led them to the second floor.

The archives were in a high-ceilinged room at the head of the stairs. They entered the room to find themselves facing two bookcases of seven shelves each. Each file-book contained materials relating to forty cases, and at first glance there seemed to be thousands of file-books. Asakawa didn't notice Ryuji's reaction, he was too busy turning pale himself. *If we spend time on this, we could well die here in this gloomy room. There's got to be another way!*

Ryuji, unfazed, asked, "Do you mind if we have a look?"

"Go right ahead." Tetsuaki stayed and watched them for a little while, half out of astonishment and half out of curiosity to see just what they thought they'd find. But eventually he seemed to have given up on them. "I've got work to do," he said, leaving.

When they were alone, Asakawa turned to Ryuji and spoke. "So, want to tell me what's going on?" His voice was a bit thick, because he was still craning his neck looking at all the files. These were the first words he'd spoken since entering the Hall. The files were arranged in chronological order, beginning with 1956 and ending in 1988. 1988—that was the year Miura had died. Only death had brought down the curtain on his thirty-two-year quest.

"We don't have much time, so I'll tell you while we look. I'll start with 1956. You start with 1960."

Asakawa tentatively pulled out a file and flipped through it. Each page contained at least one photo and a piece of paper on which was written a short description as well as a name and an address.

"What am I looking for?"

"Pay attention to names and addresses. We're trying to find a woman from Izu Oshima Island."

"A woman?" asked Asakawa, cocking his head questioningly.

"Remember that old woman on the video? She told somebody they were going to give birth. Think she was talking to a man?"

Ryuji was right. Men could not bear children.

So they started searching. It was a simple, repetitive task, and since Asakawa asked why these files existed in the first place, Ryuji explained.

Professor Miura had always been interested in supernatural phenomena. In the '50s, he'd begun experiments with paranormal powers, but he hadn't gotten any results reliable enough to allow him to formulate a scientific theory. Clairvoyants would find themselves unable to do in front of an audience what they had done easily before. It took a lot of concentration to be able to display these powers. What Professor Miura was searching for was the kind of person who could exert his or her power at any time, under any circumstances. He could see that if the person failed in front of witnesses, then Miura himself would be called a fraud. He was convinced that there must be more people out there with paranormal powers than he knew about, so he set about finding them. But how was he to do this? He couldn't interview everybody to check for clairvoyance, second sight, telekinesis. So he came up with a method. To anybody who might possibly have such powers, he sent a piece of film in a securely sealed envelope and asked them to imprint upon it with their minds a certain pattern or image, and then send it back to him, still sealed. In this way he could test the powers of people even at great distances. And since such psychic photography seemed to be a fairly basic power, people who possessed it often seemed to be clairvoyant as well. In 1956, he'd begun to recruit paranormals from all over the country, with the help of former students of his who had gone to work for publishers and newspapers. These former students helped set up a network which would report any rumor of supernatural powers straight back to Professor Miura. However, an examination of the film returned to him suggested that no more than a tenth of claimants actually had any power. The rest had skillfully broken the seal and replaced the film. Obvious cases of deception were weeded out at this point, but cases where it wasn't clear one way or the other were kept, ultimately resulting in the unmanageable collection Asakawa saw before him. In the years since Miura had started, the network had been perfected through the development of the mass media and an increase in the number of participating former students; the data had piled up year after year until the man died.

"I see," murmured Asakawa. "So that's the meaning of this

collection. But how do you know that the name of the person we're looking for is in here?"

"I'm not saying it definitely is. But there's a strong possibility it's here. I mean, look at what she did. You know yourself that there are a few people who can actually produce psychic photos. But there can't be too many paranormals who can actually project images onto a television tube without any equipment whatsoever. That's power of the very highest order. Someone with that kind of power would stand out, even if they didn't try to. I don't think Miura's network would have let someone like that slip through."

Asakawa had to admit that the possibility was genuine. He redoubled his efforts.

"By the way, why am I looking at 1960?" Asakawa suddenly looked up.

"Remember the scene on the video that shows a television? It was a rather old model. One of the early sets, from the '50s or early '60s."

"But that doesn't necessarily mean..."

"Shut up. We're talking probabilities here, right?"

Asakawa chided himself for being so irritated this last little while. But he had good reason to be. Given the limited time-frame, the number of files was huge. It would have been more unnatural to be calm about it.

At that moment, Asakawa saw the words "Izu Oshima" in the file he was holding.

"Hey! Got one," he yelled, triumphantly. Ryuji turned around, surprised, and peered at the file.

Motomachi, Izu Oshima. Teruko Tsuchida, age 37. Postmarked February 14, 1960. A black-and-white photograph showing a white lightning-like slash against a black background.

The description read: *Subject sent this with a note predicting a cross-shaped image. No traces of substitution.*

"How about that?" Asakawa trembled with excitement as he waited for Ryuji's response.

"It's a possibility. Take down the name and address, just in case." Ryuji turned back to his own search. Asakawa felt better for having found a likely candidate so soon, but at the same time he was a bit dissatisfied with Ryuji's brusque reaction.

Two hours passed. They didn't find another woman from Izu Oshima. Most of the submissions were either from Tokyo itself or the surrounding Kanto region. Tetsuaki appeared, offering them tea and two or three possibly sarcastic comments before leaving. Their hands on the files were getting slower and slower; they'd been at it for two hours and hadn't even polished off a year's worth.

Finally, somehow, Asakawa got through 1960. As he went to start on 1961 he happened to glance at Ryuji. Ryuji was sitting cross-legged on the floor, motionless, face buried in an open file. *Is he asleep, the idiot?* Asakawa reached out his hand, but then Ryuji emitted a stifled groan.

"I'm so hungry I could die. How about you go buy us some takeout and oolong tea? Oh, and make reservations for this evening at *Le Petit Pension Soleil.*"

"What the hell?"

"That's the inn the guy runs."

"I know that. But why would I want to stay there with you?"

"You'd rather not?"

"For starters, we haven't got time to lounge around at an inn."

"Even if we find her now, there's no way to get to Izu Oshima right now. We can't go anywhere today. Don't you think it'd be better to get a good night's sleep and marshal our energies for tomorrow?"

Asakawa felt an indescribable aversion to spending the night with Ryuji at an inn. But there was no alternative, so he gave up and went out to buy food and tell Tetsuaki Miura they'd be staying the night. Then he and Ryuji ate their takeout and drank their oolong tea. It was seven in the evening. A brief respite.

His arms were tired and his shoulders stiff. His eyes swam, he took off his glasses. Instead, he held the files close enough to his face that he could lick them if he wanted. He had to use all his concentration or he was afraid he'd miss something, which tired him even more.

Nine o'clock. The silence of the archives was broken by Ryuji's mad screech. "I've found it, finally! So that's where she was hiding."

Asakawa felt himself drawn to the file. He sat down next to Ryuji and put his glasses back on to look at it. It said:

Izu Oshima, Sashikiji. Sadako Yamamura. Age 10. The envelope was postmarked August 29, 1958. *Subject sent this with a note predicting it would be imprinted with her own name. She's the real thing, without a doubt.* Attached was a photograph showing the character *yama,* "mountain," in white against a black background. Asakawa had seen that character somewhere before.

"That's...that's it." His voice trembled. On the video, the scene of the eruption of Mt. Mihara had been followed immediately by a shot of the character for "mountain," identical to this one. Not only that, the screen of the old television in the tenth scene had displayed the character *sada.* This woman's name was Sadako Yamamura.

"What do you think?" asked Ryuji.

"No question about it. This is it."

At long last Asakawa found hope. The thought crossed his mind that maybe, just maybe, they'd beat the deadline.

6

October 16—Tuesday

10:15 a.m. Ryuji and Asakawa were on a high-speed passenger boat that had just left port at Atami. There was no regular ferry linking Oshima and the mainland, so they'd had to leave the car in the parking lot next to the Atami Korakuen Hotel. Asakawa was still clutching the key in his left hand.

They were scheduled to arrive on Oshima in an hour. A strong wind blew and it looked like rain. Most of the passengers hadn't ventured out onto the deck, but stayed huddled in their reserved seats. Asakawa and Ryuji had been in too much of a hurry to check before buying their tickets, but it looked like a typhoon was approaching. The waves were large, and the rocking of the boat was worse than normal.

Sipping a can of hot coffee, Asakawa went over the whole chain of events again in his mind. He wasn't sure if they should congratulate themselves for having come this far, or reproach themselves for not having found out about "Sadako Yamamura" and set out for Oshima Island earlier. Everything had hung on noticing that the black curtain flashing momentarily over the images on the video was eyelids, blinking. The images had been recorded not by machine but by the human sensory apparatus. Essentially, the person had focused her energies on the video deck at cabin B-4 while it was recording, and created not a psychic photo but a psychic video. This surely indicated paranormal powers of immeasurable proportions. Ryuji had assumed that such a person would stand out from the crowd, and gone looking for her, and had ultimately found out her name. Not that they knew for sure that "Sadako Yamamura" was, in fact, the culprit. She was still just a suspect. They were heading to Oshima in order to follow up on their suspicions.

The sea was rough, causing the boat to pitch and roll violently. Asakawa felt an ugly premonition come over him. Maybe it hadn't been such a good idea for both of them to go to Oshima. What if they got tied down by the typhoon and couldn't leave the island? Who'd save his wife and daughter? The deadline was almost at hand. 10:04 p.m., the day after tomorrow.

Asakawa warmed his hands with the coffee can and shrank down into his seat. "I still can't believe it, you know. That a human being could really do something like that."

"It doesn't matter if you believe it or not, now, does it?" Ryuji answered without taking his eyes from his map of Oshima. "Anyway, it's a reality staring you in the face. You know, all we're seeing is one small part of a continuously changing phenomenon."

Ryuji set the map down on his knee. "You know about the Big Bang, right? They believe that the universe was born in a tremendous explosion twenty billion years ago. I can mathematically express the form of the universe, from its birth to the present. It's all about differential equations. Most phenomena in the universe can be expressed with differential equations, you know. Using them, you can figure out what the universe looked like a hundred million years ago, ten billion years ago, even a second or a tenth of a second after that initial explosion. But. *But.* No matter how far we go back, no matter how we try to express it, we just can't know what it looked like at *zero*, at the very moment *of* the explosion. And there's another thing. How is our universe going to end? Is the universe expanding or contracting? See, we don't know the beginning and we don't know the end; all we can know about is the in-between stuff. And that, my friend, is what life is like."

Ryuji poked Asakawa in the arm.

"I guess you're right. I can look at photo albums and get a reasonable idea of what I was like when I was three years old, or when I was a newborn."

"See what I mean? But what's before birth, what's after death—these are things we just don't know."

"After death? When you die, that's the end, you just disappear. That's all, right?"

"Hey, have you ever died?"

"No, I haven't." Asakawa shook his head with utter earnestness.

"Well then you don't know, do you? You don't know where you go after you die."

"Are you saying there's such a thing as spirits?"

"Look, all I can say is, I just don't know. But when you're talking about the birth of life, I think things go a lot smoother when you posit the existence of a soul. None of the claptrap of modern molecular biologists actually sounds real. What are they really saying? 'Take hundreds each of twenty-odd different amino acids, put them in a bowl, mix them all together, add a little electrical energy, and *voilà*, protein, the building block of life.' And they really expect us to believe that? Might as well tell us we're all children of God—at least that'd be easier to swallow. What I think is that there's a completely different kind of energy involved at the moment of birth; almost like there's a certain will at work."

Ryuji seemed to lean in a little closer to Asakawa, but then he suddenly changed the subject. "By the way, I couldn't help but notice you were engrossed in the Professor's *oeuvre* back at the Memorial Hall. Come across anything interesting?"

Now that he mentioned it, Asakawa remembered that he had started to read something. *Thoughts have energy, and that energy...*

"I think it said something about thoughts being energy."

"What else?"

"I didn't have time to finish reading it."

"Heh, heh, that's too bad. You were just getting to the good part. The Professor could really make me laugh, the way he'd set out in all seriousness things that would shock normal people. What the old man was saying, basically, is that ideas are life forms, with energy of their own."

"Huh? You mean, the thoughts in our heads can turn into living beings?"

"That's about the size of it."

"Well, that's a rather extreme suggestion."

"It is indeed, but similar ideas have been propounded since before the time of Christ. I suppose you could just look at it as a different theory of life."

Having said this much, Ryuji suddenly seemed to lose interest in the conversation, returning his gaze to the map.

Asakawa understood what Ryuji was saying, most of it anyway, but it didn't sit very well with him. *We may not be able to scientifically explain what we're facing. But it's real, and because it's real we have to face it as a real phenomenon and deal with it as such, even if we don't understand its cause or effect. What we need to concentrate on right now is figuring out the riddle of the charm and saving our own asses, not unlocking all the secrets of the supernatural.* Ryuji might have some good points. But what Asakawa really needed from him were clearer answers.

The farther out to sea they went the worse the motion of the boat, and Asakawa began to worry he'd get seasick. The more he thought about it the more he thought he felt an unsettled feeling in his chest. Ryuji, who had been nodding off, suddenly raised his head and looked outside. The sea was throwing up dark gray waves, and in the distance they could see the dim shadow of an island.

"You know, Asakawa, something's worrying me."

"What?"

"The four kids who stayed at the log cabin. Why didn't they try to carry out the charm?"

That again.

"Isn't it obvious? They didn't believe the video."

"Well, that's what I thought. It explains why they pulled a prank like erasing the charm. But I was just remembering a trip I took with the track team back in high school. In the middle of the night, Saito comes bursting into the room. You remember Saito, right? Kind of not quite all there. There were twelve of us on the team, and we were all sleeping together in one room. And that idiot comes running in, teeth chattering, and screams, 'I've seen a ghost!' He opened the bathroom door and saw a little girl crouched behind the trash can by the sink—she was crying. Now, aside from me, how do you think the other ten guys reacted to this?"

"They probably half believed and half laughed it off."

Ryuji shook his head. "That's how it'd work in a horror movie, or on TV. At first no one takes it seriously, and then one by one, they're picked off by the monster, right? But it's different in real life. Every single one of them, without exception, believed him. All ten of them. And not because all ten of them were especially chicken, either. You could try it on any group of people and get the same results. A fundamental sense of terror is built into us humans, on the instinctual level."

"So what you're saying is, it's strange that those four didn't believe the video."

As he listened to Ryuji's story, Asakawa was recalling the face of his daughter, crying from seeing the demon mask. He remembered how puzzled he'd been—how had she known the demon mask was supposed to be scary?

"Hmm. Well, the scenes on that video don't tell a story, and they're not all that frightening to just look at. So I suppose it's possible to disbelieve it. But weren't they at least bothered, those four? What would you do? If you were told that carrying out a charm would save your life, even if you didn't believe in it, wouldn't you feel you ought to give it a try anyway? I would have expected at least one of them to break rank. I mean, even if he or she insisted on putting on a brave face in front of the others, he or she could always perform the charm in secret after getting back to Tokyo."

Asakawa's bad feeling grew stronger. He had actually wondered the same thing himself. *What if the charm turns out to be something impossible?*

"So maybe it was something they couldn't carry out, and so they convinced themselves they didn't believe it anyway...." An example occurred to Asakawa. What if a woman who had been murdered left a message in the world of the living in an effort to get someone else to avenge her, so that she could be at peace?

"Heh, heh. I know what you're thinking. What would you do if that turned out to be the case?"

Asakawa asked himself: if the charm included a command to kill someone, would he be able to do it? Would he be able to kill a perfect stranger to save his own life? But what worried him more was, if it came to that, who would be the one to carry out the charm? He shook his head furiously. *Stop thinking such stupid things.* All he could do at the moment was pray that this Sadako Yamamura person's desire was something that anybody could fulfill.

The outlines of the island were becoming clearer; the wharf at Motomachi Harbor was slowly coming into view.

"Listen, Ryuji. I have a favor to ask." Asakawa spoke fervently.

"What's that?"

"If I don't make it in time...that is..." Asakawa couldn't bring himself to say the word "die." "If you figure out the charm the very next day, could you...Well, there's my wife and daughter...."

Ryuji cut in. "Of course. Leave it to me. I'll be responsible for saving wifey and babykins."

Asakawa took out one of his business cards and wrote a phone number on the back. "I'm going to send them to her parents' house in Ashikaga until we solve this thing. This is the number there. I'm going to give it to you now, before I forget."

Ryuji put the card in his pocket without even glancing at it.

Just then came the announcement that the ship had docked at Motomachi on Oshima Island. Asakawa intended to call home from the waterfront and convince his wife to go home to her parents' for a while. He didn't know when he'd get back to Tokyo. Who knew? Time might run out for him here on Oshima. He couldn't stand the thought of his family alone and terrified in their little condo.

As they walked down the gangway, Ryuji asked: "Hey, Asakawa. Do a wife and kid really mean that much?"

It was a very un-Ryuji-like question. Asakawa couldn't help but laugh as he replied, "You'll find out, one of these days."

But Asakawa didn't really think Ryuji was capable of starting a normal family.

7

The wind was stronger here on the pier at Oshima than it had been on the wharf at Atami. Overhead the clouds were scurrying from west to east, while underfoot the concrete jetty shook with the force of waves breaking against it. The rain wasn't falling that hard, but the raindrops, borne by the wind, were hitting Asakawa's face head-on. Neither of them had umbrellas. They jammed their hands into their pockets and hunched forward as they walked quickly along the pier over the ocean.

Islanders holding placards for car-rental companies or banners for inns were there to greet the tourists. Asakawa lifted his head and looked for the person who was supposed to meet them. Before getting on the boat at the harbor in Atami, Asakawa had contacted his office and asked for the phone number of the Oshima office, ultimately enlisting the help of a correspondent named Hayatsu. None of the national news organizations had full-fledged bureaus on Oshima; instead they hired locals as stringers. These correspondents kept an eye on island doings, watching for any noteworthy incidents or interesting episodes and reporting them to the main office; they were also responsible for assisting any reporters dispatched to the island on stories. Hayatsu had worked for the *Daily News* before retiring here to Oshima. His territory included not just Oshima itself but all seven islands in the Izu chain, and when anything happened he didn't have to wait for a reporter to arrive from headquarters, but could file his own articles. Hayatsu had a network of contacts on the island, so his cooperation promised to speed up Asakawa's investigation.

On the phone, Hayatsu himself had responded positively to Asakawa's request, promising to meet him at the jetty. Since they'd never met, Asakawa had described himself and said he was traveling with a friend.

Now he heard a voice from behind. "Excuse me, are you Mr. Asakawa?"

"Yes."

"I'm Hayatsu, the Oshima correspondent." He held out umbrellas and smiled good-naturedly.

"Sorry to impose on you so suddenly like this. We really appreciate your help."

As they hurried to Hayatsu's car, Asakawa introduced Ryuji. The wind was so loud they could hardly speak over it until they'd climbed inside the vehicle. It was a compact, but surprisingly spacious inside. Asakawa rode in front, Ryuji in the back.

"Shall we go straight to Takashi Yamamura's house?" asked Hayatsu, both hands on the steering wheel. He was over sixty, and had a full head of hair, though much of it was gray.

"So, you've already found Sadako Yamamura's family?" Asakawa had already told Hayatsu on the phone that they were coming to investigate someone by that name.

"It's a small town. Once you said it was a Yamamura from Sashikiji, I knew right away who it was. There's only one family by that name here. Yamamura's a fisherman who runs his house as a bed-and-breakfast in the summertime. What do you think? We could have him put you up there tonight. Of course you're welcome at my place, too, but it's a little small and rundown. I'm sure having you stay there would be an imposition on you." Hayatsu laughed. He and his wife lived alone, but he wasn't exaggerating: they really didn't have room to sleep two guests.

Asakawa looked back at Ryuji.

"I'm fine with that."

Hayatsu's little car sped toward the Sashikiji district, on the southern tip of the island. Sped as much as it could, that is: the Oshima Ring Road circling the island was too narrow and winding to go very fast on. The vast majority of the cars they passed were also compacts. At times their field of vision opened up to their right, to reveal the ocean, and when it did the sound of the wind would change. The sea was dark, reflecting the deep leaden color of the sky, and it heaved violently, throwing up whitecaps. If it hadn't been for those brief flashes of white, it would have been difficult to tell where the sky stopped and the sea began, or where the sea stopped and the land began. The longer they gazed at it the more depressing it seemed. The radio blared a typhoon alert, and their surroundings became that much darker. They veered right at a fork in the road and immediately entered a tunnel of camellias. They could see bare roots beneath the camellias, tangled and wizened; long years of exposure to wind and rain had eroded some of the plants' soil. Now they were wet and slick with rain—it looked to Asakawa like they were speeding through the intestines of a huge monster.

"Sashikiji is dead ahead," said Hayatsu. "But I don't think this Sadako Yamamura woman is here anymore. You can get the details from Takashi Yamamura. From what I hear he's a cousin of her mother's."

"How old would this Sadako be now?" asked Asakawa. For

some time now Ryuji had been scrunched down in the back seat, uttering not a word.

"Hmm. I've never actually met her, you know. But if she's still alive, she must be forty-two, forty-three, maybe?"

If she's still alive? Asakawa wondered why Hayatsu had used that expression. Maybe she was missing? Suddenly he was filled with misgivings. What if they'd come all this way to Oshima only to find no one knew if she was dead or alive? What if this was a dead end?

Finally the car pulled up in front of a two-story house bearing the sign *Yamamura Manor*. It stood on a gentle slope with a commanding view of the ocean. No doubt in good weather the scenery was splendid. In the offing they could make out the triangular shape of an island. That was Toshima.

"When the weather is nice, you can see Nijima, Shikinejima and even Kozushima from here," said Hayatsu proudly, pointing south over the sea.

8

"Investigate? What is it exactly I should investigate about this woman?"

She joined the troupe in '65? You've got to be kidding—that's twenty-five years ago. Yoshino was ranting to himself. *It's hard enough to trace a criminal's steps a year after the fact. But twenty-five?*

"We need anything and everything you can find out. We want to know what kind of life this woman's led, what she's doing right now, what she wants."

Yoshino could only sigh. He wedged the receiver between his ear and his shoulder and pulled a notepad over from the edge of the desk.

"...and how old was she at the time?"

"Eighteen. She graduated from high school on Oshima and went straight to Tokyo, where she joined a theater group called Theater Group Soaring."

"Oshima?" Yoshino stopped writing and frowned. "Hey, where are you calling from, anyway?"

"From a place called Sashikiji, on Izu Oshima Island."

"And when do you plan on coming back?"

"As soon as I can."

"You realize there's a typhoon heading your way?"

Of course there was no way Asakawa could be ignorant of it,

being right there in the middle of it, but to Yoshino the whole thing had taken on an unreal quality that he had begun to find amusing. The "deadline" was the night after next, and yet Asakawa himself was holed up on Oshima, possibly unable to escape.

"Have you heard any travel advisories?" Asakawa still didn't know many details.

"Well, I'm not sure, but the way it looks now, I imagine they'll be grounding all flights and suspending ocean transport."

Asakawa had been too busy chasing down Sadako Yamamura to pick up any reliable information about the typhoon. He'd had a bad feeling ever since stepping onto the Oshima pier, but now that the possibility of being stranded here had been voiced, he suddenly felt a sense of urgency. Receiver still in hand, he fell silent.

"Hey, hey, don't worry. They haven't cancelled anything yet." Yoshino tried to sound positive. Then he changed the subject. "So, this woman...Sadako Yamamura. You've checked her history out up to the age of eighteen?"

"More or less," Asakawa answered, conscious of the sound of the wind and waves outside the phone booth.

"This isn't your only lead, right? You've got to have something besides this Theater Group Soaring."

"Nope, that's it. Sadako Yamamura, born in Sashikiji on Izu Oshima Island in 1947 to Shizuko Yamamura...hey, make a note of that name. Shizuko Yamamura. She was twenty-two in '47. She left her new baby, Sadako, with her grandmother and ran off to Tokyo."

"Why did she leave the baby on the island?"

"There was a man. Make a note of this, too: Heihachiro Ikuma. At the time he was Assistant Professor of Psychiatry. He was

Shizuko Yamamura's lover."

"So does that mean Sadako is Shizuko and Ikuma's child?"

"I haven't been able to find proof, but I think it's safe to assume that."

"And they weren't married, right?"

"Exactly. Heihachiro Ikuma already had a family."

So it had been an illicit affair. Yoshino licked the tip of his pencil.

"Okay, I'm with you. Go on."

"Early in 1950 Shizuko suddenly revisits her hometown for the first time in three years. She's reunited with her daughter Sadako, and lives here for a while. But by the end of the year she's absconded again, this time taking Sadako with her. For the next five years, nobody knows where Shizuko and Sadako are or what they're doing. But in the mid '50s, Shizuko's cousin, still living here on the island, hears a rumor that Shizuko has become famous doing something or other."

"Was she involved in some sort of incident?"

"It's unclear. The cousin just says that he started hearing things about Shizuko, through the grapevine. But when I gave him my card, he saw I work for a newspaper publisher and said, 'If you're a reporter you probably know more about it than me.' From the way he was talking it sounds like from about 1950 to 1955 Shizuko and Sadako were involved in something that caused a stir in the media. But news from the mainland was hard to come by on the island...."

"And so you'd like me to check and see what it was that got them in the news?"

"You read my mind."

"Idiot. It was obvious."

"There's more. In '56, Shizuko comes back to the island, dragging Sadako with her. The mother's so worn down that she looks like a different person, and she won't answer any of her cousin's questions. She just closes up, mumbling incoherently. And then one day she throws herself into Mt. Mihara, the volcano, and kills herself. She was thirty-one."

"So I'm also finding out why Shizuko committed suicide."

"If you would." Still holding the receiver, Asakawa bowed. If he ended up stranded on this island, then Yoshino would be his only hope. Asakawa regretted that both he and Ryuji had so blithely come here. Ryuji could have easily investigated a little hamlet like Sashikiji all by himself. It would have been more efficient for Asakawa to stay in Tokyo and wait for Ryuji to contact him, and then team up with Yoshino to check things out on that end.

"Alright, I'll do what I can. But I think I'm a little understaffed here."

"I'll call Oguri and ask him to send some people your way."

"That'd be great."

It was one thing to say it, of course, but Asakawa didn't have much confidence in the idea. His editor was always complaining about being short-handed. Asakawa seriously doubted he'd spare valuable manpower for something like this.

"So, her mother kills herself, and Sadako stays on in Sashikiji, taken care of by her mother's cousin. That cousin has turned his house into a bed-and-breakfast now." He was about to say that he and Ryuji were now staying in that very house, but decided it was an unnecessary detail.

"The following year, Sadako, who's a fourth-grader now, makes a name for herself at school by predicting the eruption of

Mt. Mihara. Did you get that? Mt. Mihara erupted in 1957, on the very day and time Sadako had predicted."

"Now that's impressive. If we had a woman like that we wouldn't need the Coordinating Committee for Earthquake Prediction."

As a result of her prediction's coming true, her fame had spread throughout the island, and was picked up by Professor Miura's network. But Asakawa figured he didn't need to explain all that. What was important now was...

"After that, islanders kept coming to Sadako asking her to predict their futures. But she turned down every single request. She just kept saying she didn't have that kind of power."

"Out of modesty?"

"Who knows? Then, when she finishes high school, she takes off for Tokyo like she just couldn't wait to get away. The relatives who'd been taking care of her got exactly one postcard from her. It said she'd passed the test and had been accepted into Theater Group Soaring. They haven't heard from her again to this day. There's not a soul on the island who knows where she is or what she's up to."

"In other words, the only clue we have, the only trace she left, is this Theater Group Soaring."

"I'm afraid so."

"Okay, let me make sure I have this straight. What I'm supposed to find out is: what Shizuko Yamamura was in the news for, why she jumped into a volcano, and where her daughter went and what she did after joining a theater troupe at age eighteen. In other words, all about the mother and all about the daughter. Just those two things."

"Right."

"Which first?"

"Huh?"

"I'm asking you whether you want me to start with the mother or the daughter. You don't have much time left, you know."

The most pressing issue, clearly, was what had become of Sadako.

"Could you start with the daughter?"

"Gotcha. I guess first thing tomorrow I'll pop in to the office of Theater Group Soaring."

Asakawa looked at his watch. It was only a little past six in the evening. Still plenty of time before a rehearsal space would be closing.

"Hey, Yoshino. Not tomorrow. Say you'll do it tonight."

Yoshino heaved a sigh and shook his head slightly. "Now look, Asakawa. I have my own work to do, you know—did you ever think of that? I've got a mountain of things I've got to write up before morning. Even tomorrow's a little..." Yoshino trailed off. If he said any more it would look like he was trying to make Asakawa feel too much in his debt. He always took the greatest care to appear manly in situations like this.

"Please, I'm begging you. I mean, my deadline is the day after tomorrow." He knew how things worked in their business, and he was afraid to put it any more strongly. All he could do was to wait quietly for Yoshino's decision.

"But... Ah, what the hell. I'll try to get to it tonight. I'm not making any promises, mind you."

"Thanks. I owe you." Asakawa bowed and started to hang up.

"Hey, hang on a second. There's something important I haven't asked you yet."

"What's that?"

"What possible relationship could there be between what you saw on that video and this Sadako Yamamura?"

Asakawa paused. "You wouldn't believe it even if I told you."

"Try me."

"No video camera recorded those images." Asakawa paused for a good long moment to allow his meaning to sink into Yoshino's brain. "Those images are things that Sadako saw with her eyes and things she imagined in her head, fragments presented one after another with nothing to contextualize them."

"Huh?" Yoshino was momentarily at a loss for words.

"See. I told you you wouldn't believe it."

"You mean they're like psychic photos?"

"The phrase doesn't even begin to cover it. She actually caused these images to appear on a TV tube. She's projecting moving images onto a TV."

"So, what, she's a production agency?" Yoshino laughed at his own joke. Asakawa didn't get angry. He understood why Yoshino had to joke. He listened silently to his friend's carefree laughter.

9:40 p.m. As he climbed the stairs out of Yotsuya Sanchome Station on the Marunouchi subway line, a gust of wind threatened to blow Yoshino's hat off, and he had to hold it down onto his head with both hands. He looked around him for the fire station he was supposed to use as a landmark. It was right there on the corner. A minute's walk down the street took him to his destination.

A sign stood on the sidewalk, reading Theater Group Soaring; next to it a flight of stairs led down to a basement, from the depths of which came the voices of young men and women, raised in mingled singing and recitation. They probably had a performance coming up and were planning to rehearse until the trains stopped running. He didn't have to be an arts reporter to figure that out. But he spent most of his time chasing after crime stories. He had to admit it felt a little weird visiting the rehearsal space of a repertory theater company.

The stairs to the basement were made of steel and every step clanged. If the founding members of the company had no recollection of Sadako Yamamura, then the thread would snap, and that psychic's life, on which all their hopes rested, would sink back into the darkness. Theater Group Soaring had been founded in 1957, and Sadako had joined in 1965. There were only four founding members still around today, including a guy named Uchimura, a playwright and director who spoke for the group.

Yoshino gave his card to a twenty-something intern standing at the entrance to the rehearsal hall and asked him to call Uchimura.

"You have a visitor from the *Daily News*, sir." The intern spoke in a resonant, actorly voice, calling to the director, who sat by the wall watching over everyone's performances. Uchimura turned around in surprise. Realizing his visitor was from the press, he was all smiles as he approached Yoshino. Theater companies all treated the press with great politeness. Even the smallest mention in a newspaper's arts column could make a big difference in ticket sales. With only a week left until opening night, he assumed the reporter had come to take a peek at the rehearsals. The *Daily News* had never paid much attention to him before, so Uchimura poured on the charm, determined to make the most of the chance. But the minute he learned the real reason for Yoshino's visit, Uchimura abruptly seemed to lose all interest in him. Suddenly he was extremely busy. He looked around the hall until he spied a smallish actor in his fifties, seated on a chair. "Over here, Shin," he said in a shrill voice, summoning the man. Something in the overly familiar tone he used when addressing the middle-aged actor—or maybe it was his womanish voice itself, combined with his ungainly long arms and legs—gave the brawny Yoshino the creeps. This guy is *different*, he thought.

"Shin baby, you don't go on until the second act. Be a dear and talk to this man about Sadako Yamamura. You remember that creepy girl, don't you?"

Shin's voice was one Yoshino had heard before, dubbing Japanese dialogue onto Western movies shown on TV. Shin Arima was better known as a voice actor than for his work onstage. He was one of the other original members still in the troupe.

"Sadako Yamamura?" Arima scratched his balding head as he tried to reel in quarter-century-old memories. "Oh, *that* Sadako Yamamura." He grimaced. Evidently the woman had left a deep impression on him.

"You remember? Well, then, I'm rehearsing here, so take him up to my room, won't you?" Uchimura bowed slightly and walked back toward the assembled players; by the time he reached the place he'd been sitting, he was once more every inch the lordly director.

Opening a door marked *President*, Arima pointed to a leather sofa set and said, "Have a seat." If this was the President's office, it meant that the troupe was organized like a business. No doubt the director doubled as CEO.

"So what brings you out in the middle of a storm like this?" Arima's face glistened red with sweat from rehearsing, but a kindly smile lurked in the depths of his eyes. The director looked like the type of person who was always weighing the other's motives while conversing, but Arima was the kind of guy who answered everything you asked him honestly, without covering anything up. Interviews could either be easy or painful, depending on the subject's personality.

"I'm sorry to bother you when you're so busy like this." Yoshino sat down and took out his notepad. He assumed his usual pose, pen clutched in his right hand.

"I never expected to hear the name Sadako Yamamura, not now. That was ages ago."

Arima was recalling his youth. He missed the youthful energy he'd had then, running away from the commercial theater company he'd originally belonged to and founding a new troupe with his friends.

"Mr. Arima, when you placed her name a few minutes ago you said, '*that* Sadako Yamamura.' What exactly did you mean by that?"

"That girl—let me see, when was it she joined, anyway? I believe we'd only been around a few years. The company was really taking off then, and we had more kids wanting to join every year. Anyway, that Sadako, she was a strange one."

"In what way was she strange?"

"Hmm." Arima put his hand to his jaw and thought for a while. *Come to think of it, why do I have the impression that she was strange?*

"Was there something in particular about her, something that stood out?"

"No, to look at her, she was just an ordinary girl. A little tall, but quiet. She was always alone."

"Alone?"

"Well, usually the interns become quite close to each other.

But she never tried to get involved with the others."

There was always someone like that in any group. It was hard for Yoshino to imagine that this alone had made her stand out.

"How would you describe her, say, in a word?"

"In a word? Hmm. Eerie, I'd have to say." Without hesitating, he called her "eerie." And Uchimura had called her "that creepy girl." Yoshino couldn't help but feel sorry for a maiden of eighteen whom everybody characterized as eerie. He began to imagine some grotesque figure of a woman.

"What was it about her that made her seem eerie?"

Now that he stopped to examine, it seemed odd to Arima that his impressions of an intern who'd been around for no longer than a year, and twenty-five years ago at that, should still seem so fresh. There was something tugging at the back of his mind. Something had happened, something that had served to fix her name in his memory.

"Oh, yes, now I remember. It was right in this room." Arima looked around the president's office. Thinking back on the incident, he could vividly recall even how the furniture had been arranged in those days, when this room was still being used as the main office.

"You see, we've rehearsed in this space since the beginning, but it used to be a lot smaller. This room we're in now used to be our main office. There were lockers over there, and we had a frosted-glass divider standing right about here.... Right, and there used to be a TV right there—well, we have a different one there now." Arima pointed as he spoke.

"A TV?" Yoshino narrowed his eyes and adjusted his grip on his pen.

"Right. One of those old black and white jobs."

"Okay. So what happened?" Yoshino urged him to go on.

"Rehearsal had just ended and nearly everybody had gone home. I wasn't happy with one of my lines, and I came up here to go over my part one more time. I was right over there, see..." Arima pointed to the door. "I was standing there, looking into the room, and through the frosted glass I could see the TV screen flickering. I thought, well, someone's watching TV. Mind you, I wasn't mistaken. It was on the other side of the divider, so I couldn't actually see what was on the screen, but I could see the quavering black and white light. There was no sound. The room was dim, and as I came around the divider, I wondered who was in front of the TV, and I peered at the person's face. It was Sadako Yamamura. But when I came around to the other side of the divider and stood beside her, there was nothing on the screen. Of course, I just automatically assumed that she'd just switched it off. At that point, I had no doubts yet. But..."

Arima seemed reluctant to continue.

"Please, go on."

"I spoke to her. I said, 'You'd better hurry home before the trains stop running.' And I turned on the desk lamp. But it wouldn't turn on. I looked and saw that it wasn't plugged in. I crouched down to plug it in, and that's when I noticed it: the television wasn't plugged in, either."

Arima vividly recalled the chill that had run up his spine when he saw the plug lying there on the floor.

Yoshino wanted to confirm what he'd just heard. "So even though it wasn't plugged in, the television was definitely on?"

"That's right. It made me shudder, let me tell you. I raised my head without thinking and looked at Sadako. What was she doing sitting there in front of an unplugged television set? She didn't meet my gaze, but just kept staring at the screen, with a faint smile on her lips."

Arima seemed to remember the smallest detail. The episode had obviously made a deep impression on him.

"And did you tell anyone about this?"

"Naturally. I told Uchy—that is, Uchimura, the director, whom you just met—and also Shigemori."

"Mr. Shigemori?"

"He was the real founder of the company. Uchimura is actually our second leader."

"Ah-ha. So how did Mr. Shigemori react to your story?"

"He was playing mah-jongg at the time, but he was fascinated. He always did have a weakness for women, and it seemed he'd had his eye on her for a while, planning to make her his. Then that evening, after he'd had a few, he started talking crazy, saying 'tonight I'm going to storm Sadako's apartment.' We didn't know what to do. It was just drunken babbling—we couldn't take it too seriously, but we couldn't go along with it, either. After a while, everybody went home, and Shigemori was left alone. And in the end we never knew if he actually went to Sadako's apartment that night or not. Because the next day, when Shigemori showed up at the rehearsal space, he looked like a completely different person. He was pale and silent, and he just sat in his chair saying absolutely nothing. Then he died, right there, just like going to sleep."

Startled, Yoshino looked up. "What was the cause of death?"

"Cardiac paralysis. Today they'd call it 'sudden heart failure,' I guess. He was pushing himself pretty hard to get ready for a premiere, and I think he just overdid it."

"So basically, nobody knows if something happened between

Sadako and Shigemori."

Yoshino pressed the point, and Arima gave a definite nod. No wonder she'd left such a strong impression, Yoshino thought.

"What happened to her after that?"

"She quit. I think she was only with us for a year or two."

"And then what did she do, after she quit?"

"I'm afraid I can't help you there."

"What do most people do after they quit the troupe?"

"People who are really dedicated try to join another company."

"Do you think Sadako Yamamura might have done that?"

"She was a bright girl, and her acting instincts weren't bad at all. But she had such personality defects. I mean, this business is all about personal relationships. I don't think she was really cut out for it."

"So you're saying there's a possibility she left the theater world altogether?"

"I really couldn't say."

"Isn't there anybody who might know what happened to her?"

"Maybe one of the other interns who was here at the time."

"Would you happen to have any of their names and addresses?"

"Hold on." Arima stood up and walked over to the shelves built into the wall. Bound files were lined up from one end of the shelf to the other; he took one down. It contained the portfolios applicants submitted when they took the entrance exam.

"Including her, there were eight interns who joined in 1965." He waved their portfolios in the air.

"May I have a look?"

"Go right ahead."

Each portfolio had two photos attached, a head shot and a full-body shot. Trying to remain calm, Yoshino pulled out Sadako Yamamura's portfolio. He looked at her photos.

"Hey, didn't you say she was 'eerie' a few minutes ago?" Yoshino was confused. There was too much of a gap between the Sadako he'd imagined from Arima's description and the Sadako in the photos. "Eerie? You've got to be kidding me. I've never seen such a pretty face."

Yoshino wondered why he had phrased it that way—why he'd said "pretty face" instead of "pretty girl." Certainly her facial features were perfectly regular. But she lacked a certain womanly roundness. But looking at the full-body shot, he had to admit that her slender waist and ankles were strikingly feminine. She was beautiful—and yet, the passage of twenty-five years had corroded their impressions of her, until they remembered her as "eerie," as "that creepy girl." Normally they should have recalled her as "that wonderfully beautiful young woman." Yoshino's interest was piqued by this "eeriness" that seemed to elbow out the salient prettiness of her face.

9

October 17—Wednesday

Standing at the intersection of Omotesando and Aoyama-dori, Yoshino once more took out his notebook. *6-1 Minami Aoyama, Sugiyama Lodgings.* That had been Sadako's address twenty-five years before. The address had him worried. He followed Omotesando as it curved, and sure enough, 6-1 was the block opposite the Nezu Museum, one of the posher districts in the city. Just as he'd feared, there were nothing but imposing red-brick condos where the cheap Sugiyama Lodgings should have been.

Aw, who were you kidding anyway? How were you supposed to follow this woman's tracks twenty-five years later?

His only remaining lead was the other kids who'd joined the theater group at the same time as Sadako. Of the seven who'd come in that year, he'd only been able to find contact information for four. If none of them knew anything about Sadako's whereabouts, then the trail would have gone dead. And Yoshino had a feeling that was exactly what would happen. He looked at his watch: eleven in the morning. He dashed into a nearby stationery shop to send a fax to the Izu Oshima bureau. He might as well tell Asakawa everything he'd found out up to this point.

At that very moment, Asakawa and Ryuji were at that

"bureau," Hayatsu's home.

"Hey, Asakawa, calm down!" Ryuji yelled toward Asakawa, who was pacing around the room with his back turned. "Panicking won't help, you know."

The typhoon warnings flowed steadily from the radio: maximum wind velocity, barometric pressure near the eye of the storm, millibars, north-northeasterly winds, areas of violent winds and rain, heaving swells... It all rubbed Asakawa the wrong way.

At the moment, Typhoon No. 21 was centered on a point in the sea roughly a hundred and fifty kilometers south from Cape Omaezaki, advancing in a north-northeasterly direction at a speed of roughly twenty kilometers an hour, maintaining wind speeds of forty meters per second. At this rate it would hit the sea just south of Oshima by evening. It would probably be tomorrow—Thursday—before air and sea travel was restored. At least, that was Hayatsu's forecast.

"Thursday, he says!" Asakawa was seething. *My deadline is tomorrow night at ten! You damn typhoon, hurry up and blow through, or turn into a tropical depression, or something.* "When the hell are we going to be able to catch a plane or a boat off this island?" Asakawa wanted to get angry at someone, but he didn't even know who. *I never should've come here. I'll regret it forever. And that's not all—I don't even know where to begin regretting. I never should have watched that video. I never should have gotten curious about Tomoko Oishi and Shuichi Iwata's deaths. I never should have taken a cab that day... Shit.*

"Don't you know how to relax? Complaining to Mr. Hayatsu isn't going to get you anywhere." Ryuji grabbed Asakawa's arm, with an unexpected gentleness. "Think about it this way. Maybe the charm is something that can only be carried out here on the island. It's at least possible. Why didn't those brats use the charm? Maybe they didn't have the money to come to Oshima. It's plausible. Maybe these stormclouds'll have a silver lining—at least try to believe it, and maybe you'll be able to calm down."

"That's *if* we can figure out what the charm is!" Asakawa brushed away Ryuji's hand. Asakawa saw Hayatsu and his wife Fumiko exchange a glance, and it seemed to him they were laughing. Two grown men going on about charms.

"What's so funny?" He started to advance on them, but Ryuji grabbed his arm, with more force than before, and pulled him back.

"Knock it off. You're wasting your energy."

Seeing Asakawa's irritation, the kind-hearted Hayatsu had begun to feel almost responsible for transportation being disrupted on account of the typhoon. Or perhaps he was just sympathetic at the sight of people suffering so because of the storm. He prayed for the success of Asakawa's project. A fax was due to arrive from Tokyo, but waiting seemed only to ratchet up Asakawa's annoyance. Hayatsu tried to defuse the situation.

"How is your investigation coming?" Hayatsu asked gently, seeking to calm Asakawa.

"Well..."

"One of Shizuko Yamamura's childhood friends lives right nearby. If you'd like, I can call him over and you can hear what he has to say. Old Gen won't be out fishing on a day like this. I'm sure he's bored—he'd be happy to come over."

Hayatsu figured that if he gave Asakawa something else to investigate it would be bound to distract him. "He's nearing seventy, so I don't know how well he'll be able to answer your questions, but it has to be better than just waiting."

"Alright..."

Without even waiting for the answer, Hayatsu turned around and called to his wife in the kitchen: "Hey, call Gen's place and have him get over here right away."

Just as Hayatsu had said, Genji was happy to talk to them. He seemed to like nothing better than talking about Shizuko Yamamura. He was sixty-eight, three years older than Shizuko would have been. She'd been his childhood playmate, and also his first love. Whether it was because the memories became clearer as he talked about them or just because he was stimulated by having an audience, the recollections came pouring out of him. For Genji, talking about Shizuko was talking about his own youth.

Asakawa and Ryuji learned a certain amount from his rambling, occasionally tearful stories about Shizuko. But they were aware that they could only trust Old Gen so far. Memories were always liable to being prettified, and all of this had happened over forty years ago. He might even be getting her confused with another woman. Well, maybe not—a man's first love was special, not someone he'd mix up with someone else.

Genji wasn't exactly eloquent. He used a lot of roundabout expressions, and Asakawa soon got tired of listening. But then he said something that had Asakawa and Ryuji listening intently. "I think that what made Shizu change was that stone statue of the Ascetic we pulled up out of the sea. There was a full moon that night...." According to the old man, Shizuko's mysterious powers were somehow connected to the sea and the full moon. And on the night it happened, Genji himself had been beside her, rowing the boat. It was 1946, on a night toward the end of summer; Shizuko was twenty-one and Genji was twenty-four.

It was hot for so late in the season, and even nightfall brought no relief. Genji spoke of these events of forty-four years ago as though they had happened last night.

That sweltering evening, Genji was sitting on his front porch lazily fanning himself, gazing at the night sky calmly reflected on the moonlit sea. The silence was broken when Shizu came running up the hill to his house. She stood in front of him, tugging at his sleeve, and cried, "Gen, get your boat! We're going fishing." He asked her why, but all she would say was, "We'll never have another moonlit night like this." Genji just sat there as if in a daze, looking at the most beautiful girl on the island. "Wipe that stupid look off your face and hurry up!" She pulled at his collar until he got to his feet. Genji was used to having her push him around and tell him what to do, but he asked her anyway, "What in the world are we going fishing for?" Staring at the ocean, she gave a brisk reply: "For the statue of the Ascetic."

"Of the Ascetic?"

With raised eyebrows and a note of regret in her voice, Shizuko explained that earlier in the day, some Occupation soldiers had hurled the stone statue of the Ascetic into the sea.

In the middle of the island's eastern shore there was a beach called the Ascetic's Beach, with a small cave called the Ascetic's Grotto. It contained a stone statue of En no Ozunu, the famed Buddhist ascetic, who had been banished here in the year 699. Ozunu had been born with great wisdom, and long years of discipline had given him command of occult and mystic arts. It was said that he could summon gods and demons at will. But Ozunu's power to foretell the future had made him powerful enemies in the world of books and weapons, and he'd been judged a criminal, a menace to society, and exiled here to Izu Oshima. That had been almost thirteen hundred years ago. Ozunu holed himself up in a small cave on the beach and devoted himself to even more strenuous disciplines. He also taught farming and fishing to the people of the island, earning respect for his virtue. Finally he was pardoned and allowed to return to the mainland, where he founded the Shugendo monastic tradition. He was thought to have spent three years on the island, but stories of his time there abounded, including the legend that he had once shod himself with iron clogs and flown off to Mt. Fuji. The islanders still retained a great deal of affection for En no Ozunu, and the Ascetic's Grotto was considered the holiest place on the island. A festival, known as the Festival of the Ascetic, was held every year on June 15th.

Right after the end of World War II, however, as part of their policy toward Shintoism and Buddhism, the Occupation forces had taken En no Ozunu's statue from where it was enshrined in the cave and tossed it into the ocean. Shizuko, who had deep faith in Ozunu, had evidently been watching. She had hid herself in the shadow of the rocks at Worm's Nose Point and watched carefully as the statue was cast from the American patrol boat. She memorized the exact spot.

Genji couldn't believe his ears when he heard that they were going fishing for the statue of the Ascetic. He was a good fisherman with strong arms, but he'd never tried to catch a stone statue. But there was no way he could just turn Shizuko down, given the secret feelings he nursed for her. He launched his boat into the night, thinking to take this opportunity to put her in his debt. And truth be told, being out on the sea under a beautiful moon like this, just the two of them, promised to be a wonderful thing.

They'd built fires on Ascetic's Beach and at Worm's Nose as landmarks, and now they rowed farther and farther out to sea. Both of them were quite familiar with the ocean here—the lie of the seafloor, the depth, and the schools of fish that swam here. But now it was nighttime, and no matter how bright the moon was, it illuminated nothing beneath the surface. Genji didn't know how Shizuko intended to find the statue. He asked her, while working the oars, but she didn't answer. She just checked their position again by the bonfires on the beach. One might have been able to get a pretty good idea of where they were by gazing over the waves at the fires on the beach, and estimating the distance between them. After they'd rowed several hundred meters, Shizuko cried, "Stop here!"

She went to the stern of the boat, leaned down close to the surface of the water, and peered into the dark sea. "Look the other way," she commanded Genji. Genji guessed what Shizuko was about to do, and his heart leapt. Shizuko stood up and took off her splash-patterned kimono. His imagination aroused by the sound of the robe slipping across her skin, Genji found it hard to breathe. Behind him he heard the sound of her jumping into the sea. As the spray hit his shoulders he turned around and looked. Shizuko was treading water, her long black hair tied back with a rag and one end of a slender rope clenched between her teeth. She thrust her upper body out of the water, took two deep breaths, then dived to the bottom of the sea.

How many times did her head pop up from the surface of the water to gasp for air? The last time, she no longer had the end of the rope in her mouth. *I've tied it fast to the Ascetic. Go ahead and pull him up*, she said in a trembling voice.

Gen shifted his body to the bow of the boat and pulled on the rope. In no time Shizuko climbed aboard, draped her kimono around her body, and came up beside Genji in time to help him haul up the statue. They placed it in the center of the boat and headed back to the shore. The whole way back, neither Genji nor

Shizuko said a word. There was something in the atmosphere that quashed all questions. He found it mysterious that she'd been able to locate the statue in the darkness at the bottom of the sea. It was only three days later that he was able to ask her. She said that the Ascetic's eyes had called to her on the ocean floor. The green eyes of the statue, master of gods and demons, had glowed at the bottom of the deep dark sea.... That's what Shizuko had said.

After that, Shizuko began to feel physical discomfort. She'd never even had a headache up until then, but now she often experienced searing pains in her head, accompanied by visions of things she'd never seen before flashing across her mind's eye. And it happened that these scenes she had glimpsed very soon manifested themselves in reality. Genji had questioned her in some detail. It seemed that when these future scenes inserted themselves into her brain, they were always accompanied by the same citrus fragrance in her nostrils. Genji's older sister had gotten married and moved to Odawara, on the mainland; when she died, the scene had presented itself to Shizuko beforehand. But it didn't sound like she could actually, consciously predict things that would happen in the future. It was just that these scenes would flash across her mind, with no warning, and with no inkling of why she'd witnessed those exact scenes. So Shizuko never allowed people to ask her to predict their futures.

The following year she went up to Tokyo, despite Genji's efforts to stop her. She came to know Heihachiro Ikuma, and conceived his child. Then, at the end of the year, she went back to her hometown and gave birth to a baby girl. Sadako.

They didn't know when Genji's tale would end. Ten years later Shizuko jumped into the mouth of Mt. Mihara, and to judge by the way Genji related the event, it seemed he had decided to blame it on her lover, Ikuma. It was perhaps a natural thought, as he had been Genji's rival in love, but his obvious resentment made his account hard to sit through. All they'd gleaned from him was the knowledge that Sadako's mother had been able to see the future, and the possibility that this power had been given her by a stone statue of En no Ozunu.

Just then the fax machine began to hum. It printed out an enlargement of the head shot of Sadako Yamamura that Yoshino had gotten from Theater Group Soaring.

Asakawa was strangely moved. This was the first actual look he'd gotten of this woman. Even though it had only been for the briefest moment, he'd shared the same sensations as this woman, seen the world from the same vantage point. It was like catching the first glimpse of a lover's face in the dim morning light, finally seeing what she looks like, after a night of entwined limbs and shared orgasms in the dark.

It was odd, but he couldn't think of her as hideous. But that was only natural; although the photo that came through the fax machine was somewhat blurred around the edges, still it fully communicated the allure of Sadako's beautifully regular features.

"She's a fine woman, isn't she?" Ryuji said. Asakawa suddenly recalled Mai Takano. If you compared them purely on the basis of looks, Sadako was far more beautiful than Mai. And yet the scent of a woman was much more powerful with Mai. And what about that "eerie" quality that was supposed to characterize Sadako? It didn't come through in the photograph. Sadako had powers that ordinary people didn't have; they must have influenced the people around her.

The second page of the fax summarized information about Shizuko Yamamura. It picked up right where Genji's story had left off just now.

In 1947, having left behind her hometown of Sashikiji for the capital, Shizuko suddenly collapsed with head pains and was taken to a hospital. Through one of the doctors, she came to know Heihachiro Ikuma, an assistant professor in the psychiatry department of Taido University. Ikuma was involved in trying to find a scientific explanation for hypnotism and related phenomena, and he became very interested in Shizuko when he discovered that she had startling powers of clairvoyance. The finding went so far as to change the thrust of his research. Thereafter Ikuma would immerse himself in the study of paranormal powers, with Shizuko as the subject of his research. But the two soon progressed beyond a mere researcher-subject relationship. In spite of his having a family, Ikuma began to have romantic feelings toward Shizuko. By the end of the year she was pregnant with his child, and to escape the eyes of the world she went back home, where she had Sadako. Shizuko immediately returned to Tokyo, leaving Sadako in Sashikiji, but three years later she returned to reclaim her child. From then until the time of her suicide, evidently, she never let Sadako leave her side.

When the 1950s dawned, the duo of Heihachiro Ikuma and Shizuko Yamamura was a sensation in the pages of the newspapers and the weekly newsmagazines. They provided a sudden insight into the scientific underpinnings of supernatural powers. At first, perhaps dazzled by Ikuma's position as a professor at such a prestigious university, the public unanimously believed in Shizuko's powers. Even the media wrote her up in a more-or-less favorable light. Still, there were persistent claims that she could only be a fake, and when an authoritative scholarly association weighed in with the one-word comment "questionable," people began to shift their support away from the pair.

The paranormal powers Shizuko exhibited were mainly ESP-related, such as clairvoyance or second sight, and the ability to produce psychic photographs. She didn't display the power of telekinesis, the ability to move things without touching them. According to one magazine, simply by holding a piece of film in a tightly sealed envelope against her forehead, she could psychically imprint upon it a specified design; she could also identify the image on a similarly concealed piece of film a hundred times out of a hundred. However, another magazine maintained that she was nothing more than a con-woman, claiming that any magician, with some training, could easily do the same things. In this way the tide of public opinion began to rise against Shizuko and Ikuma.

Then Shizuko was visited by misfortune. In 1954 she gave birth to her second baby, but it took sick and died at only four months of age. It had been a boy. Sadako, who was seven at the time, seemed to have showered a special affection on her newborn little brother.

The following year, in 1955, Ikuma challenged the media to a public demonstration of Shizuko's powers. At first Shizuko didn't want to do it. She said that it was hard to concentrate her awareness the way she wanted to among a mass of spectators; she was afraid she'd fail. But Ikuma was unyielding. He couldn't stand being labeled a charlatan by the media, and he couldn't think of a better way to outwit them than by offering clear proof of her authenticity.

On the appointed day, Shizuko reluctantly mounted the dais in the lab theater, under the watchful eyes of nearly a hundred scholars and representatives of the press. She was mentally exhausted, to boot, so these were hardly the best conditions for her to work under. The experiment was to proceed along quite simple lines. All she had to do was identify the numbers on a pair of dice inside a lead container. If she had just been able to exert her powers normally, it would have been no problem. But she *knew* that each one of the hundred people surrounding her was waiting and hoping for her to fail. She trembled, she crouched down on the floor, she cried out in anguish, "Enough of this!" Shizuko herself explained it this way: everybody had a certain degree of psychic power. She just had more of it than others did. But surrounded by a hundred people all willing her to fail, her power was disrupted—she couldn't get it to work. Ikuma went even further: "It's not just a hundred people. No, now the whole population of Japan is trying to stamp out the fruits of my research. When public opinion, fanned by the media, begins to turn, then the media says nothing the people don't want to hear. They should be ashamed!" Thus the great public display of clairvoyance ended with Ikuma's denunciation of the mass media.

Of course, the media interpreted Ikuma's diatribe as an attempt to shift the blame for the failed demonstration, and that's how it was written up in the next day's newspapers. *A FAKE AFTER ALL...THEIR TRUE COLORS REVEALED...TAIDO UNIVERSITY PROFESSOR A FRAUD...FIVE YEARS OF DEBATE ENDED...VICTORY FOR MODERN SCIENCE.* Not a single article defended them.

Toward the end of the year, Ikuma divorced his wife and resigned from the university. Shizuko began to become increasingly paranoid. After that, Ikuma decided to acquire paranormal abilities himself, and he retreated deep into the mountains and stood under waterfalls, but all he got was pulmonary tuberculosis. He had to be committed to a sanatorium in Hakone. Meanwhile

Shizuko's psychological state was becoming more and more precarious. Eight-year-old Sadako convinced her mother to go back home to Sashikiji, to escape the eyes of the media and the ridicule of the public, but then Shizuko slipped her daughter's gaze and jumped into the volcano. And so three people's lives crumbled.

Asakawa and Ryuji finished reading the two-page printout at the same time.

"It's a grudge," muttered Ryuji. "Imagine how Sadako must have felt when her mom threw herself into Mt. Mihara."

"She hated the media?"

"Not just the media. She resented the public at large for destroying her family, first treating them like darlings, and then when the wind changed scorning them. Sadako was with her mother and father between the ages of three and ten, right? She had first-hand knowledge of the vagaries of public opinion."

"But that's no reason to arrange an indiscriminate attack like this!" Asakawa's objection was made in full consciousness of the fact that he himself belonged to the media. In his heart he was making excuses—he was pleading. *Hey, I'm just as critical of the media's tendencies as you are.*

"What are you mumbling about?"

"Huh?" Asakawa realized that unknowingly he had been voicing his complaints, as if they were a Buddhist chant.

"Well, we've begun to illuminate the images on that video. Mt. Mihara appears because it's where her mother killed herself, and also because Sadako herself had predicted its eruption. It must have made a particularly strong psychic impression on her. The next scene shows the character for 'mountain,' *yama*, floating into view. That's probably the first psychic photograph Sadako succeeded in making, when she was very small."

"Very small?" Asakawa didn't see why it had to be from when she was very small.

"Yes, probably from when she was four or five. Next, there's the scene with the dice. Sadako was present during her mother's public demonstration; this scene means that she was watching, worried, as her mother tried to guess the numbers on the dice."

"Hold on a minute, though. Sadako clearly *saw* the numbers on the dice in that lead bowl."

Both Asakawa and Ryuji had watched that scene *with their own eyes*, so to speak. There was no mistaking.

"And?"

"Shizuko couldn't see them."

"Is it so strange that the daughter could do what the mother couldn't? Look, Sadako was only seven then, but her power already far outstripped her mother's. So much so that the combined unconscious will of a hundred people was nothing to her. Think about it: this is a girl who could project images onto a cathode-ray tube. Televisions produce images by an entirely different mechanism from photography—it's not just a matter of exposing film to light. A picture on TV is composed of 525 lines, right? Sadako could manipulate those. This is power of a completely different order here."

Asakawa still wasn't convinced. "If she had so much power, what about the psychic photo she sent to Professor Miura? She should have been able to produce something much more impressive."

"You're even dumber than you look. Her mother had gained nothing but unhappiness by letting people know about her power. Her mother probably didn't want her to make the same mistake.

She probably told Sadako to hide her abilities and just lead a normal life. Sadako probably carefully restrained herself so as to produce only an average psychic photo."

Sadako had stayed in the rehearsal hall alone after everyone else had left, so that she could test her powers on the television set, still a rarity in those days. She was trying to be careful not to let anyone know what she could do.

"Who's the old woman who appears in the next scene?" asked Asakawa.

"I don't know who that is. Perhaps she came to Sadako in a dream or something, whispered prophecies in her ear. She was using an old dialect. I'm sure you've noticed that everyone here now speaks pretty standard Japanese. That old lady was pretty old. Maybe she lived in the twelfth century, or maybe she has some connection to En no Ozunu."

... Next year you're going to have a child.

"I wonder if that prediction really came true?"

"Oh, that? Well, there's the scene with the baby boy right after that. So I originally thought it meant that Sadako had given birth to a boy, but according to this fax, that doesn't appear to be the case."

"There's her brother who died at four months old..."

"Right. I think that's it."

"But what about the prediction? The old woman is definitely speaking to Sadako—she says *you*. Did Sadako have a baby?"

"I don't know. If we believe the old lady, then I guess she did."

"Whose child was it?"

"How should I know? Listen, don't think I know everything. I'm just speculating here."

If Sadako Yamamura did have a child, who was the father? And what was the child doing now?

Ryuji stood up suddenly, banging his knees on the table as a result.

"I thought I was getting hungry. Look—it's way past noon. Say, Asakawa, I'm going to get something to eat." So saying, Ryuji headed for the door, rubbing his kneecaps. Asakawa had no appetite, but something still bothered him, and he decided to tag along. He'd just remembered something Ryuji had told him to investigate, something he'd had no clue how to approach and so hadn't done anything about. This was the question of the identity of the man in the video's last scene. It might be Sadako's father, Heihachiro Ikuma, but there was too much enmity in the way Sadako looked at him for that. When he'd seen the man's face on the screen, Asakawa had felt a dull, heavy pain somewhere deep inside his body, accompanied by a strong feeling of antipathy. He was a rather handsome man, particularly around the eyes; he wondered why she hated him so. No matter what, that kind of gaze was not one Sadako would have turned on a relative. There was nothing in Yoshino's report to suggest that she had squared off against her father. Rather, he got the impression that she was close to her parents. Asakawa suspected it would be impossible to discover the identity of this man. Nearly thirty years had undoubtedly changed his looks considerably. Still, just on the off-chance, maybe he should ask Yoshino to dig up a photo of Ikuma. He wondered what Ryuji would think about this. Wanting to take the matter up with him, Asakawa followed Ryuji outside.

The wind blew loudly. There was no point in using an umbrella. Asakawa and Ryuji hunched their shoulders and ran down the street to a bar in front of the harbor.

"How about a beer?" Without waiting for a reply, Ryuji turned to the waitress and called out, "Two beers."

"Ryuji, to go back to our earlier conversation, what do you think the images on that video are, finally?"

"Don't know."

Ryuji was too busy eating his Korean barbecue lunch special to even look up, so he gave a curt answer. Asakawa stabbed a sausage with his fork and took a swallow of his beer. Out the window they could see the pier. There was nobody at the ticket window for the Tokai Kisen ferry line. Everything was silent. No doubt all the tourists trapped on the island were sitting at the windows of their hotels or B&B's, looking worriedly at this same dark sea and sky.

Ryuji looked up. "I imagine you've probably heard what people say goes though a person's mind at the moment of death, right?"

Asakawa returned his gaze to the scene in front of him. "The scenes from your life that have made the deepest impression on you are replayed, sort of like a flashback." Asakawa had read a book in which the author described an experience along those lines. The author had been driving his car along a mountain road when he lost control of the steering wheel, plunging the car into a deep ravine. During the split second that the car hung in the air after leaving the road, the author realized that he was going to die. And at the instant he realized that, a bunch of different scenes from throughout his life came pitter-pattering up and flashed through his brain, so clearly that he could see every detail. In the end, miraculously, the writer had survived, but the memory of that instant remained vivid for him.

"You can't be suggesting... Is *that* what this is?" Asakawa asked. Ryuji raised a hand and signaled the waitress to bring him another beer.

"All I'm saying is, that's what the video reminds me of. Each one of those scenes represents a moment of extreme psychic or emotional engagement for Sadako. It's not too much of a stretch to think that they were the scenes in her life that left the deepest impression, is it?"

"I get it. But hey, does that mean that..."

"Right. There's a strong possibility that that's the case."

So Sadako Yamamura is no longer of this world? She died, and the scenes which flitted through her mind at the moment of death had taken this shape and remained in the world of the living—was that it?

"So why did she die? And another thing, what was her relationship with the man in the last scene of the video?"

"I told you to stop asking me so many questions. There's a lot I don't understand about it, either."

Asakawa looked unconvinced.

"Hey, try using your head for a change. You rely too much on other people. What would you do if something happened to me and you were stuck trying to figure out the charm all by yourself?"

That hardly seemed likely. Asakawa might die, and Ryuji might solve the riddle alone, but the opposite would never happen. Asakawa was sure of that, if of nothing else.

They went back to the "bureau" where Hayatsu was waiting for them. "You had a call from a fellow named Yoshino. He wasn't at his office, so he said he'd call back in ten minutes."

Asakawa sat in front of the phone and prayed for good news. The phone rang. It was Yoshino.

"I've been trying to call you. Where were you?" There was a note of reproach in his voice.

"Sorry about that. We went out to get a bite to eat."

"Okay. Now, did you get my fax?" Yoshino's tone changed.

The note of criticism disappeared, and his voice became gentler. Asakawa felt something unpleasant coming.

"Yes, thanks. It was very helpful." Asakawa switched the receiver from his left hand to his right. "And, so? Did you find out what happened to Sadako after that?" Asakawa asked enthusiastically.

There was a pause before Yoshino replied, however. "No. I hit a dead end."

The second he heard this, Asakawa's face crumpled as if he were about to burst into sobs. Ryuji watched as if he found it amusing to see a man's expression turn from hope to despair before his eyes. Then he plopped himself down on the floor facing the garden and stretched his legs out in front of him.

"What do you mean, a dead end?" Asakawa's voice had risen several notes.

"I was only able to locate four of the interns who joined the troupe with Sadako. I called them, but none of them know anything. They're all middle-aged guys of around fifty now. All any of them could tell me was they hadn't seen her since shortly after the death of Shigemori, the company's representative. There's no more information to be had about Sadako Yamamura."

"Nonsense. This can't be the end of it."

"Well, how does it look on your end?"

"How does it look on my end? I'll tell you how it looks. It looks like I'm going to die tomorrow night at ten o'clock. And not just me—my wife and daughter are going to die on Sunday morning at eleven. That's how it looks."

Ryuji called out from behind him, "Hey, don't forget about me! You'll make me feel bad."

Asakawa ignored him and continued. "There've got to be other things you can try. Maybe there's someone besides the interns who would know what happened to Sadako. Listen, my family's lives depend on it."

"Not necessarily, though."

"What are you talking about?"

"Maybe you'll still be alive after the deadline passes."

"You don't believe me. I get it." Asakawa could feel the whole world go dark before his eyes.

"Well…I mean, how could I really believe a hundred percent in a story like this?"

"Now, look, Yoshino." How should he put it? What did he need to say to convince him? "I don't even believe the half of it myself. It's stupid. A charm? Come on! But you see, if there's even a one-in-six chance that it's all true… It's like Russian roulette. You've got a gun with one bullet in it, and you know that there's only one chance in six that when you pull the trigger it'll kill you. But could *you* pull that trigger? Would you risk your family on those odds? No, you wouldn't. You'd move the muzzle away from your temple—if you could you'd throw the whole damned gun into the ocean. Right? It's only natural."

Asakawa was all wound up now. Behind him Ryuji was wailing, "We're idiots! Both of us, idiots!"

"Shut up!" Asakawa shielded the receiver with the palm of his hand as he turned to yell at Ryuji.

"Something wrong?" Yoshino lowered the tone of his voice.

"No, it's nothing. Listen, Yoshino, I'm begging you. You're the only one I can count on." Suddenly Ryuji grabbed Asakawa's arm. Giving way to anger, Asakawa spun around, but when he did he saw that Ryuji was looking unexpectedly earnest.

"We're idiots. You and I both have lost our cool," he said, quietly.

"Could you hold on a minute?" Asakawa lowered the receiver. Then, to Ryuji, "What's the matter?"

"It's so simple. Why didn't we think of it before? There's no need to follow Sadako's trail chronologically. Why can't we work our way backwards? Why did it have to be cabin B-4? Why did it have to be Villa Log Cabin? Why did it have to be South Hakone Pacific Land?"

Asakawa's expression changed in a heartbeat as he came to a realization. Then, in a much calmer mood, he picked up the receiver again.

"Yoshino?"

Yoshino was still waiting on the other end of the line.

"Yoshino, forget about the theater company lead for a while. There's something else I urgently need you to check on. It's just come up. I believe I've already told you about South Hakone Pacific Land..."

"Yeah, you did. It's a resort club, right?"

"Right. As I recall, they built a golf course there about ten years ago, and then gradually expanded into what they are now. Now, listen, what I need you to look up is, what was there before Pacific Land?"

He could hear the scratching of pen on paper.

"What do you mean, what was there before? Probably nothing but mountain meadows."

"You may be right. But then again, you may be wrong."

Ryuji tugged at Asakawa's sleeve again. "And a layout. If there was something standing on that land before the resort, tell your gentleman caller to get a map that shows the layout of the buildings and the grounds."

Asakawa relayed the request to Yoshino and hung up the phone, willing him to come up with something, anything, by way of a lead. It was true: everybody had a little psychic power.

10

October 18—Thursday

The wind was a little stronger, and low white clouds raced by in the otherwise clear sky. Typhoon No. 21 had passed by the previous evening, grazing the Boso Peninsula to the northeast of Oshima before dissipating over the ocean. In its wake it left painfully dazzling blue seas. In spite of the peaceful autumn weather, as Asakawa stood on the deck of the boat watching the waves he felt like a condemned man on the eve of his execution. Raising his eyes he could see the gentle slope of the Izu highlands in the middle distance. Today, at last, he would face his deadline. It was now ten in the morning; in another twelve hours, it would come, unerringly. It had been a week since he watched the video in cabin B-4. It seemed like ages ago. Of course it felt long: in just one week he'd experienced more terror than most people experience in a lifetime.

Asakawa wasn't sure how being cooped up on Oshima all day Wednesday would hurt him. On the phone yesterday he'd gotten excited and accused Yoshino of dragging his feet, but now that he thought about things calmly, he was actually very grateful to his colleague for doing so much for him. If Asakawa had been running around chasing down leads himself, he probably would have gotten excited and missed something, or gone down a blind alley.

This is fine. The typhoon was on our side. If he didn't think that way, he'd never make it. Asakawa was starting to prepare his mind so that when his time came to die he wouldn't be consumed with regrets about what he had or hadn't done.

Their last clue was the three-page printout he held in his hand. Yoshino had spent half the previous day tracking down the information before faxing it. Before South Hakone Pacific Land had been built, the land had been occupied by a rather unusual facility. Unusual these days, that is—at the time, establishments like it were perfectly run-of-the-mill. It was a tuberculosis treatment facility—a sanatorium.

Nowadays few people lived in fear of TB, but if one read much prewar fiction, one couldn't help but come across mention of it. It was the tuberculosis bacillus that gave Thomas Mann the impetus to write *The Magic Mountain*, that allowed Motojiro Kajii to sing with piercing clarity of his decay. However, the discovery of streptomycin in 1944, and hydrazide in 1950 stole TB's literary cachet, reducing its status to that of just another communicable disease. In the '20s and '30s, as many as 200,000 people a year were dying from it, but the number dropped drastically after the war. Even so, the bacillus didn't become extinct. Even now, it still kills around five thousand people a year.

In the days when TB ran rampant, clean, fresh air and a quiet, peaceful environment were deemed essential for recovery. Thus, sanatoriums were built in mountainous areas. But as progress in medicinal treatments produced a corresponding drop in the number of patients, these facilities had to adjust their range of services. In other words, they had to start treating internal ailments, even performing surgeries, or else they wouldn't be able to survive financially. In the mid-1960s, the sanatorium in South Hakone was faced with just this choice. But its situation was even more critical than most, due to its extreme remoteness. It was just too hard to get to. With TB, once patients checked in they usually didn't check back out again, so ease of access wasn't much of an issue. But it proved to be a fatal flaw in the plan to transform the place into a general hospital. The sanatorium ended up shutting down in 1972.

Waiting in the wings was Pacific Resorts, which had been looking for a suitable location to build a golf course and resort. In 1975, Pacific Resorts bought a section of alpine land which included the old sanatorium site and immediately set about developing their golf course. Later they built summer homes to sell, a hotel, a swimming pool, an athletic club, and tennis courts—the whole line of resort facilities. And in April of this year, six months ago, they'd put the finishing touches on Villa Log Cabin.

"What kind of place is it, then?" Ryuji was supposed to be on deck, but he suddenly appeared in the seat next to Asakawa.

"Huh?"

"South Hakone Pacific Land, of course."

That's right. He's never been there.

"It's got a nice view at night." Asakawa recalled the curiously lifeless atmosphere, the tennis balls with their hollow echo under the orange lights.... *Where does that atmosphere come from anyway? I wonder how many people died there when it was a sanatorium.* Asakawa pondered this as he remembered how the beautiful evening lights of Numazu and Mishima had spread out at his feet.

Asakawa put the first page of the printout on the bottom and spread the other two pages out on his lap. The second page was a simple diagram showing the layout of the sanatorium grounds; the third showed the building as it was today, an elegant three-story building containing an information center and a restaurant. This was the building Asakawa had entered to ask directions to Villa Log Cabin. Asakawa shifted his gaze back and forth between the two pages. The passage of nearly thirty years was embodied in those two pieces of paper. If it wasn't for the fact that the access road was in the same place, he'd have no idea what on one map corresponded to what on the other. Mentally reconstructing the layout as he knew it, he looked at the second page to try to find out what had originally stood where the cabins were now. He couldn't be absolutely sure, but when he lay one page on top of the other, it certainly seemed as if there had been nothing there before. Just thick woods covering the side of a valley.

He went back to the first page. It contained one more very important piece of information, besides the story of the sanatorium's transformation into a resort. Jotaro Nagao, 57. A doctor, a GP and pediatrician, with a private practice in Atami. For five years, from 1962 to 1967, Nagao had worked at the South Hakone sanatorium. He'd been young, just past his internship. Of the doctors who'd been there at the time, the only ones still alive were Nagao and Yozo Tanaka, who was retired now, living with his daughter and her husband in Nagasaki. All the rest, including the head of the facility, were dead. Therefore, Dr. Nagao was their only chance to find out anything about the sanatorium in South Hakone. Yozo Tanaka was already 80, and Nagasaki was much too far away—they wouldn't have time to visit him.

Asakawa had pleaded desperately with Yoshino to find a living witness, and Yoshino, gritting his teeth to keep from yelling back at Asakawa, had come up with Dr. Nagao. He'd sent not only the man's name and address, but also an intriguing summary of his career. It was probably just something Yoshino had happened to come across in his research, and he'd decided to append it, not actually meaning anything by it. Dr. Nagao had been at the sanatorium from 1962 to 1967, but he hadn't spent the entirety of those five years in the performance of his duties. For two weeks—a short time, to be sure, but significant—he'd gone from doctor to patient, and been housed in an isolation ward. In the summer of 1966, while visiting an isolation ward up in the mountains, he'd carelessly allowed himself to contract the smallpox virus from a patient. Fortunately, he had been inoculated a few years previously, so it didn't turn into anything major: no visible outbreak, no recurrence of the fever, only minor symptoms. But they'd put him in isolation to keep him from infecting anyone else. What was so interesting was that this had assured Nagao a place in medical history. He had been the last smallpox patient in Japan. It wasn't necessarily something that would get him into the Guinness Book, but Yoshino seemed to have thought it was interesting. For people of Asakawa and Ryuji's generation, the word "smallpox" didn't even register.

"Ryuji, have you ever had smallpox?"

"Idiot. Of course not. It's extinct."

"Extinct?"

"Yes. Eradicated through human ingenuity. Smallpox no longer exists in this world."

The World Health Organization had made a dedicated effort to wipe out small pox through vaccinations, and as a result it had all but disappeared from the face of the earth by 1975. There are records of the last small pox patient in the world: a Somalian youth who came down with it on October 26, 1977.

"Can a virus become extinct? Is that possible?" Asakawa didn't know much about viruses, but he couldn't shake the impression that no matter how much you tried to kill one, eventually it would mutate and find a way to survive.

"See, viruses kind of wander around on the border between living things and non-living things. Some people even theorize that they were originally human genes, but nobody really knows where they come from or how they emerged. What's certain is that they've been intimately connected with the appearance and evolution of life."

Ryuji's arms had been folded behind his head; now he stretched them wide. His eyes glittered. "Don't you find it fascinating, Asakawa? The idea that genes could escape from our cells and become another life form? Maybe all opposites were originally identical. Even light and darkness—before the Big Bang they were living together in peace, with no contradiction. God and the Devil, too. All the Devil is is a god who fell from grace—they're the same thing, originally. Male and female? It used to be that all living things were hermaphroditic, like worms or slugs, with both female and male sex organs. Don't you think that's the ultimate symbol of power and beauty?" Ryuji laughed as he said this. "It'd sure save a lot of time and trouble when it comes to sex."

Asakawa peered at Ryuji's face to see what was so funny. There was no way that an organism with both female and male genitalia epitomized perfect beauty.

"Are there any other extinct viruses?"

"Gee, if you're so interested I suggest you look right into it when you get back to Tokyo."

"*If* I get back."

"Heh, heh. Don't worry. You'll get back."

At that moment the high-speed boat they were on was exactly halfway through the voyage linking Oshima and Ito, on the Izu Peninsula. They could have made it back to Tokyo quicker by flying, but they wanted to visit Dr. Nagao in Atami, so they'd taken the sea route.

Straight ahead they could see the ferris wheel at the Atami Korakuen. They were arriving right on time, at 10:50. Asakawa descended the gangway and ran to the parking lot where they'd left their rental car.

"Calm down, would you?" Ryuji followed at a leisurely pace. Nagao's clinic was near Kinomiya Station on the Ito Line—not very far away at all. Asakawa watched impatiently as Ryuji climbed into the car, and then headed into Atami's maze of hills and one-way streets.

Immediately after he'd settled himself, Ryuji said, with a perfectly straight face, "Hey, I was thinking—maybe the Devil's behind this whole thing after all." Asakawa was too busy looking at street signs to answer. Ryuji continued. "The Devil always appears in the world in a different form. You know the bubonic plague that ravaged Europe in the second half of the thirteenth century? Half of the total population died. Can you believe that? Half, that's like the population of Japan being reduced to sixty million. Naturally, artists at the time likened the plague to the Devil. It's like that now, too—don't we talk about AIDS as if it were a modern Devil? But listen, devils never drive humanity to extinction. Why? Because if people cease to exist, so do devils. The same with viruses. If the host cell perishes, the virus can't survive. But humanity drove the smallpox virus to extinction. Really? Could we really do that?"

It's impossible in the modern world to even imagine the terror once inspired by smallpox, when it raged throughout the world claiming so many lives. Such was the suffering it caused that it gave rise to innumerable religious beliefs and superstitions in Japan, as well as elsewhere. People believed in gods of pestilence, and it was the God of Smallpox that brought that disease, though perhaps it should have been called a devil. In any case, could people really drive a god to the brink of extinction? Ryuji's question harbored a deep uncertainty.

Asakawa wasn't listening to Ryuji. In some corner of his mind he wondered why the guy was rambling on about this now, but mainly he was just thinking about not making any wrong turns. Every nerve focussed on getting to Dr. Nagao's clinic as fast as possible.

11

In a lane in front of Kinomiya Station was a small, one-story house with a shingle by the door that read *Nagao Clinic: Internal Medicine and Pediatrics*. Asakawa and Ryuji stood in front of the door for some time. If they couldn't pull any information out of Nagao, it'd be *sorry, time's up!* There was no more time to scare up new leads. But just what was there to find out from him? It was probably hoping for too much to think that he'd even remember much of anything about Sadako Yamamura from thirty years ago. They didn't even have any hard evidence that Sadako had any connection at all with the sanatorium in South Hakone. All of Nagao's colleagues at the sanatorium, except for Yozo Tanaka, had died of old age. They probably could have tracked down the names of some nurses if they'd tried, but it was too late for that now.

Asakawa looked at his watch. 11:30. Only a little over ten hours left until the deadline, and here he was, hesitating to open the door.

"What are you waiting for? Go on in." Ryuji gave him a shove. Of course, he could understand why Asakawa was hesitating, even though he'd been in such a hurry to get here. He was scared. No doubt he was afraid of seeing his last hope dashed, his last chance to survive eliminated. Ryuji stepped in front of him and opened the door.

A couch big enough for three people stood along one wall of

the small waiting room. Conveniently, there were no patients waiting. Ryuji bent over at the little receptionist's window and spoke to the fat middle-aged nurse behind it. "Excuse me. We'd like to see the doctor."

Without lifting her eyes from her magazine, the nurse lazily replied, "Would you like to make an appointment?"

"No, that's not it. There's something we'd like to ask him about."

She closed her magazine, looked up, and put on her glasses. "May I ask what this is in regards to?"

"Like I say, we'd just like to ask him a few questions."

Irritated, Asakawa peeked out from behind Ryuji's back and asked, "Is the doctor in?"

The nurse touched the rims of her glasses with both hands and studied the two men. "What is this about?" she asked overbearingly.

Both Ryuji and Asakawa stood up straight. Ryuji said, loudly enough to be heard, "With a receptionist like her it's no wonder there are no patients."

"*Excuse* me?" she said.

Asakawa hung his head; it wouldn't do to get her angry. But just then the door to the examination room opened and Nagao appeared, dressed in a white lab coat.

Although he was completely bald, Nagao looked rather younger than his 57 years. He frowned and fixed a suspicious gaze on the two men in his entryway.

Asakawa and Ryuji both turned at the sound of Nagao's voice, and the instant they saw his face, they gasped simultaneously.

And we thought this guy might be able to tell us something about Sadako? No kidding. As if it were an electric current coursing through his brain, Asakawa found himself replaying the final scene of the video in his head. The sweating, panting face of a man seen from close up, eyes bloodshot. A gaping wound in his exposed shoulder, from which blood ran, dripping into the viewer's eyes, clouding them over. A tremendous pressure on the viewer's chest, murderous intent in the man's face... And that face was exactly what they saw now: Dr. Nagao. He was older now, but there was no way of mistaking him.

Asakawa and Ryuji exchanged glances. Then Ryuji pointed at the doctor and began to laugh. "Heh, heh, heh. Now this is why games are interesting. Ah, who would have thought it? Imagine running into *you* here."

Nagao was obviously displeased at the way these two strange men had reacted to seeing him. He raised his voice. "Who are you?" Unfazed, Ryuji walked right up to him and grabbed him by the lapels. Nagao was several centimeters taller than Ryuji. Ryuji flexed his powerful arms and pulled the doctor's ear to his mouth, then spoke in a gentle voice that belied his strength.

"So tell me, pal, what was it you did to Sadako Yamamura thirty years ago at the South Hakone Sanatorium?"

It took a few seconds for the words to sink into the doctor's brain. Nagao's eyes darted around nervously as he searched his memories. Then they came to him, scenes of a time he'd never been able to forget. His knees sagged; all the strength seemed to go out of his body. Just as he was about to faint, Ryuji steadied him and leaned him back against the wall. Nagao wasn't shocked by the memories themselves. Rather, it was the fact that the man before him, who may or may not have even been thirty years old, knew about what had happened. Indescribable dread pierced his soul.

"Doctor!" exclaimed the nurse, Ms. Fujimura.

"I think it's about time this place closed for lunch," Ryuji said, signaling to Asakawa with his eyes. Asakawa closed the curtain over the entryway so that no patients would enter.

"Doctor!" Nurse Fujimura didn't know how to handle the situation. She just waited, dumbly, for Nagao to instruct her. Nagao somehow pulled himself together a little and thought about what to do next. Thinking that above all, he couldn't let this nosy woman find out about what had happened, he assumed a calm expression.

"Nurse Fujimura, you can take your break now. Run along now and get something to eat."

"But, doctor..."

"Just do as I say. There's no need to worry about me."

First two strange men come in and whisper something in the doctor's ear, and the next thing she knew the doctor was collapsing. She didn't know what to make of all this, and so she just stood there for a few moments. Finally, the doctor shouted, "Go, now!" She practically flew out the front door.

"Now, then. Let's hear what you have to say for yourself." Ryuji went into the examination room. Nagao followed after, looking like a patient who's just been informed he has cancer.

"I'll warn you before we start, you mustn't lie to us. I and this gentleman here know everything—we've seen it with our very eyes." Ryuji pointed first to Asakawa and then to his own eyes.

"What the...?" *Seen it? Impossible. The bushes were too thick. There was nobody else around. Not to mention, these two are too young. They would have only been...*

"I understand why you might be reluctant to believe me. But we both know your face—all too well." Suddenly Ryuji's tone changed. "In that case, why don't I tell you one of your distinguishing features? You've still got a scar on your right shoulder, haven't you?"

Nagao's eyes grew wide with astonishment, and his jaw started to quiver. After a pregnant pause, Ryuji said, "Now, shall I tell you why you have that scar on your shoulder?" Ryuji leaned over and stretched his neck until his lips were almost touching Nagao's shoulder. "Sadako Yamamura bit you, didn't she? Just like this." Ryuji opened his mouth and pretended to bite through the white cloth. Nagao's trembling grew worse, and he desperately tried to say something, but his mouth wouldn't work. He couldn't form words.

"I think you get my point. Now, we're not going to repeat anything you tell us. We promise. All we want to know is everything that happened to Sadako."

Not that he was in any condition to think at all, but Nagao didn't think Ryuji's words quite added up. If they'd already seen everything, why did they need to hear anything from the doctor's mouth? *But wait, the whole idea that they saw anything is silly. They couldn't have seen anything. They probably weren't even born yet. So what's going on here? What do they think they've seen?* The more he thought about it the less sense it made, until his head felt like it was ready to burst.

"Heh, heh, heh." Ryuji chuckled and looked at Asakawa. The man's eyes said it all. *Frighten him like this and he'll come clean. He'll tell us anything.*

And indeed, Nagao began to talk. He himself was puzzled as to why he remembered everything so clearly. And as he spoke, every sensory organ in his body began to recall the excitement of that day. The passion, the heat, the touch, the glossy shine of her skin, the song of the locusts, the mingled smells of sweat and grass, and the old well....

"I don't even know what caused it. Maybe the fever and headache robbed me of my ordinary good judgment. Those were the early symptoms of smallpox—which meant I had already passed through the incubation period. But I didn't dream that I had caught the disease myself. Fortunately, I managed not to infect anyone else in the sanatorium. To this day I'm haunted by the thought of what would have happened if the tuberculosis patients had been attacked by smallpox as well.

"The day was a hot one. I'd been examining the tomograms of a newly-admitted patient, and I had found a hole the size of a one-yen coin in one of his lungs. I'd told him to resign himself to spending a year with us, and then I'd given him a copy of the diagnosis to give his company. Then I couldn't take it anymore—I just had to get outside. But even breathing the fresh mountain air didn't make the pain in my head go away. So I went down the stone steps beside the ward, thinking to take shelter in the shade of the garden. There I noticed a young woman leaning against a tree trunk, gazing at the world down below. She wasn't one of our patients. She was the daughter of a patient who'd been there long before I arrived, a man named Heihachiro Ikuma, a former assistant professor at Taido University. Her name was Sadako Yamamura. I remember the name well: her family name was different from her father's. For about a month she had been making frequent visits to the sanatorium, but she didn't spend much time with her father. Nor would she ask the doctors much about his condition. All I could assume was that she was there to enjoy the alpine scenery. I sat down next to her and smiled at her, asking her how her father was doing. But she didn't look like she even wanted to know much about his illness. On the other hand, it was clear that she knew he didn't have much longer. I could tell by the way she spoke. She knew the day her father was going to die, with more certainty than any doctor's educated guess.

"Sitting there beside her like that, talking to her about her life and her family, I suddenly became aware that my headache, so unbearable a little while ago, had retreated. In its place appeared a fever accompanied by an odd feeling of excitement. I felt vitality well up within me, as if the temperature of my blood had been raised. I gazed at her face. I felt what I always felt, a sense of wonder that a woman with such perfect features should exist in the world. I'm not exactly sure what defines beauty, but I know that Dr. Tanaka, who was twenty years older than me, used to say the same thing. That he'd never seen anyone more beautiful than Sadako Yamamura. My breathing was choked with fever, but somehow I controlled it enough to softly put a hand on her shoulder and say to her, 'Let's go somewhere cooler to talk, in the shade.'

"She suspected nothing. She nodded once and started to get to her feet. And as she stood up, and bent over, I saw—down the front of her white blouse—her perfectly-formed little breasts. They were so white that my whole mind was suddenly dyed milky white, and it was as if my reason was taken from me in the shock.

"She paid no attention to my agitation, but just brushed the dust from her long skirt. Her gestures seemed so innocent and adorable.

"We strolled on and on through the lush forest, surrounded by the droning of the cicadas. I hadn't decided on any particular destination, but my feet kept heading in a certain direction. Sweat ran down my back. I took off my shirt, leaving only my undershirt. We followed an animal track until it opened up onto the side of a valley where there stood a dilapidated old house. It had probably been at least ten years since anyone had lived there. The walls were rotting and the roof looked like it could collapse at any moment. There was a well on the other side of the house, and when she saw it she ran toward it, saying, 'Oh, I'm so thirsty.' She bent over to look in. Even from the outside it was obvious that the well wasn't used anymore. I ran to the well, too. But not to look inside. What I wanted to see was Sadako's chest as she bent over again. I placed both hands on the lip of the well and got a close look. I could feel cool, damp air rising from the dark depths of the earth to caress my face, but it couldn't take away the burning urge I felt. I didn't know where the urge came from. I think now that the smallpox fever had taken away my mechanism of control. I swear to you, I had never experienced such sensual temptation before in my life.

"I found myself reaching out to touch that gentle swelling. She looked up in shock. Something snapped inside me. My memories of what happened next are hazy. All I can recall are fragmentary scenes. I found myself pressing Sadako to the ground. I pulled her blouse up over her breasts, and then... My memory skips to her resisting, violently, and then biting my shoulder; it was the intense pain that brought me to my senses. I saw the blood flowing from my shoulder drip onto her face. Blood dripped into her eyes, and she shook her head in revulsion. I adjusted my body to that rhythmic movement. What did my face look like then? What did she see when she looked at me? The face of a beast, I'm sure. That's what I was thinking as I finished.

"When it was over, she fixed me with an implacable gaze. Still lying on her back, she raised her knees and skillfully used her elbows to scoot backwards. I looked at her body again. I thought my eyes had deceived me. Her wrinkled gray skirt had bunched up around her waist, and she made no move to cover her breasts as she backed up. A ray of sunlight fell on the point where her thighs converged, clearly illuminating a small, blackish lump. I raised my eyes to her chest—beautifully-shaped breasts. Then I looked down again. Within her pubic mound, covered with hair, was a pair of perfectly developed testicles.

"Had I not been a doctor, I probably would have been shocked silly. But I knew of cases such as this from photos in medical texts. Testicular feminization syndrome. It's an extremely rare syndrome. I never thought I'd see one outside of a textbook—much less in a situation such as that. Testicular feminization is a type of male pseudohermaphroditism. Externally the person seems completely female, having breasts and a vagina, but usually not a uterus. Chromosomally the person is XY, however—male. And for some reason people with this condition are all beautiful.

"Sadako was still staring at me. I was probably the first person outside her family to discover the secret of her body. Needless to say, she had been a virgin up until a few minutes previous. It had been a necessary trial if she were to go on living as a woman. I was trying to rationalize my actions. Then, suddenly, words flew into my head.

"I'll kill you.

"As I reeled from the strength of will behind the words, I instantaneously intuited that her telepathic message was no lie. There was no room within it for even a sliver of doubt; my body accepted it as a certainty. She'd do me, if I didn't do her first. My body's instinct for self-preservation gave me an order. I climbed back on top of her, placed both hands on her slender neck, and pressed with my full weight. To my surprise, there was less resistance this time. She narrowed her eyes with pleasure and relaxed her body, almost as if she wanted to die.

"I didn't wait to see if she'd stopped breathing. I picked her body up and went to the well. I think my actions were still beyond my will at this point. In other words, I didn't pick her up intending to drop her into the well, but rather, the moment I picked her up, the round black mouth of the well caught my eye, and put it in my mind to do it. Everything felt as if it was working out perfectly for me. Or, rather, I felt as if I was being moved by a will beyond my own. I had a general idea of what was going to happen next. I could hear a voice in the back of my head saying this was all a dream.

"The well was dark, and from where I stood at the top I couldn't see the bottom very well. From the smell of soil wafting up, it seemed that there was a shallow accumulation of water at the bottom. I let go. Sadako's body slid down the side of the well into the earth, hitting the bottom with a splash. I stared into the well until my eyes got used to the dark, but I still couldn't see her curled up down there. Even so, I couldn't shake my uneasiness. I flung rocks and dirt into the well, trying to hide her body forever. I threw in armfuls of dirt and five or six fist-sized rocks before I just couldn't do any more. The rocks hit her body, making a dull thud at the bottom of the well and stimulating my imagination. When I thought of that sickly beautiful body being broken by those stones, I couldn't go through with it. I know that doesn't make any sense. On the one hand I desired the destruction of her body, but on the other hand I didn't want her body to be marred."

When Nagao had finished speaking, Asakawa handed him the map of South Hakone Pacific Land.

"Where on this map would that well be?" Asakawa asked,

urgently. It took Nagao a few moments to understand what he was being shown, but after he was told that what had once been the sanatorium was now a restaurant, he seemed to regain his orientation.

"I think it was right about here," he said, pointing to a point on the map.

"No doubt about it. That's where Villa Log Cabin is," Asakawa said, rising. "Let's go!"

But Ryuji was calm. "Don't go rushing off just yet. We still have some things we need to ask this old fart. Now, this syndrome you mention..."

"Testicular feminization syndrome."

"Can a woman with this bear children?"

Nagao shook his head. "No, she can't."

"One other thing. When you raped Sadako Yamamura, you had already contracted smallpox, right?"

Nagao nodded.

"In which case, the last person in Japan to be infected with smallpox was Sadako Yamamura, no?"

It was certain that just before her death, Sadako Yamamura's body had been invaded by the smallpox virus. But she had died immediately afterward. If its host perishes, a virus can't go on living. Nagao didn't know how to answer and looked down, avoiding Ryuji's gaze. He gave only a vague reply.

"Hey! What are you doing? We've got to get going!" Asakawa was in the doorway, urging Ryuji to hurry.

"Shit. Hope you're happy," said Ryuji, flicking the tip of the doctor's nose with his index finger before following Asakawa.

12

He couldn't explain it logically, but from his experience reading novels and watching trashy TV shows, he felt like he had a good idea of the kind of plot device called for now, based on the way the story had unfolded. There was a certain tempo to the unfolding. They hadn't been searching for Sadako's hiding place, but in the blink of an eye they'd stumbled upon the tragedy that had befallen her and the spot where she was buried. So when Ryuji told him to "stop in front of a large hardware store," Asakawa was relieved: *he's thinking the same thing I am*. Asakawa still couldn't imagine what a horrible task this would be. Unless it had been completely buried, finding the old well in the vicinity of Villa Log Cabin shouldn't be too difficult. And once they found it, it should be easy to bring up Sadako's remains. It all sounded pretty simple—and he wanted to think it would be. It was one in the afternoon; the mid-day sun reflected brilliantly from the hilly streets in this hot-spring resort town. The brightness, and the neighborhood's laid-back weekday mood, clouded his imagination. It didn't occur to him that even if it were only four or five meters deep, the bottom of a well was bound to be an entirely different world from the well-lit ground above.

Nishizaki Hardware. Asakawa saw the sign and braked. There were stepladders and lawn mowers lined up in front of the store. They should be able to get everything they needed here.

"I'll let you do the shopping," Asakawa said, running to a nearby phone booth. He paused before entering it to take a phone card from his wallet.

"Hey, we don't have time to waste on phone calls." But Asakawa wasn't listening. Grumbling, Ryuji went into the store and grabbed rope, a bucket, a shovel, a pulley block, and a high-powered flashlight.

Asakawa was desperate. This might be his last chance to hear their voices. He knew full well how little time he had to waste. He only had nine hours left until his deadline. He slipped his card into the phone and dialed the number of his wife's parents' house in Ashikaga. His father-in-law answered.

"Hello, it's Asakawa. Could you call Shizu and Yoko to the phone?" He knew he was being rude, skipping the customary exchange of pleasantries. But he didn't have time to worry about his father-in-law's feelings. The man started to say something, but then seemed to sense the urgency of the situation, and immediately summoned his daughter and granddaughter. Asakawa was extremely glad his mother-in-law hadn't been the one to answer. He'd never have gotten a word in edgewise then.

"Hello?"

"Shizu, is that you?" Hearing her voice, he missed her already.

"Where are you?"

"Atami. How's everything there?"

"Oh, about the same. Yoko's having a great time with Grandma and Grandpa."

"Is she there?" He could hear her voice. No words, just sounds as she struggled to climb up on her mother's lap to get to her father.

"Yoko, it's Daddy." Shizu put the receiver to Yoko's ear.

"Dada, Dada..." He could barely hear the words, if words they were. They were all but drowned out by the sounds of her breathing into the phone, or rubbing the mouthpiece against her cheek. But these noises only made him feel that much closer to her. He was overcome with the desire to leave all this behind him and hug her.

"Yoko, you wait there, ok? Daddy's coming soon to get you in the vroom-vroom."

"Really? When are you getting here?" Shizu had taken the phone without him realizing it.

"On Sunday. Right, I'll be renting a car and driving up, so let's all take a drive into the mountains, to Nikko or something."

"Really? Yoko, isn't that great? Daddy's going to take us for a drive in a car on Sunday!"

He felt his ears burning. Was he really in a position to make that kind of promise? A doctor was never supposed to say anything to give his patient false hope; he was supposed to do things to minimize the eventual shock as much as possible.

"It sounds like you've got this thing you're working on straightened out."

"Well, it's coming along."

"You promised me that when all this is over you'd tell me the whole thing from the beginning."

He had promised that. In exchange for her not asking any questions right now, he'd said he'd tell her all about it once it was taken care of. His wife had kept her end of the bargain.

"Hey, how long are you going to keep talking?" Ryuji said from behind him. Asakawa turned around. Ryuji had the trunk open and was loading his purchases into the car.

"I'll call again. I might not be able to tonight, though." Asakawa placed his hand on the hook. If he pushed, the connection would be broken. He didn't even know why he'd called. Was it just to hear their voices, or did he have something more important to tell them? But he knew that even if he'd been able to talk to her for an hour, when it came time to hang up he'd still feel constrained, as if he'd only said half of what he wanted to say. It'd just be the same thing. He pressed down on the hook, and then let go. In any case, everything would be clear tonight at ten. Tonight at ten....

Driving up in the daytime like this, South Hakone Pacific Land felt like a typical mountain resort. The creepy mood he'd felt last time he came was hidden by the sunlight. Even the sound of bouncing tennis balls was normal, not sluggish and sonorous like before, but crisp and light. They could see Mt. Fuji, hazy and white, and below them in the distance scattered flashes of sun from greenhouse roofs.

It was a weekday afternoon and Villa Log Cabin appeared deserted. It seemed that the only time the rental units were fully occupied was weekends and the summer vacation season. B-4 was vacant today, too. Leaving Ryuji to check in, Asakawa unloaded the car and changed into lighter clothes.

He looked carefully around the room. A week ago this evening Asakawa had fled in fear from this haunted house. He remembered running into the bathroom to throw up, feeling that he was about to piss himself. He could even remember, quite vividly, the graffiti he'd seen on the bathroom wall when he'd knelt down in front of the toilet. Now he opened the bathroom door. The same graffiti in the same place.

It was just after two. They went out onto the balcony and ate the box lunches they'd bought on the way while gazing over the grassy meadow surrounding the cabins. The fretful mood that had shadowed them here from Nagao's clinic subsided a bit. Even amidst the worst panic, there are still scattered moments like this, when time flows leisurely by. Even when trying to finish a story by an impending deadline, Asakawa would sometimes find himself aimlessly watching coffee drop from the spout of the coffee maker, and later he'd reflect on how elegantly he'd wasted precious time.

"Eat up. We'll need our strength," said Ryuji. He'd bought two lunches just for himself. Asakawa meanwhile didn't seem to have much appetite; from time to time he'd rest his chopsticks and look back inside the cabin.

Suddenly, he spoke, as if it had just occurred to him. "Maybe we'd better get this straight. What exactly are we doing here?"

"We're going to look for Sadako, of course."

"And what do we do once we've found her?"

"Take her back to Sashikiji and lay her to rest."

"So that's the charm. You're saying that's what she wants."

Ryuji chewed loudly for a while on a big mouthful of rice, eyes staring straight ahead, unfocused. Asakawa could tell from the look on his face that Ryuji wasn't entirely convinced, either. Asakawa was scared. It was his last chance, and he wanted some sort of assurance that they were doing the right thing. There were to be no do-overs.

"There's nothing else we can do now," said Ryuji, tossing away his empty lunch box.

"What about this possibility? Maybe she wants us to clear away her resentment toward the person who killed her."

"You mean Jotaro Nagao? You mean if we exposed him, Sadako would be appeased?"

Asakawa looked deep into Ryuji's eyes, trying to figure out

what he really thought. If they dug up the remains and laid them to rest and it still didn't save Asakawa's life, maybe Ryuji was planning to kill Dr. Nagao. Maybe he was using Asakawa as a test case, trying to save his own skin....

"Come on. Don't be stupid," said Ryuji with a laugh. "First of all, if Nagao had really incurred Sadako's resentment, he'd already be dead."

True. She definitely had that kind of power.

"So why did she let herself be killed by him?"

"I can't say. But look: she was surrounded by the deaths of people close to her. She knew nothing but frustration. Even disappearing from the theater company like that was essentially a frustration of her goals, right? Then she visits her father at the sanatorium and finds out that he's near death."

"A person who's given up on the world harbors no resentment toward the person who takes her out of it, is that what you're saying?"

"Not exactly. Rather, I think it's possible that Sadako herself caused those impulses in Old Man Nagao. In other words, maybe she killed herself, but borrowed Nagao's hands to do it."

Her mother had thrown herself into a volcano, her father was dying of tuberculosis, her own dreams of becoming an actress had been shattered, and then there was her congenital handicap. She had any number of reasons to commit suicide. And there were things that just didn't add up unless one assumed she'd killed herself. Yoshino's report had mentioned Shigemori, founder of Theater Group Soaring. He'd gotten drunk and dropped in on Sadako, and died the next day of cardiac paralysis. It was almost certain that Sadako had killed him using some abnormal ability of hers. She had that kind of power. She could easily kill a man or two without leaving any evidence. So why was Nagao still alive? It made no sense, unless one decided that she must have guided his will in order to kill herself.

"Well, okay, let's say it was suicide. But why did she have to be raped before she died? And don't tell me it's because she didn't want to die a virgin."

Asakawa had hit the nail on the head, and as a result Ryuji was at a loss for an answer. That was exactly what he was going to say.

"Is that really so stupid?"

"Huh?"

"Is it really so foolish to not want to die a virgin?" Ryuji pressed his point with a desperate earnestness. "If it were me...if by some chance it were me, that's how I'd feel. I wouldn't want to die a virgin."

This wasn't like Ryuji, Asakawa felt. Asakawa couldn't explain it logically, but neither the words nor the facial expression were like Ryuji at all.

"Are you serious? Men and women are different. Especially in the case of Sadako Yamamura."

"Heh, heh. Just kidding. Sadako didn't want to be raped. Of course she didn't. I mean, who'd want a thing like that to happen to oneself? Plus, she bit Nagao's shoulder down to the bone. It was only after it had happened that the thought of dying occurred to her, and without even considering it she guided Nagao in that direction. I think that's probably what happened."

"But then, wouldn't you still expect her to have a lingering resentment toward Nagao?" Asakawa still wasn't convinced.

"But aren't you forgetting? We need to imagine the spear-tip of her resentment being pointed, not at any one individual, but at society in general. Compared to that, her hatred of Nagao was as insignificant as a fart in a windstorm."

If hatred toward society in general was what was incorporated into that video, then what was the charm? What could it be? The phrase *indiscriminate attack* came into Asakawa's mind, before Ryuji's thick voice interrupted his thoughts.

"Enough already. If we have time to think about crap like this, we should be spending it trying to find Sadako. She's the one who'll solve every riddle."

Ryuji drained the last of his oolong tea and then stood up and tossed the empty can out toward the valley floor.

They stood on the gentle hillside looking around at the tall grass. Ryuji handed Asakawa a sickle and pointed with his chin to the slope on the left side of B-4. He wanted him to cut away the tangles of grass and examine the contours of the ground there. Asakawa bent down, dropped his knee, and began to swing the sickle in an arc parallel to the ground. Grass began to fall.

Thirty years before a dilapidated house had stood here, with a well in its front yard. Asakawa stood up again. He looked around again, wondering where he'd build his dwelling if he were to live here. He'd probably choose a site with a nice view. There was no other reason to build a house up here. Where was the best view? Eyes trained on the greenhouse roofs shining far below, Asakawa walked around a bit, paying attention to the shifting perspective. The view didn't seem to change much no matter where he went. But he thought that if he were building a house, it would be easier to build it where cabin A-4 stood than where B-4 was. When he bent down to the ground and looked he realized that was the only level patch of ground. He crawled around in the space between A-4 and B-4, cutting the grass and feeling the earth with his hands.

He had no memory of ever drawing water from a well. He realized that he'd never even seen a real well. He had no idea what one really looked like, especially one in a mountainous area such as this. Was there really groundwater here? But then, a few hundred meters east along the floor of the valley there was a patch of marsh, surrounded by tall trees. Asakawa's thoughts weren't coming together. What was he supposed to concentrate on during a task such as this? No idea. He felt the blood rush to his head. He looked at his watch: almost three o'clock. Seven hours left. Would all this effort get them any closer to meeting the deadline? The thought sent his mind into further disarray. His image of the well was hazy. What would remain to mark the site of an old well? A bunch of stones piled up in a circle? What if they'd collapsed and fallen into the earth? No way. Then they'd never make it in time. He looked at his watch again. Exactly three now. He'd just drunk 500 milliliters of oolong tea on the balcony, but already his throat was dry again. Voices echoed in his head: *look for a bulge in the earth, look for rocks*. He jabbed the shovel into the exposed dirt. Time and blood assaulted his brain. His nerves were shot, but he didn't feel fatigued. Why was time flowing so differently now than it had on the balcony, when they were eating lunch? Why had he started to panic so much the minute he'd set to work? Was this the right thing to do, really? Weren't there a lot of other things they should be doing?

He'd dug a cave once as a child. He must have been in the fourth or fifth grade. He laughed weakly as he recalled the episode.

"What in the world are you doing?" At the sound of Ryuji's voice, Asakawa's head jerked up. "What've you been up to, crawling around over here. We've got to search a wider area."

Asakawa gaped up at Ryuji. Ryuji had the sun at his back, his face was shadowy. Drops of sweat from his dark face fell to the grass by his feet. *What was I up to?* A little hole had been dug in the ground right in front of him. Asakawa had dug it.

"You digging a pit or something?"

Ryuji sighed. Asakawa frowned and moved to look at his watch.

"And stop looking at your fucking watch!" Ryuji slapped his hand away. He glared at Asakawa for a little while, then sighed again. He squatted and whispered, calmly, "Maybe you ought to take a break."

"No time."

"I'm telling you, you need to get a hold of yourself. Panicking won't get you anywhere." Asakawa was crouching, too, and Ryuji poked him lightly in the chest. Asakawa lost his balance and fell over backwards, feet up in the air.

"That's it, lie down just like that, just like a baby."

Asakawa squirmed, trying to get to his feet.

"Don't move! Lie down! Don't waste your strength." Ryuji stepped on Asakawa's chest until he stopped struggling. Asakawa closed his eyes and gave up resisting. The weight of Ryuji's foot receded into the distance. When he gently opened his eyes again, Ryuji was moving his short, powerful legs, crossing over into the shade of B-4's balcony. His gait was eloquent. He'd had an inspiration as to where they could find the well, and his sense of desperation had faded.

After Ryuji had left, Asakawa lay still for a while. Flat on his back, spread-eagled, he gazed up into the sky. The sun was bright. How weak his spirit was compared to Ryuji's. Disgusting. He regulated his breathing and tried to think coolly. He wasn't confident he could keep himself together as the next seven hours ticked away. He'd just follow Ryuji's every order. That'd be best. Lose himself, place himself under the sway of someone with an unyielding spirit. *Lose yourself! You'll even be able to escape the terror then. You're going to be buried in the earth—you'll become one with nature.* As if in answer to his wish, he was suddenly overcome by drowsiness and began to lose consciousness. At the very threshold of sleep, in the midst of a daydream about lifting Yoko high into the air, he remembered once again that episode from his grade-school days.

There was a municipal sports ground on the outskirts of the town where he'd grown up. There was a cliff at its edge, and at the foot of the cliff was a swamp with crayfish in it. When he was a schoolboy, Asakawa often went there with his buddies to catch crayfish. On that particular day, the sun shining on the exposed red earth of the cliff next to the swamp was like a challenge. He was tired of sitting there holding his fishing pole anyway, so he went over to where the sun was shining on the cliff and began to dig a hole in its steep face. The dirt was soft clay, and it crumbled away at his feet when he thrust in an old piece of board he'd found. Before long his friends joined him. There'd been three of them, he seemed to recall, or maybe four. Just the perfect number for digging a cave. Any more and they would have been bumping heads, any fewer and it would have been too much work for each of them.

After an hour of digging they'd made a hole just the right size for one of them to crawl into. They kept going. They'd originally been on their way home from school, and soon one of his friends said he had to be getting home. Only Asakawa, whose idea it had been in the first place, kept at it silently. And by the time the sun set the cave had grown large enough for all the boys who were left to squeeze into. Asakawa had hugged his knees; he and his friends giggled at each other. Curled up in the red clay like that, they felt like the Stone Age people at Mikkabi, whose remains they'd just learned about in Social Studies.

However, after a little while the entrance to the hole was blocked by a lady's face. The setting sun was at her back, so her face was in shadow and they couldn't make out her expression, but they realized it was a fiftyish housewife from the neighborhood.

"What are you boys doing digging a hole here? It'd be pretty disgusting if you got buried alive in there," the lady said, peering into the cave. Asakawa and the two other boys exchanged glances. Young though they were, they still noticed something odd about her warning. Not, "Cut it out—that's dangerous," but, "Cut it out, because if you got buried alive in there and died it would be disgusting to people in the neighborhood, such as me." She was cautioning them purely for her own good. Asakawa and his friends began to giggle again. The lady's face blocked the entrance like a figure in a shadow play.

Ryuji's face gradually superimposed itself over the lady's.

"Now you're a bit too relaxed. Imagine being able to go night-night in a place like this. Hey, you jerk, what are you giggling at?"

Ryuji woke him up. The sun was nearing the western horizon, and darkness was fast approaching. Ryuji's face and figure against the weakening sunlight were even blacker than before.

"Come over here a minute." Ryuji pulled Asakawa to his feet and then silently crawled back under the balcony of B-4. Asakawa followed. Under the balcony, one of the boards between the supporting pillars had been peeled partway back. Ryuji stuck his hand in behind the board and pulled it out with all his might. With a loud *snap* the board broke in half diagonally. The decor inside the cabin was modern, but these boards were so flimsy you could break them by hand. The builders had thoroughly skimped on the parts you couldn't see. Ryuji poked the flashlight inside and shined it around under the cabin. He nodded as if to say, *come look at this*. Asakawa fixed his gaze on the gap in the wall and looked inside. The flashlight beam was trained on a black protrusion over by the west side. As he stared at it he noticed that the sides seemed to have an uneven texture, like a pile of rocks. The top was covered with a concrete lid; blades of grass poked out of cracks in the concrete and between the stones. Asakawa immediately realized what was directly overhead. The living room of the cabin. And directly over the round rim of the well were the television and VCR. A week ago, when he'd watched that video, Sadako Yamamura had been this close, hiding, watching what went on above.

Ryuji pulled off more boards until there was an opening large enough for a man to pass through. They both ducked through the hole in the wall and crawled to the rim of the well. The cabin was built on a grade, and they'd entered from the downhill end, so the further they went the lower the floorboards got, creating a sense of something pressing down on them. Even though there should be plenty of air in the dark crawl space, Asakawa began to find it hard to breathe. The soil here was clammier than outside. Asakawa knew full well what they must do now. He knew, but he felt no fear yet. He felt claustrophobic just from the floorboards over his head, but maybe he'd have to go down into the bottom of the well, into a place ruled by an even deeper darkness.... Not *maybe*. To pull Sadako out, they'd almost certainly have to descend into the well.

"Give me a hand here," said Ryuji. He'd grabbed a piece of rebar poking out from a crack in the concrete lid and was trying to pull the lid onto the downhill slope. But the ceiling was too low, and he couldn't get much leverage. Even someone like Ryuji who could bench 120 kilos was down to half strength if he didn't have the right footing. Asakawa went around the well until he was uphill from it and lay down on his back. He placed both hands on a support column to brace himself and then pushed against the lid with his feet. There was an ugly sound as concrete scraped against stone. Asakawa and Ryuji began to chant in order to synchronize their efforts. The lid moved. How many years had it been since the well's face was exposed? Had the well been capped when Villa Log Cabin was built, or when Pacific Land was established, or when the sanatorium closed? They could only guess, based on the strength of the seal between the concrete and the stones, on the almost-human screech as the lid was torn away. Probably more than just six months or a year. But no longer than twenty-five years. In any case, the well had now started to open its mouth. Ryuji stuck the blade of the shovel into the space they'd made so far and pushed.

"Okay, when I give the signal, I want you to lean on the handle."

Asakawa turned around.

"Ready? One, two, three, push!"

As Asakawa leaned on the makeshift lever, Ryuji pushed on the side of the cap with both hands. With an agonized shriek, the lid fell to the ground.

The lip of the well was faintly damp. Asakawa and Ryuji picked up their flashlights, placed their other hands on the wet rim, and pulled themselves up. Before shining light into the well, they moved their heads and shoulders into the roughly fifty-centimeter gap between the top of the well and the floor above. A putrid smell arose on the cold air. The space inside the well was so dense that they felt if they let go their hands they'd be sucked in. She was here, all right. This woman with extraordinary supernatural power, with testicular feminization syndrome... "Woman" wasn't even the right word. The biological distinction between male and female depended on the structure of the gonads. No matter how beautifully feminine the body, if those gonads were in the form of testes it was a male. Asakawa didn't know whether he should consider Sadako Yamamura a man or a woman. Since her parents had named her Sadako, it seemed they had intended to raise her as a woman. This morning, on the boat to Atami, Ryuji had said, *Don't you think a person with both male and female genitals is the ultimate symbol of power and beauty?* Come to think of it, Asakawa had once seen something in an art book that had made him doubt his eyes. A perfectly mature female nude was reclining on a slab of stone, with a splendid example of the male genitalia peeking out from between her thighs....

"Can you see anything?" asked Ryuji. The beams of their flashlights showed that water had collected in the bottom of the well, about four or five meters down. But they didn't know how deep the water was.

"There's water down there." Ryuji scuffled around, tying the end of the rope to a post.

"Okay, point your flashlight downward and hold it over the edge. Don't drop it, whatever you do."

He's planning to go down in there. As he realized this, Asakawa's legs began to shake. *What if I have to go down...* Now, finally, with the narrow, vertical tunnel staring him in the face, Asakawa's imagination started to work on him. *I can't do it. Go into that black water and do what? Fish around for bones, that's what. There's no way I can do that, I'll go crazy.* As he gratefully watched Ryuji lower himself into the hold, he prayed to God that his turn would never come.

His eyes were accustomed to the dark now, and he could see the moss covering the inner surface of the well. The stones of the wall, in the orange beam of his flashlight, seemed to turn into eyes and noses and mouths, and when he couldn't tear his gaze away, the patterns of the stones transformed into dead faces, distorted with demonic cries at their moment of death. Innumerable evil spirits undulated like seaweed, hands outstretched toward the exit. He couldn't drive away the image. A pebble fell into the ghastly shaft, barely a meter across, echoed against the sides of the well, and was swallowed into the gullets of the evil spirits.

Ryuji wormed his body into the space between the top of the well and the floorboards, wrapped the rope around his hands, and slowly let himself down. Soon he was standing on the bottom. His legs were submerged up to his knees. It wasn't very deep.

"Hey, Asakawa! Go get the bucket. Oh, and the thin rope, too."

The bucket was where they'd left it, on the balcony. Asakawa crawled out from underneath the cabin. It was dark outside. But it still felt far brighter than under the foundation. What a feeling of release! So much pure air! He looked around at the cabins: only A-1, by the road, emitted any light. He made a point of not looking at his watch. The warm, friendly voices spilling from A-1 seemed to constitute a separate world, floating in the distance. They were the sounds of dinnertime. He didn't have to look at his watch to know what time it must be.

He returned to the lip of the well, where he tied the bucket and shovel to the end of the rope and lowered them down. Ryuji shoveled earth from the bottom of the well into the bucket. From time to time he'd crouch and run his fingers through the mud, searching for something, but he didn't find anything.

"Haul the bucket up!" he shouted. With his belly braced against the edge of the well, Asakawa pulled up the bucket, then dumped the mud and rocks out on the ground before lowering the empty bucket back down into the well. It seemed that quite a bit of dirt and sand had drifted into the well before it had been sealed. Ryuji dug and dug, but without turning up Sadako's beautiful limbs.

"Hey, Asakawa." Ryuji paused in his labors and looked up. Asakawa didn't reply. "Asakawa! Something wrong up there?"

Asakawa wanted to reply: *Nothing's wrong. I'm fine.*

"You haven't said a word this whole time. At least, you know, call out encouragement or something. I'm getting a bit melancholy down here."

Asakawa said nothing.

"Well, then, how about a song? Something by Hibari Misora, maybe."

Asakawa still said nothing.

"Hey! Asakawa. Are you still there? I know you didn't faint on me."

"I'm...I'm fine," he managed to mutter.

"You're a pain in the ass, that's what you are." Ryuji spat out the words and jammed the tip of the shovel into the water. How many times had he done this now? The water level was slowly dropping, but still there were no signs of what they were looking for. He could see the bucket climbing more and more slowly. Then, finally, it stopped. Asakawa let it slip out of his hands. He'd had it raised about half the height of the well, and now it plunged back down again. Ryuji managed to avoid a direct hit, but he got splashed from head to toe with muddy water. Along with anger came the realization that Asakawa was at the limit of his strength.

"Sonofabitch! Are you trying to kill me?" Ryuji climbed up the rope. "Your turn."

My turn! Shocked, Asakawa stood up, banging his head hard on the floorboards in the process. "Wait, Ryuji, it's okay, I'm alright, I've still got some strength left," Asakawa stammered. Ryuji poked his head out of the well.

"No you haven't, not an ounce. Your turn."

"Just, just hold on. Let me catch my second wind."

"We'd be here 'til dawn."

Ryuji shined the light in Asakawa's face. There was a strange look in his eyes. Fear of death had stolen his reason. One look told Ryuji that Asakawa was no longer capable of rational judgment. Between shoveling muddy water into a bucket and hauling that bucket four or five meters straight up, it didn't take much to see which was the harder job.

"Down you go." Ryuji pushed Asakawa toward the well.

"No—wait—I—it's..."

"What?"

"I'm claustrophobic."

"Don't be silly."

Asakawa continued to cringe, unmoving. The water at the bottom of the well trembled slightly.

"I can't do it. I can't go down there."

Ryuji grabbed Asakawa by the collar and slapped him twice. "Snap out of it. 'I can't go down there.' You've got death staring you in the face, and you might be able to do something about it, and now you say you can't do it? Don't be a worm. It's not just your own life at stake here, you know. Remember that phone call? You ready to take sweet babykins down into the darkness with you?"

He thought about his wife and daughter. He couldn't afford to be a coward. He held their lives in his hands. But his body wouldn't obey him.

"Is this really going to work, though?" But there was no purpose in his voice; he knew it was pointless to even ask the question now. Ryuji relaxed his grip on his collar.

"Shall I tell you a little more about Professor Miura's theory? There are three conditions that have to be met in order for a malevolent will to remain in the world after death. An enclosed space, water, and a slow death. One, two, three. In other words, if someone dies slowly, in an enclosed space, with water present, then usually that person's angry spirit will haunt the place. Now, look at this well. It's a small, enclosed space. There's water. And remember what the old lady in the video said."

...How has your health been since then? If you spend all your time playing in the water, monsters are bound to get you.

Playing in the water. That was it. Sadako was down there under that black muddy water *playing*, even now. An endless, watery, underground game.

"You see, Sadako was still alive when she was dropped into this well. And while she waited for death she coated the very walls with her hatred. All three conditions were met in her case."

"So?"

"So, according to Professor Miura, it's easy to exorcise such a curse. We just free her. We take her bones out of this nasty old well, have a nice memorial service, and lay her to rest in the soil of her native place. We bring her up into the wide, bright world."

A while before, when he'd crawled out from under the cabin to get the bucket, Asakawa had felt an indescribable sense of liberation. Were they supposed to provide Sadako with the same thing? Was that what she wanted?

"So that's the charm?"

"Maybe it is and maybe it isn't."

"That's pretty vague."

Ryuji grabbed Asakawa's collar again. "Think! There's nothing certain in our future! All we can hope for is a vague future. But in spite of that, you're going to keep on living. You can't give up on life just because it's vague. It's a question of possibilities. The charm... There might be a lot of other things Sadako wants. But there's a good possibility that taking her remains out of here will break the curse of the video."

Asakawa twisted his face and screamed silently. *Enclosed space, water, and slow death, he says. Those three conditions allow the strongest survival of an evil spirit, he says. Where's the proof that anything that fraud Miura said is true?*

"If you understand me, you'll go down into the well."

But I don't understand. How can I understand something like this?

"You don't have time to dawdle. Your deadline is almost here." Ryuji's voice grew gradually kinder. "Don't think you can overcome death without a fight."

Asshole! I don't want to hear your philosophy of life!

But he finally began to climb over the rim of the well.

"Attaboy. You finally think you can do it?"

Asakawa clung to the rope and lowered himself down the inner wall of the well. Ryuji's face was before his eyes.

"Don't worry. There's nothing down there. Your biggest enemy is your imagination."

When he looked up, the beam of the flashlight hit him full in the face, blinding him. He pressed his back against the wall; his grip on the rope began to loosen. His feet slipped against the stones, and he suddenly dropped about a meter. His hands burned from the friction.

He was dangling just above the surface of the water, but couldn't make himself go in. He extended one foot, putting it in the water up to his ankle, as if he were testing the temperature of a bath. With the cold touch of the water came gooseflesh, from the tips of his toes to his spine, and he immediately retracted his foot. But his arms were too tired to keep hanging onto the rope. His weight pulled him slowly down, and eventually he couldn't endure anymore so he planted both feet. Immediately the soft dirt below the water enveloped his feet, submerging them. Asakawa still clung to the rope in front of his eyes. He started to panic. He felt as if a forest of hands were reaching up from the earth to pull him into the mud. The walls were closing in on all sides, leering at him: *there's no escape.*

Ryuji! He tried to scream, but he couldn't find his voice. He couldn't breathe. Only a faint, dry sound escaped his throat, and he looked upward like a drowning child. He felt something warm trickle down the insides of his thighs.

"Asakawa! Breathe!"

Overcome by the pressure, Asakawa had forgotten to breathe.

"It's alright. I'm here." Ryuji's voice echoed down to him, and Asakawa managed to suck in a lungful of air.

He couldn't control the pounding of his heart. He couldn't do what he needed to do down here. He desperately tried to think of something else. Something more pleasant. If this well had been outside, under a sky full of stars, it wouldn't be this horrible. It was because it was covered by cabin B-4 that it was so hard to take. It cut off the escape route. Even with the concrete lid gone, there were only floorboards and spiderwebs above. *Sadako Yamamura has lived down here for twenty-five years. That's right, she's down here. Right under my feet. This is a tomb, that's what it is. A tomb.* He couldn't think of anything else. Thought itself was closed off to him, as was any kind of escape. Sadako had tragically ended her life down here, and the scenes that had flashed through her mind at her moment of death had remained here, still strong, through the power of her psyche. And they'd matured down here in this cramped hole, breathing like the ebb and flow of the tide, waxing and waning in strength according to some cycle that had at some point coincided in frequency with the television placed directly overhead; and then they'd made their appearance in the world. Sadako was breathing. From out of nowhere, the sound of breathing enclosed him. *Sadako Yamamura, Sadako Yamamura.* The syllables repeated themselves in his brain, and her terrifyingly beautiful face came to him out of the photographs, shaking her head coquettishly. Sadako Yamamura was here. Asakawa recklessly began to dig through the earth beneath him, searching for her. He thought of her pretty face and her body, trying to maintain that image. *That beautiful girl's bones, covered in my piss.* Asakawa moved the shovel, sifting through the mud. Time no longer mattered. He'd taken off his watch before coming down here. Extreme fatigue and stress had deadened his vexation, and he forgot the time limit he was laboring under. It felt like being drunk. He had no sense of time. Only by the number of times the bucket came back down the well to him, and by the beating of his heart, did he have any way of measuring time.

Finally, Asakawa grasped a large, round rock with both hands.

It was smooth and pleasant to the touch, with two holes in its surface. He lifted it out of the water. He washed the dirt out of its recesses. He picked it up by what must once have been earholes and found himself face to face with a skull. His imagination clothed it with flesh. Big, clear eyes returned to the deep, hollow sockets, and flesh appeared above the two holes in the middle, forming itself into an elegant nose. Her long hair was wet, and water dripped from her neck and from behind her ears. Sadako Yamamura blinked her melancholy eyes two or three times to shake the water from her eyelashes. Squeezed between Asakawa's hands, her face looked painfully distorted. But still, her beauty was unclouded. She smiled at Asakawa, then narrowed her eyes as if to focus her vision.

I've been wanting to meet you. As he thought this, Asakawa slumped down right where he was. He could hear Ryuji's voice from far overhead.

Asakawa! Wasn't your deadline 10:04? Rejoice! It's 10:10!

Asakawa, can you hear me? You're still alive, right? The curse is broken. We're saved. Hey, Asakawa! If you die down there you'll end up just like her. If you die, just don't put a curse on me, okay? If you're going to die, die nice, would you? Hey, Asakawa! If you're alive, answer me, dammit!

He heard Ryuji, but he didn't really feel saved. He just curled up as if in a dream, as if in another world, clutching Sadako Yamamura's skull to his chest.

PART FOUR *Ripples*

1

October 19—Friday

A phone call from the manager's office woke Asakawa from his slumber. The manager was reminding them that checkout was at 11 a.m., and asking if they'd prefer to stay another night. Asakawa reached out with his free hand and picked up his watch beside his pillow. His arms were tired, just lifting them was an effort. They didn't hurt yet, but they'd probably ache like hell tomorrow. He wasn't wearing his glasses, so he couldn't read the time until he brought the watch right up to his eyes. A few minutes past eleven. Asakawa couldn't think of how to reply right away. He didn't even know where he was.

"Will you be staying another night?" asked the manager, trying to suppress his annoyance. Ryuji groaned right beside him. This wasn't his own room, that was for sure. It was as if the whole world had been repainted without his knowing it. The thick line connecting past to present and present to future had been cut into two: before his sleep and after it.

"Hello?"

Now the manager was worried that there was nobody on the other end of the line. Without even knowing why, Asakawa felt joy flood his breast. Ryuji rolled over and opened his eyes slightly. He was drooling. Asakawa's memories were hazy; all he found when he searched his recollections was darkness. He could more or less remember visiting Dr. Nagao and then heading for Villa Log Cabin, but everything after that was vague. Dark scenes came to him, one after another, and his breath caught in his throat. He felt like he did after waking up from a powerful dream, one that left a strong impression even though he'd forgotten what it was about. But for some reason, his spirits were high.

"Hello? Can you hear me?"

"Uh, yeah." Asakawa finally managed to reply, adjusting his grip on the receiver.

"Check-out time is eleven o'clock."

"Got it. We'll get our things together and leave right away." Asakawa adopted an officious tone to match the manager's. He could hear a faint trickle of water from the kitchen. It seemed someone hadn't turned the faucet tight last night before going to sleep. Asakawa hung up the phone.

Ryuji had closed his eyes again. Asakawa shook him. "Hey, Ryuji. Get up."

He had no idea how long they'd slept. Ordinarily, Asakawa slept no more than five or six hours a night, but now he felt like he'd been asleep for much longer than that. It had been a long time since he'd been able to sleep soundly, untroubled.

"Hey, Ryuji! If we don't get out of here they're going to charge us for another night." Asakawa shook Ryuji harder, but he didn't wake up. Asakawa raised his eyes and saw the milky-white plastic bag on the dining room table. Suddenly, as if some chance happening had brought back a fragment of a dream, he remembered what was inside it. *Calling Sadako's name. Pulling her out of the cold earth under the floor, stuffing her into a plastic bag.* The sound of running water... It had been Ryuji, last night, who had gone to the sink and washed the mud from Sadako. The water was still running. By then, the appointed time had already passed. And even now, Asakawa was still alive. He was overjoyed. Death had been breathing down his neck, and now that it had been cleared away, life seemed more concentrated; it began to glow. Sadako's skull was beautiful, like a marble sculpture.

"Hey, Ryuji! Wake up!"

Suddenly, he got a bad feeling. Something caught in a corner of his mind. He put his ear to Ryuji's chest. He wanted to hear Ryuji's heart beating through his thick sweatshirt, to know he was still alive. But just as his ear was about to touch Ryuji's chest, Asakawa suddenly found himself in a headlock, held by two powerful hands. Asakawa panicked and started to struggle.

"Gotcha! Thought I was dead, didn't you?" Ryuji released his grip on Asakawa's head and laughed an odd, childlike laugh. How could he joke around after what they'd just been through? Anything was liable to happen. If at that instant he'd seen Sadako Yamamura alive and standing by the table, and Ryuji tearing at his hair dying, Asakawa would have believed his eyes. He suppressed his anger. He owed Ryuji a great deal.

"Stop fooling around."

"It's payback time. You scared the bejeezus out of me last night." Still on his side, Ryuji began to chuckle.

"What did I do?"

"You collapsed down there at the bottom of the well. I really thought you'd gone and died. I was worried. Time was up. I thought you were out of the game."

Asakawa said nothing, just blinked several times.

"Hah. You probably don't even remember. Ungrateful bastard."

Now that he thought about it, Asakawa couldn't remember crawling out of the well on his own. Finally he recalled dangling from the rope, his strength totally spent. Hauling his sixty kilogram frame four or five meters straight up couldn't have been easy, even for someone of Ryuji's strength. The image of himself hanging suspended reminded him somehow of the stone statue of En no Ozunu being pulled up from the bottom of the sea. Shizuko had gained mysterious powers for fishing out the statue, but all Ryuji had to show for his troubles were aches and pains.

"Ryuji?" asked Asakawa in a strangely altered voice.

"What?"

"Thanks for everything you've done. I really owe you."

"Don't start getting mushy on me."

"If it hadn't been for you, I'd be...well, you know. Anyway, thanks."

"Cut the crap. You're going to make me puke. Gratitude isn't worth a single yen."

"Well then, how about some lunch? I'm buying."

"Oh, well in that case." Ryuji pulled himself to his feet, staggering a little. All of his muscles were stiff. Even Ryuji was having trouble making his body do what he wanted it to.

From the South Hakone Pacific Land rest house, Asakawa called his wife in Ashikaga and told her he'd pick her up in a rental car Sunday morning, as promised. *So, everything's all taken care of?* she asked. All Asakawa could say was, "Probably." From the fact that he was still here, alive, he could only guess that things were resolved. But as he hung up the phone, something still bothered him deeply. He couldn't quite get over it. Just from the mere fact that he was alive, he wanted to believe that everything was wrapped up neatly, but... Thinking that Ryuji might have the same doubts, Asakawa walked back to the table and asked, "This is really the end, right?"

Ryuji had wolfed down his lunch while Asakawa was on the phone.

"Your family doing alright?" Ryuji wasn't going to answer Asakawa's question right away.

"Yeah. Hey, Ryuji, are you feeling like it's not all over yet?"

"You worried?"

"Aren't you?"

"Maybe."

"About what? What bothers you?"

"What the old woman said. *Next year you're going to have a child*. That prediction of hers."

The moment he realized Ryuji had exactly the same doubts, Asakawa turned to trying to dispel those doubts.

"Maybe the 'you,' just that once, was referring to Shizuko instead of Sadako."

Ryuji rejected this straightaway. "Not possible. The images on that video come from Sadako's own eyes and mind. The old woman was talking to her. 'You' can only refer to Sadako."

"Maybe her prediction was false."

"Sadako's ability to foresee the future should have been infallible, one hundred percent."

"But Sadako was physically incapable of bearing children."

"That's why it's so strange. Biologically, Sadako was a man, not a woman, so there was no way she could have a kid. Plus, she was a virgin until right before she died. And..."

"And?"

"Her first sexual experience was Nagao. The last smallpox victim in Japan. Quite a coincidence."

It was said that in the distant past God and the Devil, cells and viruses, male and female, even light and darkness had been identical, with no internal contradiction. Asakawa began to feel uneasy. Once the discussion moved into the realm of genetic structures, or the cosmos before the creation of the Earth, the answers were beyond the pale of individual questioning. All he could do at this point was to persuade himself to dispel niggling uncertainties in his heart and tell himself that it was all over.

"But I'm alive. The riddle of the erased charm is solved. This case is closed."

Then Asakawa realized something. Hadn't the statue of En no Ozunu *willed* itself to be pulled up from the bottom of the ocean? That will had worked on Shizuko, guiding her actions, and as a result she was given her new power. Suddenly that pattern looked awfully familiar. Bringing Sadako's bones up from the bottom of the well, fishing En no Ozunu's statue up from the ocean floor... But what bothered him was the irony: the power Shizuko was given brought her only misery. But that was looking at things the wrong way. Maybe in Asakawa's case, simply being released from the curse was the equivalent of Shizuko's receiving power. Asakawa decided to make himself think so.

Ryuji glanced at Asakawa's face, reassuring himself that the man before him was, indeed, alive, then nodded twice. "I suppose you do have a point." Exhaling slowly, he sank back into his chair. "And yet..."

"What?"

Ryuji sat up straight and asked, as if to himself, "What did Sadako give birth to?"

2

Asakawa and Ryuji parted company at Atami Station. Asakawa intended to take Sadako's remains back to her relatives in Sashikiji and have them hold a memorial service for her. They probably wouldn't even know what to do with her, a distant relative they hadn't heard a peep out of in nearly thirty years. But, things being what they were, he couldn't just abandon her. If he hadn't known who she was, he could have had her buried as a Jane Doe. But he knew, and so all he could do was hand her over to the people in Sashikiji. The statute of limitations was long past, and it would be nothing but trouble to bring up a murder now, so he decided to say she'd probably been a suicide. He wanted to hand her off and then return immediately to Tokyo, but the boat didn't depart that often. Leaving now, he'd end up having to spend the night on Oshima. Since he'd have to leave the rental car in Atami, flying back to Tokyo would just make things more complicated.

"You can deliver her bones all by yourself. You don't need me for that." As he'd said this, getting out of the car in front of Atami Station, Ryuji seemed to be laughing at Asakawa. Sadako's bones were no longer in the plastic bag. They were wrapped neatly in a black cloth in the back seat of the car. To be sure, it was such a small bundle that even a child could have delivered it to the Yamamura house in Sashikiji. The point was to get them to accept her. If they refused, then Asakawa wouldn't have anywhere to take her. That would be troublesome. He had the feeling that the charm would only be completely fulfilled when someone close to her held services for her. But still: why should they believe him when he showed up on their doorstep with a bag of bones, saying this is your relative whom you haven't heard from in twenty-five years? What proof did he have? Asakawa was still a little worried.

"Well, happy trails. See you in Tokyo." Ryuji waved and went through the ticket gate. "If I didn't have so much work, I wouldn't mind tagging along, but you know how it is." Ryuji had a mountain of work, scholarly articles and the like, that needed immediate attention.

"Let me thank you again."

"Forget about it. It was fun for me, too."

Asakawa watched until Ryuji disappeared into the shadow of the stairs leading to the platform. Just before disappearing from view, Ryuji stumbled on the steps. Although he quickly regained his balance, for a brief moment as he swayed Ryuji's muscular form seemed to go double in Asakawa's vision. Asakawa realized he was tired, and rubbed his eyes. When he took his hands away, Ryuji had disappeared up the stairs. A curious sensation pierced his breast, and somewhere he detected the faint scent of citrus....

That afternoon, he delivered Sadako's remains to Takashi Yamamura without incident. He'd just returned from a fishing voyage, and as soon as he saw the black wrapped bundle he seemed to know what it was. Asakawa held it out in both hands and said, "These are Sadako's remains."

Takashi gazed at the bundle for a while, then narrowed his eyes tenderly. He shuffled over to Asakawa, bowed deeply, and accepted the bones, saying, "thank you for coming all this way."

Asakawa was a bit taken aback. He didn't think the old man would accept it that easily. Takashi seemed to guess what he was thinking, and he said, in a voice full of conviction, "It's definitely Sadako."

Up until age three, and then from age nine to age eighteen, Sadako had lived here, at the Yamamura estate. Takashi was sixty-one now. What exactly did she mean to him? Guessing from his expression as he received her remains, Asakawa imagined that he must have loved her dearly. He didn't even ask for assurance that this was Sadako. Perhaps he didn't need to. Perhaps he knew intuitively that it was her inside the black cloth. The way his eyes had flashed when he'd first seen the bundle attested to that. There must be some sort of power at work here, too.

Having completed his errand, Asakawa wanted to get away from Sadako as quickly as possible. So he beat a hasty retreat, lying that "I'll miss my flight if I don't leave now." If the family changed their minds and suddenly decided they wouldn't accept the remains as Sadako's without proof, all would be lost. If they started asking him for details, he didn't know what he'd say. It would be a long time before he'd be able to tell anyone the whole story. He particularly didn't feel up to telling her relatives.

Asakawa stopped by Hayatsu's "bureau" to say thanks for all his help the other day, and then he headed for the Oshima Hot Springs Hotel. He wanted to soak away all his fatigue in a hot bath and then write up the whole sequence of events.

3

Just about the time Asakawa was settling into bed at the Oshima Hot Springs Hotel, Ryuji was dozing at his desk in his apartment. His lips rested on a half-written essay, his spittle smudging the dark blue ink. He was so tired that his hand still clutched his beloved Montblanc fountain pen. He hadn't switched over to a word processor yet.

Suddenly his shoulders jerked and his face contorted unnaturally. Ryuji leapt up. His back went ramrod-straight, and his eyes opened far wider than they usually did when he woke up. His eyes were normally slightly slanted, and when they were wide open like this he looked different, somehow cuter than usual. His eyes were bloodshot. He'd been dreaming. Ryuji, normally not afraid of anything, was shaking through and through. He couldn't remember the dream. But the tautness of his body, and his trembling, bore witness to the terror of the dream. He couldn't breathe. He looked at the clock. 9:40. He couldn't immediately figure out the significance of the time. The lights were on—the overhead fluorescent bulb and the desk lamp in front of him—and there was plenty of light, but things still felt too dark. He felt an instinctual fear of the dark. His dream had been ruled by a darkness like no other.

Ryuji swiveled in his chair and looked at the video deck. The fateful tape was still in it. For some reason, he couldn't look away again. He kept staring at it. His breathing became rough. Misgiving showed on his face. Images raced through his mind, leaving no room for logical thought.

"Shit. You've come...."

He placed both hands on the edge of the desk and tried to figure out what was behind him. His apartment was in a quiet place just off a main street, and all sorts of indistinct sounds came in from the street. Occasionally the revving of an engine or the squeal of tires would stand out, but other than that the sounds from outside were just a dull, solid mass stretching out behind him to the left and right. Pricking up his ears, he could figure out what was making some of the noises. Among them were the voices of insects. This mixed-up herd of sounds now started to float and flutter like a ghost. Reality seemed to recede—that was Ryuji's impression. And as reality receded it left an empty space around him, in which some sort of spirit matter hovered. The chilly night air and the moisture clinging to his skin turned into shadows and closed in on him. The beating of his heart grew faster, outstripping the ticking of the clock. The signs were pressing down on his chest. Ryuji looked again at the clock. 9:44. Every time he looked, he gulped.

A week ago, when I watched that video at Asakawa's, what time was that? He said his brat always goes to sleep at around nine....Assuming we hit 'play' after that, we would have finished at....

He couldn't figure out exactly when they'd finished watching the video. But he could tell that the time was fast approaching. He was well aware that these indications that were now closing in on him were no counterfeit. This was different from when one's imagination magnified one's fears. This was no imaginary pregnancy. *It* was definitely coming steadily closer. What he didn't know was...

Why's it only coming for me? Why is it coming for me, when it didn't come for Asakawa? It's not fair.

His mind overflowed with confusion.

What the hell's going on? Didn't we figure out the charm? So why? Why? WHY?

His chest was beating an alarm. It felt like something had reached inside his breast and was squeezing his heart. Pain shot through his spine. He felt a cool touch on his neck, and, startled, he tried to get up from his chair, but instead he was overcome by severe pain in his waist and back. He collapsed on the floor.

Think! What should you do now?

Somehow his remaining consciousness managed to give orders to his body. *Stand! Stand and think!* Ryuji crawled over the floor mats to the video deck. He pushed eject and took out the tape. *Why am I doing this?* There was nothing else he could do but take a good long look at this tape that was behind everything. He looked at it back and front, and then went to put it back in the video deck, but stopped. There was a title written on the label on the spine of the tape. Asakawa's handwriting. *Liza Minnelli, Frank Sinatra, Sammy Davis, Jr./1989.* It must have had some music program recorded on it, before Asakawa had used it to dub *that* video. An electric jolt ran down his spine. A single thought swiftly took shape in his otherwise blank mind. *Nonsense,* he told himself, putting the thought from his mind, but when he turned the tape over, that momentary jolt changed to a certainty. Suddenly Ryuji understood many things. The riddle of the charm, the old woman's prophecy, and another power hidden in the images on that tape... Why had those four kids in Villa Log Cabin run off without trying to carry out the charm? Why was Ryuji facing death when Asakawa's life had been spared? What had Sadako given birth to? The hint was right here, so close at hand. He hadn't realized that

Sadako's power had become fused with another power. She'd wanted to have a child, but her body couldn't bear one. So she'd made a bargain with the devil—for lots of children. *What effect is this going to have?* Ryuji wondered. He laughed through his pain, an ironic laugh.

You've got to be kidding. I wanted to watch the end of mankind. And here I am, in the vanguard....

He crawled to the telephone and started to dial Asakawa's home number, but then he remembered: he was on Oshima.

Sonofabitch'll sure be surprised when he hears I'm dead. The terrific pressure in his chest made his ribs creak.

He dialed Mai Takano's number. Ryuji wasn't sure whether it was a fierce attachment to life or just a desire to hear her voice one last time which had given rise to this impulse to summon Mai; he couldn't tell the difference anymore. But a voice came to him.

Give it up. It wouldn't be right to get her messed up in this.

But on the other hand, he still had a smidgen of hope—he might still be in time.

The clock on the desk caught his eye. 9:48. He put the receiver to his ear and waited for Mai to come to the phone. His head suddenly felt unbearably itchy. He put his hand to his head and scratched furiously, and felt several strands of hair come out. On the second ring, Ryuji lifted his face. There was a horizontal mirror on the chest of drawers in front of him, and he could see his face reflected in it. Forgetting that he had the phone wedged between his shoulder and his head, he brought his face in close to the mirror. The receiver fell, but he didn't care; he just stared at his face in the mirror. Somebody else was reflected in the mirror. The cheeks were yellowish, dried and cracked, and hair was falling out in clumps to reveal brown scabs. *A hallucination, it's got to be a hal-*

lucination, he told himself. Even so, he couldn't control his emotions. A woman's voice came from the receiver where it lay on the floor: "Hello? Hello?" Ryuji couldn't stand it. He screamed. His screams overlapped with Mai's words, and in the end he wasn't able to hear his beloved's voice. The face in the mirror was none other than his own, a hundred years in the future. Even Ryuji hadn't known it would be so terrifying to meet himself transformed into someone else.

Mai Takano picked up the phone on the fourth ring and said "hello." The only answer was a ghastly scream. A shudder came over the line. Fear itself came through the line from Ryuji's apartment to Mai's. Surprised, Mai held the receiver away from her ear. The moans continued. The first scream had been one of shock, and the subsequent moans held incredulity. She'd received harassing phone calls several times before, but she immediately realized that this was different, and brought the phone back to her ear. The voice ceased. It was followed by dead silence.

9:49 p.m. His wish to hear the voice of the woman he loved one last time had been cruelly shattered. Instead, all he'd done was drown her in his death cries. Now he breathed his last. Nothingness enveloped his consciousness. Mai's voice came again from the receiver near his hand. His legs were splayed out on the floor, his back was up against the bed, his left arm was thrown back across the mattress, his right hand was stretched out toward the receiver which still whispered "hello?" and his head was bent backwards, eyes wide open, staring at the ceiling. Just before he slipped into the void, Ryuji realized he wouldn't be saved, and he remembered to wish with all his might that he could teach that asshole Asakawa the secret of the videotape.

Mai called "hello, hello," over and over again. No reply. She put the receiver back in the cradle. Those groans had sounded familiar. A premonition crept into her breast, and she picked up the receiver again to dial her esteemed professor's number. She got a busy signal. She pressed down the hook with her finger and dialed again. Still busy. And she knew that it had been Ryuji calling, and that something horrible had happened to him.

4

October 20—Saturday

He was happy to be home again at last, but with his wife and child gone, the place seemed lonely. How long had it been since he was home? He tried to count on his fingers. He'd spent one night in Kamakura, gotten stuck on Oshima for two nights, spent the following night in Villa Log Cabin, and then another night on Oshima. He'd only been away for five nights. But it felt as if he'd been gone from home for much longer. He often went away for four or five nights to research articles, but when he came home it always felt like the time had flown by.

Asakawa sat down at the desk in his study and turned on his word processor. His body still ached here and there, and his back hurt when he stood up or sat down. Even the ten hours he'd slept last night couldn't make up for all the sleepless nights of the last week. But he couldn't stop and rest now. If he didn't take care of the work that had piled up, he wouldn't be able to keep his promise to take them on a drive to Nikko tomorrow—Sunday.

He sat right down in front of the word processor. He'd already saved the first half of the report on a floppy disk. Now he needed to add the rest, everything that had happened since Monday, when they had learned the name of Sadako Yamamura. He wanted to finish this document as quickly as possible. By dinnertime he'd written five pages. It was a pretty good pace. The pace of Asakawa's writing usually picked up as the night wore on. At this rate, he'd be able to relax and enjoy seeing his wife and daughter tomorrow. Then, on Monday, he'd go back to his normal life. He couldn't predict how his editor would react to what he was writing now, but he'd never know until he'd finished writing it. Knowing it was probably fruitless effort, Asakawa went through and put the events of the second half of the week in order. Only when the manuscript was finished would he feel that the episode was really and truly over.

Sometimes his fingers stopped over the keyboard. The printout containing Sadako's photo was sitting by the desk. He felt as if that terrifyingly beautiful girl were watching him, and it ruined his concentration. He'd seen the same things she'd seen, through those beautiful eyes. He still had the feeling that part of her had entered into his body. Asakawa put the photo out of sight. He couldn't work with Sadako staring at him.

He ate dinner at a local diner, and then he suddenly wondered what Ryuji was doing right now. He wasn't really worried—somehow he just remembered Ryuji's face. And as he went back to his room and continued working, that face floated at the edge of his consciousness, gradually becoming clearer.

I wonder what he's up to right now?

His mental image of Ryuji's face drifted in and out of focus. He felt strangely agitated, and reached out for the phone. After seven rings, he heard the receiver being picked up, and he felt relieved. But it was a woman's voice he heard.

"...Hello?" The voice was faint and thin. Asakawa had heard it before.

"Hello. This is Asakawa."

"Yes?" came the faint reply.

"Ah, you must be Mai Takano, right? I should thank you for the lunch you made the last time we met."

"Don't mention it," she whispered, and waited.

"Is Ryuji there?" Asakawa wondered why she didn't just turn the phone over to Ryuji right away.

"Is Ryuji—"

"The Professor is dead."

"...What?" How long was he speechless? All he could say, stupidly, was, "What?" His eyes stared blankly at a point on the ceiling. Finally, when the phone felt ready to slip out of his hands, he managed to ask, "When?"

"Last night, at around ten o'clock."

Ryuji had finished watching the video at Asakawa's condominium last Friday night at 9:49. He'd died right on schedule.

"What was the cause of death?" He didn't need to ask.

"Sudden heart failure...but they haven't determined an exact cause of death."

Asakawa barely managed to stay on his feet. This wasn't over. They'd just entered the second round.

"Mai, are you going to be there for a while?"

"Yes. I need to put the Professor's papers in order."

"I'll be over right away. Wait for me."

Asakawa hung up the phone and sank to the floor. His wife and daughter's deadline was tomorrow morning at eleven. Another race against time. And this time, he was alone in the fight. Ryuji was gone. He couldn't stay on the floor like this. He had to take action. Quickly. Right now.

He stepped out onto the street and gauged the traffic situation. It looked like driving would be faster than taking the train. He crossed at the crosswalk and climbed into the rental car, parked at the curb. He was glad he'd extended the rental another day so he could pick up his family.

What did this mean? Hands gripping the wheel, he tried to get his thoughts together. Scene after scene flashed back to him, but none of them made any sense. The more he thought, the less his mind could absorb, and the thread connecting events got more and more tangled until it seemed ready to snap. *Calm down! Calm down and think!* He lectured himself. Finally, he realized what he had to focus on.

First of all, we didn't really figure out the charm—the way to escape death. Sadako didn't want her bones to be found and laid to rest with an appropriate memorial service. She wanted something entirely different. What? What is it? And why am I still alive like this if we didn't figure out the charm? What does that mean? Tell me that! Why did only I survive?

At eleven o'clock next morning, Shizu and Yoko would face their deadline. It was already nine in the night. If he didn't do something, he'd lose them.

He'd been thinking of this from the perspective of a curse pronounced by Sadako, a woman who'd met an unexpected death, but he began to doubt that approach now. He had a premonition of a bottomless evil, sneering at human suffering.

Mai was kneeling formally in the Japanese-style room with an unpublished manuscript of Ryuji's on her lap. She was turning the pages, casting her eyes over each one, but it was a difficult subject at the best of times, and now nothing was sinking in. The room felt cavernous. Ryuji's parents had picked up his body early this morning and taken it back home to Kawasaki. He was gone.

"Tell me everything about last night."

His friend was dead. Ryuji was like a brother-in-arms to him. He grieved. But he hadn't time now to wallow in sentiment. Asakawa sat next to Mai and bowed.

"It was after nine-thirty at night. I got a call from the Professor...." She told him the details. The scream that had come from the phone, the silence that had followed. Then when she'd rushed to Ryuji's apartment she'd found him leaning against the bed, legs spread wide. She fixed her gaze on the spot where Ryuji's corpse had been, and as she described the scene tears came to her eyes.

"I called and called, but the Professor didn't respond."

Asakawa didn't give her time to cry. "Was there anything different about the room?"

"No," she said shaking her head. "Only that the telephone was off the hook and making an ear-splitting sound."

At the moment of death, Ryuji had called Mai. Why? Asakawa pressed further. "He didn't tell you anything there at the end? No last words? Nothing, say, about a videotape?"

"A videotape?" Mai's expression showed that she couldn't see any possible connection between her professor's death and a videotape. There was no way for Asakawa to know whether or not Ryuji had figured out the true nature of the charm just before he'd died.

But why did he call Mai? He must have done it knowing his death was at hand.... Was it just that he wanted to hear a loved one's voice? Isn't it possible that he'd figured out the charm and needed her help in carrying it out? And that's why he called her? In which case, it takes another person to make the charm work.

Asakawa started to leave. Mai walked him to the door.

"Mai, will you be staying here tonight?"

"Yes. I need to take care of his manuscript."

"Well, I'm sorry to have bothered you when you're so busy." He went to leave.

"Um..."

"Yes?"

"Mr. Asakawa, I'm afraid you have the wrong idea about the Professor and me."

"What do you mean?"

"You think we were having a relationship...as a man and a woman."

"No, well, I mean..."

Mai could spot a man who thought they were lovers—the way he looked at them. Asakawa looked at them that way. It bothered Mai.

"The first time I met you, the Professor introduced you as his best friend. That surprised me. I had never heard the Professor talk like that about anyone before. I think you were very special to him. So..." She hesitated before continuing. "So, I wish you could understand him a little better, as his best friend. The Professor...as far as I know he never knew a woman." She lowered her eyes.

You mean he died a virgin?

Asakawa had nothing to say to that. He remained quiet. The Ryuji that Mai remembered sounded like a completely different person from the one he knew. Were they talking about the same man?

"But..."

But you don't know what he did as a junior in high school, was what he wanted to say, but he stopped himself. He had no desire to dredge up a dead man's crimes, and he didn't feel like destroying Mai's cherished image of Ryuji.

Not only that, he found himself with new doubts. Asakawa believed in a woman's intuition. Mai seemed to have been pretty close to Ryuji, and if she said he was a virgin, he had to consider that a credible theory. In other words, maybe the whole thing about raping a college girl in his neighborhood had been nothing more than fiction.

"The Professor was like a child when he was with me. He told me everything. He didn't hide anything. I know almost everything there is to know about his youth. His pain."

"Is that so?" was all Asakawa could say in response.

"When he was with me he was as innocent as a ten-year old boy. When there was a third person around he was the gentleman, and with you I imagine he probably played the scoundrel. Am I right? If he hadn't..." Mai softly reached out for her white handbag, took out a handkerchief, and dabbed at her eyes. "If he hadn't put on an act like that, he would never have been able to get along in the world. Do you see what I'm saying? Can you understand that?"

Asakawa was shocked, more than anything. But then something struck him. For a guy who'd been good at his studies and excelled at sports, Ryuji had been quite a loner. He hadn't had one close friend.

"He was so pure... Not superficial, like those jerks I go to school with. They couldn't compare to him."

Mai's handkerchief was soaked with tears by now.

Standing in the doorway, Asakawa found that he had too much to think about to be able to come up with any suitable words to leave with Mai. The image of the Ryuji he'd known diverged completely from the one Mai had; his view of the man had become so unfocused now as to be unrecognizable. There was a darkness concealed within Ryuji. No matter how he struggled, Asakawa couldn't completely grasp his personality. Had he really raped that girl in high school? Asakawa had no way of knowing that, nor whether he'd continued doing things like that, as he'd said he had. And right now, with his family's deadline coming up tomorrow, Asakawa really didn't want to worry himself with anything else.

So all he said was, "Ryuji was my best friend, too."

The words must have pleased Mai. Her adorable face broke into an expression that could have been a smile or could have been more weeping, and she bowed ever so slightly. Asakawa shut the door and hurried down the stairs. As he emerged onto the street and put distance between himself and Ryuji's apartment, he was suddenly overwhelmed by the thought of this friend who'd thrown everything into this dangerous game, even sacrificing his life. Asakawa didn't bother to wipe away the tears.

5

October 21—Sunday

Midnight passed, and Sunday finally arrived. Asakawa was making notes on a sheet of paper, trying to get his thoughts in order.

Just before his death, Ryuji had figured out the charm. He telephoned Mai, possibly to summon her. Which means that he needed Mai's help to work the charm. Okay, the important question here is, why am I still alive? There's only one possible answer. At some point during the week, without even knowing it, I must have carried out the charm! What other explanation is there? The charm must be something anybody can easily do, with the help of another person.

But that brought up another problem. *Why did those four kids run out without performing the charm? If it was so easy, why couldn't at least one of them have played tough when they were together and then gone and done it in secret later? Think. What did I do this week? What did I do that Ryuji clearly didn't do?*

Asakawa let out a yell. "How the hell am I supposed to know? There must have been a thousand things I did this week that he didn't do! This isn't funny!"

He punched Sadako's photo. "Damn you! How long are you going to keep torturing me?" He hit her in the face over and over. But Sadako's expression never changed; her beauty never diminished.

He went into the kitchen and splashed some whiskey into a glass. All the blood had rushed to a single point in his head and he needed to disperse it. He went to knock it back at one gulp, but then stopped. He just might come up with the answer tonight and have to drive to Ashikaga in the middle of the night, so maybe he'd better not drink. He was mad at the way he always tried to rely on something outside himself. When he'd had to dig Sadako's bones out from under the cabin, he had given in to fear and nearly lost himself. It was only because he had Ryuji with him that he'd been able to do what he needed to do.

"Ryuji! Hey, Ryuji! I'm begging you, help me out here!"

He knew he'd never be able to go on without his wife and daughter. Never.

"Ryuji! Lend me your strength! Why am I alive? Is it because I was the one to find Sadako's remains first? If so, then there's no saving my family. That can't be right, can it, Ryuji?"

He was devastated. He knew it was no time to be wailing, but he'd lost his cool. After moaning to Ryuji for a while, his calm returned. He started making notes again on the paper. *The old woman's prophecy. Did Sadako really have a baby? Just before her death she had sex with the last smallpox victim in Japan. Does that relate somehow?* All of his notes ended with question marks. Nothing was certain. Was this going to lead him to the charm? He couldn't afford to fail.

Several more hours elapsed. It was beginning to get light outside. Lying on the floor, Asakawa could hear the sound of a man's breathing. Birds chirped. He didn't know if he was awake or dreaming. Somehow he'd wound up on the floor, asleep. He squinted against the bright morning light. The figure of a man was slowly fading in the soft light. He wasn't scared. Asakawa came to himself with a start and stared hard in the direction of the figure.

"Ryuji? Is that you?"

The figure didn't reply, but suddenly the title of a book came to Asakawa, so vividly that it might have been branded into the wrinkles of his brain.

Epidemics and Man.

The title appeared in white on the back of his eyelids when he closed his eyes, then disappeared; but it still echoed in his head. That book should be in Asakawa's study. When he'd first started to investigate the case, Asakawa had wondered if it could have been a virus that had caused four people to die simultaneously. He'd bought the book then. He hadn't read it, but he remembered putting it away on a bookshelf.

Sun was streaming in through the eastern windows, falling on him. He tried to stand up. His head throbbed.

Was it a dream?

He opened the door to his study. He took down the book that whoever-it-was had suggested to him: *Epidemics and Man.* Of course, Asakawa had a pretty good idea who it was that had made that suggestion. Ryuji. He'd returned just for a brief moment, to teach him the secret of the charm.

So where in this three-hundred-page tome did the answer lie? Asakawa had another flash of intuition. Page 191! The number was insinuated into his brain, though not quite as searingly as the last time. He opened to that page. A single word jumped out at him, and pulsed bigger and bigger.

Reproduction. Reproduction. Reproduction. Reproduction.

A virus's instinct is to reproduce. A virus usurps living structures in order to reproduce itself.

"Ooooooohhhhh!" Asakawa groaned. He'd finally grasped the nature of the charm.

It's obvious what I did this week and Ryuji didn't. I brought the tape home, made a copy, and showed it to Ryuji. The charm is simple. Anybody can do it. Make a copy and show it to somebody. Help it reproduce by showing it to somebody who hasn't seen it. Those four kids were happy with their prank and stupidly left the tape in the cabin. Nobody went to the effort of going all the way back for it so they could actually perform the charm.

No matter how he thought about it, that was the only possible interpretation. He picked up the phone and dialed Ashikaga. Shizu answered.

"Listen to me. Listen carefully to what I'm going to tell you. There's something I need your mother and father to see. Right away. I'm on my way now, so don't let them go anywhere before I get there. Do you understand? This is incredibly important."

Ah, am I selling my soul to the devil? In order to save my wife and daughter, I'm willing to put my wife's parents in danger, even if it's only temporary. But if it'll save their daughter and granddaughter, I'm sure they'll gladly cooperate. All they have to do is make copies and show them to somebody else, and they'll be out of danger. But after that...what then?

"What's this all about? I don't understand."

"Just do as I say. I'm leaving right now. Oh, right—they have a video deck, don't they?"

"Yes."

"Beta or VHS?"

"VHS."

"Great, I'm on my way. Don't, I repeat, *don't* go anywhere."

"Hold on a minute. What you want to show my mom and dad is *that* video, isn't it?"

He didn't know what to say, so he shut up.

"Right?"

"...Right."

"It's not dangerous?"

Dangerous? You and your daughter are going to be dead in five hours. Give me a break, damnit! Stop asking so many questions. I don't have time to explain it all to you from the beginning anymore. Asakawa wanted to shout at her, but he managed to restrain himself.

"Just do as I say!"

It was just before seven. If he raced there on the freeway, provided there were no traffic delays, he should get to his in-laws' house in Ashikaga by nine-thirty. Factoring in the time it would take to make a copy for his wife and another for his daughter, they should just make the eleven o'clock deadline. He hung up, opened the doors to the entertainment center, and unplugged the video deck. They needed two decks to make copies, so he had to take one of his.

As he left, he took one more look at the photo of Sadako.

You sure gave birth to something nasty.

He took the Oi ramp onto the freeway, deciding to skirt Tokyo Bay and get on the Tohoku Highway heading out of town. There wouldn't be much traffic on the Tohoku Highway. The problem was how to avoid congestion before that. As he paid the toll on the Oi on-ramp and peered at the traffic-information board, he realized for the first time that it was Sunday morning. As a result, there were hardly any cars in the tunnel under the bay, where they were usually lined up like beads on a rosary. There weren't even any jams in the big merging areas. At this rate he'd get to Ashikaga right on schedule, with plenty of time to start making copies of the video. Asakawa eased up on the accelerator. Now he was more afraid of going too fast and getting into an accident.

He sped north along the Sumida River. Glancing down, he could see neighborhoods just waking up on a Sunday morning. People were walking around with a different air than on weekday mornings. A peaceful Sunday morning.

He couldn't help but wonder. *What effect is this going to have? With my wife's copy and my daughter's copy, this virus is going to be set free in two directions—how's it going to spread from there?* He could imagine people making copies and passing them on to people who'd already seen it before, trying to keep the thing contained within a limited circle so it wouldn't spread. But that would be going against the virus's will to reproduce. There was no way of knowing yet how that function was incorporated into the video. That would take some experimenting. And it would probably be impossible to find anybody willing to risk their life to find the truth of it until it had spread pretty far and things had become quite serious. It really wasn't very difficult to make a copy and show it to someone—so that's what people would do. As the secret traveled by word of mouth, it would be added to: "You have to show it to someone who hasn't seen it before." And as the tape propagated the week's lag time would probably be shortened. People who were shown the tape wouldn't wait a week to make a copy and show it to someone else. How far would this ring expand? People would be driven by an instinctual fear of disease, and this pestilential videotape would no doubt spread throughout society in the blink of an eye. And, driven by fear, people would start to spread crazy rumors. Such as: *Once you've seen it you have to make at least two copies, and show them to at least two different people.* It'd turn into a pyramid scheme, spreading incomparably faster than it would just one tape at a time. In the space of half a year, everybody in Japan would have become a carrier, and the infection would spread overseas. In the process, of course, several people would die, and people would realize that the tape's warning wasn't a lie, and they'd start making copies even more desperately. There would be panic. Where would it all end? How many victims would this claim? Two years ago, during the boom in interest in the occult, the newsroom had received ten million submissions. Something had gone haywire. And it would happen again, allowing the new virus to run rampant.

A woman's resentment toward the masses who had hounded her father and mother to their deaths and the smallpox virus's resentment toward the human ingenuity that had driven it to the brink of extinction had fused together in the body of a singular person named Sadako Yamamura, and had reappeared in the world in an unexpected, unimagined form.

Asakawa, his family, everybody who had seen the video had been subconsciously infected with this virus. They were carriers. And viruses burrowed directly into the genes, the core of life. There was no telling yet what would result from this, how it would change human history—human evolution.

In order to protect my family, I am about to let loose on the world a plague which could destroy all mankind.

Asakawa was frightened by the essence of what he was trying to do. A voice was whispering to him.

If I let my wife and daughter die, it'll end right here. If a virus loses its host, it'll die. I can save mankind.

But the voice was too quiet.

He entered the Tohoku Highway. No congestion. If he kept going, he'd be there in plenty of time. Asakawa drove with his arms taut and both hands clutching the wheel. "I won't regret it. My family has no obligation to sacrifice themselves. There are some things you just have to protect when they're threatened."

He spoke loud enough to be heard over the engine, to renew his determination. If he were Ryuji, what would he do? He felt sure he knew. Ryuji's spirit had taught him the secret of the video. It was practically telling him to save his family. This gave him courage. He knew what Ryuji would probably say. *Be true to what you're feeling this instant! All we have in front of us is an uncertain future! The future'll take care of itself. When humanity gets around to applying its ingenuity, who knows if it won't find a solution? It's just another trial for the human species. In every age, the Devil reappears in a different guise. You can stamp it out, and stamp it out, and he'll keep coming back, over and over.*

Asakawa kept his foot steady on the accelerator and the car pointed toward Ashikaga. In his rear-view mirror he could see the skies over Tokyo, receding into the distance. Black clouds moved eerily across the skies. They slithered like serpents, hinting at the unleashing of some apocalyptic evil.

ABOUT THE AUTHOR

Koji Suzuki was born in 1957 in Hamamatsu, southwest of Tokyo. He attended Keio University where he majored in French. After graduating he held numerous odd jobs, including a stint as a cram school teacher. Also a self-described jock, he holds a first-class yachting license and crossed the U.S., from Key West to Los Angeles, on his motorcycle.

The father of two daughters, Suzuki is a respected authority on childrearing and has written numerous works on the subject. He acquired his expertise when he was a struggling writer and househusband. Suzuki also has translated a children's book into Japanese, *The Little Sod Diaries* by the crime novelist Simon Brett.

In 1990, Suzuki's first full-length work, *Paradise*, won the Japanese Fantasy Novel Award and launched his career as a fiction writer. *Ring*, written with a baby on his lap, catapulted him to fame, and the multi-million selling sequels *Spiral* and *Loop* cemented his reputation as a world-class talent. Often called the "Stephen King of Japan," Suzuki has played a crucial role in establishing mainstream credentials for horror novels in his country. He is based in Tokyo but loves to travel, often in the United States.